MASTERCRIME

Ladykillers: Crime Stories by Women

Ladykillers is a collection of crime stories by both classic and contemporary women writers – from Agatha Christie to Antonia Fraser. It is readily recognised that women are particularly adept at exposing the underlying tensions of a seemingly normal life which can often lead to a final breakdown and, sometimes, result in tragic murder. The stories collected here range from those illustrating the simple and humorous – as in Dorothy L Sayers's *The Incredible Elopement of Lord Peter Wimsey* – to the more calculated forms of blackmail shown in Elizabeth Ferrars's *Instrument of Justice* or, worse, the simple and pathetic depths of loneliness portrayed in Caroline Blackwood's *Addy*, which culminate not in crime, but in a forlorn and desperate sense of isolation.

Some of these stories have been in print elsewhere, and others – Margery Allingham's *The Black Tent* and Margaret Yorke's *The Mouse Will Play* – have never before been published. *Ladykillers* is a riveting and stimulating volume which highlights the very best crime stories and clearly demonstrates the individual and superior quality of women as crime writers.

MASTERCRIME

LADYKILLERS

Crime Stories by Women

J.M. Dent & Sons Ltd
London Melbourne

First published in Great Britain by J.M. Dent & Sons Ltd 1987
Reprinted 1987
Copyright information appears on the Acknowledgements page.

This book is set in 11/12½ Linotron 202 Garamond by
Input Typesetting Ltd, London SW19 8DR

Printed in Great Britain by Cox & Wyman Ltd, Reading for
J.M. Dent & Sons Ltd
Aldine House, 33 Welbeck Street, London W1M 8LX

British Library Cataloguing in Publication Data

Ladykillers : crime stories by women——
   (Mastercrime).
   1. Detective and mystery stories, English
   2. English fiction——20th century
   I. Taylor, Imogen
   823'.0872   PR1309.D'4

ISBN 0-460-12546-X

Contents

THE INCREDIBLE ELOPEMENT OF LORD PETER WIMSEY

'That house, señor?' said the landlord of the little *posada*. 'That is the house of the American physician, whose wife, may the blessed saints preserve us, is bewitched.' He crossed himself, and so did his wife and daughter.

'Bewitched, is she?' said Langley sympathetically. He was a professor of ethnology, and this was not his first visit to the Pyrenees. He had, however, never before penetrated to any place quite so remote as this tiny hamlet, clinging, like a rock-plant, high up the scarred granite shoulders of the mountain. He scented material here for his book on Basque folklore. With tact, he might persuade the old man to tell his story.

'And in what manner,' he asked, 'is the lady bespelled?'

'Who knows?' replied the landlord, shrugging his shoulders.

' "The man that asked questions on Friday was buried on Saturday." Will your honour consent to take his supper?'

Langley took the hint. To press the question would be to encounter obstinate silence. Later, when they knew him better, perhaps –

His dinner was served to him at the family table – the oily, pepper-flavoured stew to which he was so well accustomed, and the harsh red wine of the country. His hosts chattered to him freely enough in that strange Basque language which has no fellow in the world, and is said by some to be the very speech of our first fathers in Paradise. They spoke of the bad winter, and young Esteban Arramandy, so strong and swift at the pelota, who had been lamed by a falling rock and now halted on two sticks; of three valuable goats carried off by a bear; of the torrential rains that, after a dry summer, had scoured the bare ribs of the mountains. It was raining now, and the wind was howling unpleasantly. This did not trouble Langley; he knew and loved this haunted and impenetrable country at all times and seasons. Sitting in that rude peasant inn, he thought of the oak-panelled hall of his Cambridge college and smiled, and his eyes gleamed happily behind his scholarly pince-nez. He was a young man, in spite of his professorship and the string of letters after his name. To his university colleagues it seemed strange that this man, so trim, so prim, so early old, should spend his vacations eating garlic, and scrambling on mule-back along precipitous mountain-tracks. You would never think it, they said, to look at him.

There was a knock at the door.

'That is Martha,' said the wife.

She drew back the latch, letting in a rush of wind and rain which made the candle gutter. A small, aged woman was blown in out of the night, her grey hair straggling in wisps from beneath her shawl.

'Come in, Martha, and rest yourself. It is a bad night. The parcel is ready – oh, yes. Dominique brought it from the town this morning. You must take a cup of wine or milk before you go back.'

The old woman thanked her and sat down, panting.

'And how goes all at the house? The doctor is well?'

'He is well.'

'And *she*?'

The daughter put the question in a whisper, and the landlord shook his head at her with a frown.

'As always at this time of the year. It is but a month now to the Day of the Dead. Jesu-Maria! it is a grievous affliction for the poor gentleman, but he is patient, patient.'

'He is a good man,' said Dominique, 'and a skilful

doctor, but an evil like that is beyond his power to cure. You are not afraid, Martha?'

'Why should I be afraid? The Evil One cannot harm *me*. I have no beauty, no wits, no strength for him to envy. And the Holy Relic will protect me.'

Her wrinkled fingers touched something in the bosom of her dress.

'You come from the house yonder?' asked Langley.

She eyed him suspiciously.

'The señor is not of our country?'

'The gentleman is a guest, Martha,' said the landlord hurriedly. 'A learned English gentleman. He knows our country and speaks our language as you hear. He is a great traveller, like the American doctor, your master.'

'What is your master's name?' asked Langley. It occurred to him that an American doctor who had buried himself in this remote corner of Europe must have something unusual about him. Perhaps he also was an ethnologist. If so, they might find something in common.

'He is called Wetherall.' She pronounced the name several times before he was sure of it.

'Wetherall? Not Standish Wetherall?'

He was filled with extraordinary excitement.

The landlord came to his assistance.

'This parcel is for him,' he said. 'No doubt the name will be written there.'

It was a small package, neatly sealed, bearing the label of a firm of London chemists and addressed to 'Standish Wetherall, Esq., M.D.'

'Good heavens!' exclaimed Langley. 'But this is strange. Almost a miracle. I know this man. I knew his wife, too –'

He stopped. Again the company made the sign of the cross.

'Tell me,' he said in great agitation, and forgetting his caution, 'you say his wife is bewitched – afflicted – how is this? Is she the same woman I know? Describe her. She was tall, beautiful, with gold hair and blue eyes like the Madonna. Is this she?'

There was a silence. The old woman shook her head and muttered something inaudible, but the daughter whispered:

'True – it is true. Once we saw her thus, as the gentleman says – '

'Be quiet,' said her father.

'Sir,' said Martha, 'we are in the hand of God.'

She rose, and wrapped her shawl about her.

'One moment,' said Langley. He pulled out his note-book and scribbled a few lines. 'Will you take this letter to your master the doctor? It is to say that I am here, his friend whom he once knew, and to ask if I may come and visit him. That is all.'

'You would not go to that house, excellence?' whispered the old man fearfully.

'If he will not have me, maybe he will come to me here.' He added a word or two and drew a piece of money from his pocket. 'You will carry my note for me?'

'Willingly, willingly. But the señor will be careful? Perhaps, though a foreigner, you are of the Faith?'

'I am a Christian,' said Langley.

This seemed to satisfy her. She took the letter and the money, and secured them, together with the parcel, in a remote pocket. Then she walked to the door, strongly and rapidly for all her bent shoulders and appearance of great age.

Langley remained lost in thought. Nothing could have astonished him more than to meet the name of Standish Wetherall in this place. He had thought that episode finished and done with over three years ago. Of all people! The brilliant surgeon in the prime of his life and repu-tation, and Alice Wetherall, that delicate piece of golden womanhood – exiled in this forlorn corner of the world! His heart beat a little faster at the thought of seeing her again. Three years ago, he had decided that it would be wiser if he did not see too much of that porcelain loveliness. That folly was past now – but still he could not visualise her except against the background of the great white house in Riverside Drive, with the peacocks and the swimming-pool and the gilded tower with the roof-garden. Wetherall was a rich man, the son of old Hiram Wetherall the automobile magnate. What was Wetherall doing here?

He tried to remember. Hiram Wetherall, he knew, was dead, and all the money belonged to Standish, for there were no other children. There had been trouble when the only son had married a girl without parents or history. He had brought her from 'somewhere out west.' There had been some story of his having found her, years before, as a neglected orphan, and saved her from something or cured her of something and paid for her education, when he was still scarcely more than a student. Then, when he was a man over forty and she a girl of seventeen, he had brought her home and married her.

And now he had left his house and his money and one of the finest specialist practices in New York to come to live in the Basque country – in a spot so out of the way that men still believed in Black Magic, and could barely splutter more than a few words of bastard French or Spanish – a spot that was uncivilised even by comparison with the primitive civilisation surrounding it. Langley began to be sorry that he had written to Wetherall. It might be resented.

The landlord and his wife had gone out to see to their cattle. The daughter sat close to the fire, mending a garment. She did not look at him, but he had the feeling that she would be glad to speak.

'Tell me, child,' he said gently, 'what is the trouble which afflicts these people who may be friends of mine?'

'Oh!' She glanced up quickly and leaned across to him, her arms stretched out over the sewing in her lap. 'Sir, be advised. Do not go up there. No one will stay in that house at this time of the year, except Tomaso, who has not all his wits, and old Martha, who is –'

'What?'

'A saint – or something else,' she said hurriedly.

'Child,' said Langley again, 'this lady when I knew –'

'I will tell you,' she said, 'but my father must not know. The good doctor brought her here three years ago last June, and then she was as you say. She was beautiful. She laughed and talked in her own speech – for she knew no Spanish or Basque. But on the Night of the Dead –'

She crossed herself.

'All-Hallows Eve,' said Langley softly.

'Indeed, I do not know what happened. But she fell into the power of the darkness. She changed. There were terrible cries – I cannot tell. But little by little she became what she is now. Nobody sees her but Martha and she will not talk. But the people say it is not a woman at all that lives there now.'

'Mad?' said Langley.

'It is not madness. It is – enchantment. Listen. Two years since on Easter Day – is that my father?'

'No, no.'

'The sun had shone and the wind came up from the valley. We heard the blessed church bells all day long. That night there came a knock at the door. My father opened and one stood there like Our Blessed Lady herself, very pale like the image in the church and with a blue cloak over her head. She spoke, but we could not tell what she said. She wept and wrung her hands and pointed down the valley path, and my father went to the stable and saddled the mule. I thought of the flight from bad King Herod. But then – the American doctor came. He had run fast and was out of breath. And she shrieked at sight of him.'

A great wave of indignation swept over Langley. If the man was brutal to his wife, something must be done quickly. The girl hurried on.

'He said – Jesu-Maria – he said that his wife was bewitched. At Easter-tide the power of the Evil One was broken
and she would try to flee. But as soon as the Holy Season
was over, the spell would fall on her again, and therefore
it was not safe to let her go. My parents were afraid to
have touched the evil thing. They brought out the Holy
Water and sprinkled the mule, but the wickedness had
entered into the poor beast and she kicked my father so
that he was lame for a month. The American took his wife
away with him and we never saw her again. Even old
Martha does not always see her. But every year the power
waxes and wanes – heaviest at Hallow-tide and lifted again
at Easter. Do not go to that house, señor, if you value
your soul! Hush! they are coming back.'

Langley would have liked to ask more, but his host
glanced quickly and suspiciously at the girl. Taking up his
candle, Langley went to bed. He dreamed of wolves, long,
lean and black, running on the scent of blood.

Next day brought an answer to his letter:

> 'Dear Langley, – Yes, this is myself, and of
> course I remember you well. Only too delighted
> to have you come and cheer our exile. You will
> find Alice somewhat changed, I fear, but I will
> explain our misfortunes when we meet. Our
> household is limited, owing to some kind of super-
> stitious avoidance of the afflicted, but if you will
> come along about half-past seven, we can give
> you a meal of sorts. Martha will show you the
> way.
>
>   'Cordially,
>   Standish Wetherall.'

The doctor's house was small and old, stuck halfway up
the mountainside on a kind of ledge in the rock-wall. A
stream, unseen but clamorous, fell echoing down close at
hand. Langley followed his guide into a dim, square room

with a great hearth at one end and, drawn close before the fire, an armchair with wide, sheltering ears. Martha, muttering some sort of apology, hobbled away and left him standing there in the half-light. The flames of the wood fire, leaping and falling, made here a gleam and there a gleam, and, as his eyes grew familiar with the room, he saw that in the centre was a table laid for a meal, and that there were pictures on the walls. One of these struck a familiar note. He went close to it and recognised a portrait of Alice Wetherall that he had last seen in New York. It was painted by Sargent in his happiest mood, and the lovely wild-flower face seemed to lean down to him with the sparkling smile of life.

A log suddenly broke and fell in the hearth, flaring. As though the little noise and light had disturbed something, he heard, or thought he heard, a movement from the big chair before the fire. He stepped forward, and then stopped. There was nothing to be seen, but a noise had begun; a kind of low, animal muttering, extremely disagreeable to listen to. It was not made by a dog or a cat, he felt sure. It was a sucking, slobbering sound that affected him in a curiously sickening way. It ended in a series of little grunts or squeals, and then there was silence.

Langley stepped backwards towards the door. He was positive that something was in the room with him that he did not care about meeting. An absurd impulse seized him to run away. He was prevented by the arrival of Martha, carrying a big, old-fashioned lamp, and behind her, Wetherall, who greeted him cheerfully.

The familiar American accents dispelled the atmosphere of discomfort that had been gathering about Langley. He held out a cordial hand.

'Fancy meeting *you* here,' said he.

'The world is very small,' replied Wetherall. 'I am afraid that is a hardy bromide, but I certainly am pleased to see you,' he added, with some emphasis.

The old woman had put the lamp on the table, and now

asked if she should bring in the dinner. Wetherall replied in the affirmative, using a mixture of Spanish and Basque which she seemed to understand well enough.

'I didn't know you were a Basque scholar,' said Langley.

'Oh, one picks it up. These people speak nothing else. But of course Basque is your speciality, isn't it?'

'Oh, yes.'

'I daresay they have told you some queer things about us. But we'll go into that later. I've managed to make the place reasonably comfortable, though I could do with a few more modern conveniences. However, it suits us.'

Langley took the opportunity to mumble some sort of inquiry about Mrs. Wetherall.

'Alice? Ah, yes, I forgot – you have not seen her yet.' Wetherall looked hard at him with a kind of half-smile. 'I should have warned you. You were – rather an admirer of my wife in the old days.'

'Like everyone else,' said Langley.

'No doubt. Nothing specially surprising about it, was there? Here comes dinner. Put it down, Martha, and we will ring when we are ready.'

The old woman set down a dish upon the table, which was handsomely furnished with glass and silver, and went out. Wetherall moved over to the fireplace, stepping sideways and keeping his eyes oddly fixed on Langley. Then he addressed the armchair.

'Alice! Get up, my dear, and welcome an old admirer of yours. Come along. You will both enjoy it. Get up.'

Something shuffled and wimpered among the cushions. Wetherall stooped, with an air of almost exaggerated courtesy, and lifted it to its feet. A moment, and it faced Langley in the lamplight.

It was dressed in a rich gown of gold satin and lace, that hung rucked and crumpled upon the thick and slouching body. The face was white and puffy, the eyes vacant, the mouth drooled open, with little trickles of saliva running from the loose corners. A dry fringe of rusty hair clung to the half-bald scalp, like the dead wisps on the head of a mummy.

'Come, my love,' said Wetherall. 'Say how do you do to Mr Langley.'

The creature blinked and mouthed out some inhuman sounds. Wetherall put his hand under its forearm, and it slowly extended a lifeless paw.

'There, she recognises you all right. I thought she would. Shake hands with him, my dear.'

With a sensation of nausea, Langley took the inert hand. It was clammy and coarse to the touch and made no attempt to return his pressure. He let it go; it pawed vaguely in the air for a moment and then dropped.

'I was afraid you might be upset,' said Wetherall, watching him. 'I have grown used to it, of course, and it doesn't affect me as it would an outsider. Not that you are an outsider – anything but that – eh? Premature senility is the lay name for it, I suppose. Shocking, of course, if you haven't met it before. You needn't mind, by the way, what you say. She understands nothing.'

'How did it happen?'

'I don't quite know. Came on gradually. I took the best advice, naturally, but there was nothing to be done. So we came here. I didn't care about facing things at home where everybody knew us. And I didn't like the idea of a sanatorium. Alice is my wife, you know – sickness or health, for better, for worse, and all that. Come along; dinner's getting cold.'

He advanced to the table, leading his wife, whose dim eyes seemed to brighten a little at the sight of food.

'Sit down, my dear, and eat your nice dinner. (She understands that, you see.) You'll excuse her table-manners, won't you? They're not pretty, but you'll get used to them.'

He tied a napkin round the neck of the creature and placed food before her in a deep bowl. She snatched at it hungrily, slavering and gobbling as she scooped it up in her fingers and smeared face and hands with the gravy.

Wetherall drew out a chair for his guest opposite to where his wife sat. The sight of her held Langley with a kind of disgusted fascination.

The food – a sort of salmis – was deliciously cooked, but Langley had no appetite. The whole thing was an outrage, to the pitiful woman and to himself. Her seat was directly beneath the Sargent portrait, and his eyes went helplessly from the one to the other.

'Yes,' said Wetherall, following his glance. 'There is a difference, isn't there?' He himself was eating heartily and apparently enjoying his dinner. 'Nature plays sad tricks upon us.'

'Is it always like this?'

'No; this is one of her bad days. At times she will be – almost human. Of course these people here don't know what to think of it all. They have their own explanation of a very simple medical phenomenon.'

'Is there any hope of recovery?'

'I'm afraid not – not of a permanent cure. You are not eating anything.'

'I – well, Wetherall, this has been a shock to me.'

'Of course. Try a glass of burgundy. I ought not to have asked you to come, but the idea of talking to an educated fellow-creature once again tempted me, I must confess.'

'It must be terrible for you.'

'I have become resigned. Ah, naughty, naughty!' The idiot had flung half the contents of her bowl upon the table. Wetherall patiently remedied the disaster, and went on:

'I can bear it better here, in this wild place where everything seems possible and nothing unnatural. My people are all dead, so there was nothing to prevent me from doing as I liked about it.'

'No. What about your property in the States?'

'Oh, I run over from time to time to keep an eye on things. In fact, I am due to sail next month. I'm glad you caught me. Nobody over there knows how we're fixed, of course. They just know we're living in Europe.'

'Did you consult no American doctor?'

'No. We were in Paris when the first symptoms declared themselves. That was shortly after that visit you paid to us.' A flash of some emotion to which Langley could not put a name made the doctor's eyes for a moment sinister. 'The best men on this side confirmed my own diagnosis. So we came here.'

He rang for Martha, who removed the salmis and put on a kind of sweet pudding.

'Martha is my right hand,' observed Wetherall. 'I don't know what we shall do without her. When I am away, she looks after Alice like a mother. Not that there's much one can do for her, except to keep her fed and warm and clean – and the last is something of a task.'

There was a note in his voice which jarred on Langley. Wetherall noticed his recoil and said:

'I won't disguise from you that it gets on my nerves sometimes. But it can't be helped. Tell me about yourself. What have you been doing lately?'

Langley replied with as much vivacity as he could assume, and they talked of indifferent subjects till the deplorable being which had once been Alice Wetherall began to mumble and whine fretfully and scramble down from her chair.

'She's cold,' said Wetherall. 'Go back to the fire, my dear.'

He propelled her briskly towards the hearth, and she sank back into the armchair, crouching and complaining and thrusting out her hands towards the blaze. Wetherall brought out brandy and a box of cigars.

'I contrive just to keep in touch with the world, you see,' he said. 'They send me these from London. And I get the latest medical journals and reports. I'm writing a book, you know, on my own subject; so I don't vegetate. I can experiment, too – plenty of room for a laboratory, and no Vivisection Acts to bother one. It's a good country to work in. Are you staying here long?'

'I think not very.'

'Oh! If you had thought of stopping on, I would have offered you the use of this house while I was away. You would find it more comfortable than the *posada*, and I should have no qualms, you know, about leaving you alone in the place with my wife – under the peculiar circumstances.'

He stressed the last words and laughed. Langley hardly knew what to say.

'Really, Wetherall – '

'Though, in the old days, *you* might have liked the prospect more and *I* might have liked it less. There was a time, I think Langley, when you would have jumped at the idea of living alone with – *my wife*.'

Langley jumped up.

'What the devil are you insinuating, Wetherall?'

'Nothing, nothing. I was just thinking of the afternoon when you and she wandered away at a picnic and got lost. You remember? Yes, I thought you would.'

'This is monstrous,' retorted Langley. 'How dare you say such things – with that poor soul sitting there – ?'

'Yes, poor soul. You're a poor thing to look at now, aren't you, my kitten?'

He turned suddenly to the woman. Something in his abrupt gesture seemed to frighten her, and she shrank away from him.

'You devil!' cried Langley. 'She's afraid of you. What have you been doing to her? How did she get into this state? I *will* know!'

'Gently,' said Wetherall. 'I can allow for your natural agitation at finding her like this, but I can't have you coming between me and *my wife*. What a faithful fellow you are, Langley. I believe you still want her – just as you did before when you thought I was dumb and blind. Come now, have you got designs on *my wife*, Langley? Would you like to kiss her, caress her, take her to bed with you – my beautiful wife?'

A scarlet fury blinded Langley. He dashed an inexpert fist at the mocking face. Wetherall gripped his arm, but he broke away. Panic seized him. He fled stumbling against the furniture and rushed out. As he went he heard Wetherall very softly laughing.

The train to Paris was crowded. Langley, scrambling in at the last moment, found himself condemned to the corridor. He sat down on a suitcase and tried to think. He had not been able to collect his thoughts on his wild flight. Even now, he was not quite sure what he had fled from. He buried his head in his hands.

'Excuse me,' said a polite voice.

Langley looked up. A fair man in a grey suit was looking down at him through a monocle.

'Fearfully sorry to disturb you,' went on the fair man. 'I'm just tryin' to barge back to my jolly old kennel. Ghastly crowd, isn't it? Don't know when I've disliked my fellow-creatures more. I say, you don't look frightfully fit. Wouldn't you be better on something more comfortable?'

Langley explained that he had not been able to get a seat. The fair man eyed his haggard and unshaven countenance for a moment and then said:

'Well, look here, why not come and lay yourself down in my bin for a bit? Have you had any grub? No? That's a mistake. Toddle along with me and we'll get hold of a spot of soup and so on. You'll excuse my mentioning it, but you look as if you'd been backing a system that's come unstuck, or something. Not my business, of course, but do have something to eat.'

Langley was too faint and sick to protest. He stumbled obediently along the corridor till he was pushed into a first-class sleeper, where a rigidly correct manservant was laying out a pair of mauve silk pyjamas and a set of silver-mounted brushes.

'This gentleman's feeling rotten, Bunter,' said the man with the monocle, 'so I've brought him in to rest his aching head upon thy breast. Get hold of the commissariat and tell 'em to buzz a plate of soup along and a bottle of something drinkable.'

'Very good, my lord.'

Langley dropped, exhausted, on the bed, but when the food appeared he ate and drank greedily. He could not remember when he had last made a meal.

'I say,' he said, 'I wanted that. It's awfully decent of you. I'm sorry to appear so stupid. I've had a bit of a shock.'

'Tell me all,' said the stranger pleasantly.

The man did not look particularly intelligent, but he seemed friendly, and above all, normal. Langley wondered how the story would sound.

'I'm an absolute stranger to you,' he began.

'And I to you,' said the fair man. 'The chief use of strangers is to tell things to. Don't you agree?'

'I'd like – ' said Langley. 'The fact is, I've run away from something. It's queer – it's – but what's the use of bothering you with it?'

The fair man sat down beside him and laid a slim hand on his arm.

'Just a moment,' he said. 'Don't tell me anything if you'd rather not. But my name is Wimsey – Lord Peter Wimsey – and I am interested in queer things.'

It was the middle of November when the strange man came to the village. Thin, pale and silent, with his great black hood flapping about his face, he was surrounded with an atmosphere of mystery from the start. He settled down, not at the inn, but in a dilapidated cottage high up in the mountains, and he brought with him five mule-loads of mysterious baggage and a servant. The servant was almost as uncanny as the master; he was a Spaniard and spoke Basque well enough to act as an interpreter for his employer when necessary; but his words were few, his aspect gloomy and stern, and such brief information as he vouchsafed, disquieting in the extreme. His master, he said, was a wise man; he spent all his time reading books; he ate no flesh; he was of no known country; he spoke the language of the Apostles and had talked with blessed Lazarus after his return from the grave; and when he sat alone in his chamber by night, the angels of God came and conversed with him in celestial harmonies.

This was terrifying news. The few dozen villagers avoided the little cottage, especially at night-time; and when the pale stranger was seen coming down the mountain path, folded in his black robe and bearing one of his magic tomes beneath his arm, the women pushed their children within doors, and made the sign of the cross.

Nevertheless, it was a child that first made the personal acquaintance of the magician. The small son of the Widow Etcheverry, a child of bold and inquisitive disposition, went one evening adventuring into the unhallowed neighbourhood. He was missing for two hours, during which his mother, in a frenzy of anxiety, had called the neighbours about her and summoned the priest, who had unhappily been called away on business to the town. Suddenly, however, the child reappeared, well and cheerful, with a strange story to tell.

He had crept up close to the magician's house (the bold, wicked child, did ever you hear the like?) and climbed into a tree to spy upon the stranger (Jesu-Maria!) And he saw a light in the window, and strange shapes moving about and shadows going to and fro within the room. And then there came a strain of music so ravishing it drew the very heart out of his body, as though all the stars were singing together. (Oh, my precious treasure! The wizard has stolen the heart out of him, alas! alas!) Then the cottage door opened and the wizard came out and with him a great company of familiar spirits. One of them had wings like a seraph and talked in an unknown tongue, and another was like a wee man, no higher than your knee, with a black face and a white beard, and he sat on the wizard's shoulder and whispered in his ear. And the heavenly music played louder and louder. And the wizard had a pale flame all about his head, like the pictures of the saints. (Blessed St. James of Compostella, be merciful to us all! And what then?) Why then he, the boy, had been very much frightened and wished he had not come, but the little dwarf spirit had seen him and jumped into the tree after him, climbing – oh! so fast! And he had tried to climb higher and had slipped and fallen to the ground. (Oh, the poor, wicked, brave, bad boy!)

Then the wizard had come and picked him up and spoken strange words to him and all the pain had gone away from the places where he had bumped himself (Marvellous! marvellous!), and he had carried him into the house. And inside, it was like the streets of Heaven, all gold and glittering. And the familiar spirits had sat beside the fire, nine in number, and the music had stopped playing. But the wizard's servant had brought him marvellous fruits in a silver dish, like fruits of Paradise, very sweet and delicious, and he had eaten them, and drunk a strange, rich drink from a goblet covered with red and blue jewels. Oh, yes – and there had been a tall crucifix on the wall, big, big, with a lamp burning before it and a strange sweet perfume like the smell in church on Easter Day.

(A crucifix? That was strange. Perhaps the magician was not so wicked after all. And what next?)

Next, the wizard's servant had told him not to be afraid, and had asked his name and his age and whether he could repeat his Paternoster. So he had said that prayer and the Ave Maria and part of the Credo, but the Credo was long and he had forgotten what came after 'ascendit in cœlum.'

So the wizard had prompted him and they had finished saying it together. And the wizard had pronounced the sacred names and words without flinching and in the right order, so far as he could tell. And then the servant had asked further about himself and his family, and he had told about the death of the black goat and about his sister's lover, who had left her because she had not so much money as the merchant's daughter. Then the wizard and his servant had spoken together and laughed, and the servant had said: 'My master gives this message to your sister: that where there is no love there is no wealth, but he that is bold shall have gold for the asking.' And with that, the wizard had put forth his hand into the air and taken from it – out of the empty air, yes, truly – one, two, three, four, five pieces of money and given them to him. And he was afraid to take them till he had made the sign of the cross upon them, and then, as they did not vanish or turn into fiery serpents, he had taken them, and here they were!

So the gold pieces were examined and admired in fear and trembling, and then, by grandfather's advice, placed under the feet of the image of Our Lady, after a sprinkling with Holy Water for their better purification. And on the next morning, as they were still there, they were shown to the priest, who arrived, tardy and flustered upon his last night's summons, and by him pronounced to be good Spanish coin, whereof one piece being devoted to the Church to put all right with Heaven, the rest might be put to secular uses without peril to the soul. After which, the good padre made his hasty way to the cottage, and returned, after an hour, filled with good reports of the wizard.

'For, my children,' said he, 'this is no evil sorcerer, but a Christian man, speaking the language of the Faith. He and I have conversed together with edification. Moreover, he keeps very good wine and is altogether a very worthy person. Nor did I perceive any familiar spirits or flaming apparitions; but it is true that there is a crucifix and also a very handsome Testament with pictures in gold and colour. *Benedicite*, my children. This is a good and learned man.'

And away he went back to his presbytery; and that winter the chapel of Our Lady had a new altar-cloth.

After that, each night saw a little group of people clustered at a safe distance to hear the music which poured out from the wizard's windows, and from time to time a few bold spirits would creep up close enough to peer through the chinks of the shutters and glimpse the marvels within.

The wizard had been in residence about a month, and sat one night after his evening meal in conversation with his servant. The black hood was pushed back from his head, disclosing a sleek poll of fair hair, and a pair of rather humorous grey eyes, with a cynical droop of the lids. A glass of Cockburn 1908 stood on the table at his elbow and from the arm of his chair a red-and-green parrot gazed unwinkingly at the fire.

'Time is getting on, Juan,' said the magician. 'This business is very good fun and all that – but is there anything doing with the old lady?'

'I think so, my lord. I have dropped a word or two here and there of marvellous cures and miracles. I think she will come. Perhaps even to-night.'

'Thank goodness! I want to get the thing over before Wetherall comes back, or we may find ourselves in Queer Street. It will take some weeks, you know, before we are ready to move, even if the scheme works at all. Damn it, what's that?'

Juan rose and went into the inner room, to return in a minute carrying the lemur.

'Micky had been playing with your hair-brushes,' he said indulgently, 'Naughty one, be quiet! Are you ready for a little practice, my lord?'

'Oh, rather, yes! I'm getting quite a dab at this job. If all else fails, I shall try for an engagement with Maskelyn.'

Juan laughed, showing his white teeth. He brought out a set of billiard-balls, coins and other conjuring apparatus, palming and multiplying them negligently as he went. The other took them from him, and the lesson proceeded.

'Hush!' said the wizard, retrieving a ball which had tiresomely slipped from his fingers in the very act of vanishing. 'There's somebody coming up the path.'

He pulled his robe about his face and slipped silently into the inner room. Juan grinned, removed the decanter and glasses, and extinguished the lamp. In the firelight the great eyes of the lemur gleamed strongly as it hung on the back of the high chair. Juan pulled a large folio from the shelf, lit a scented pastille in a curiously shaped copper vase and pulled forward a heavy iron cauldron which stood on the hearth. As he piled the logs about it, there came a knock. He opened the door, the lemur running at his heels.

'Whom do you seek, mother?' he asked, in Basque.

'Is the Wise One at home?'

'His body is at home, mother; his spirit holds converse with the unseen. Enter. What would you with us?'

'I have come, as I said – ah, Mary! Is that a spirit?'

'God made spirits and bodies also. Enter and fear not.'

The old woman came tremblingly forward.

'Hast thou spoken with him of what I told thee?'

'I have. I have shown him the sickness of thy mistress – her husband's sufferings – all.'

'What said he?'

'Nothing; he read in his book.'

'Think you he can heal her?'

'I do not know; the enchantment is a strong one; but my master is mighty for good.'

'Will he see me?'

'I will ask him. Remain here, and beware thou show no fear, whatever befall.'

'I will be courageous,' said the old woman, fingering her beads.

Juan withdrew. There was a nerve-shattering interval. The lemur had climed up to the back of the chair again and swung, teeth-chattering, among the leaping shadows. The parrot cocked his head and spoke a few gruff words from his corner. An aromatic steam began to rise from the cauldron. Then, slowly into the red light, three, four, seven white shapes came stealthily and sat down in a circle about the hearth. Then, a faint music, that seemed to roll in from leagues away. The flame flickered and dropped. There was a tall cabinet against the wall, with gold figures on it that seemed to move with the moving firelight.

Then, out of the darkness, a strange voice chanted in an unearthly tongue that sobbed and thundered.

Martha's knees gave under her. She sank down. The seven white cats rose and stretched themselves, and came sidling slowly about her. She looked up and saw the wizard standing before her, a book in one hand and a silver wand in the other. The upper part of his face was hidden, but she saw his pale lips move and presently he spoke, in a deep, husky tone that vibrated solemnly in the dim room:

'ὦ πέπον, εἰ μὲν γὰρ, πόλεμον περὶ τόνδε φυγόντε,
αἰεὶ δὴ μέλλοιμεν ἀγήρω τ' ἀθανάτω τε
ἔσσεθ', οὔτε κεν αὐτὸς ἐνὶ πρώτοισι μαχοίμην,
οὔτε κέ σε στέλλοιμι μάχην ἐς κυδιάνειραν . . .'

The great syllables went rolling on. Then the wizard paused, and added, in a kinder tone: 'Great stuff, this Homer. "It goes so thunderingly as though it conjured devils." What do I do next?'

The servant had come back, and now whispered in Martha's ear.

'Speak now,' said he. 'The master is willing to help you.'

Thus encouraged, Martha stammered out her request. She had come to ask the Wise Man to help her mistress, who lay under an enchantment. She had brought an offering – the best she could find, for she had not liked to take anything of her master's during his absence. But here were a silver penny, an oat-cake, and a bottle of wine, very much at the wizard's service, if such small matters could please him.

The wizard, setting aside his book, gravely accepted the silver penny, turned it magically into six gold pieces and laid the offering on the table. Over the oat-cake and the wine he showed a little hesitation, but at length, murmuring:

'*Ergo omnis longo solvit se Teucria luctu*'

(a line notorious for its grave spondaic cadence), he meta-morphosed the one into a pair of pigeons and the other into a curious little crystal tree in a metal pot, and set them beside the coins. Martha's eyes nearly started from her head, but Juan whispered encouragingly:

'The good intention gives value to the gift. The master is pleased. Hush!'

The music ceased on a loud chord. The wizard, speaking now with greater assurance, delivered himself with fair accuracy of a page or so from Homer's Catalogue of the Ships, and, drawing from the folds of his robe his long white hand laden with antique rings, produced from mid-air a small casket of shining metal, which he proffered to the suppliant.

'The master says,' prompted the servant, 'that you shall take this casket, and give to your lady of the wafers which it contains, one at every meal. When all have been consumed, seek this place again. And remember to say three Aves and two Paters morning and evening for the intention of the lady's health. Thus, by faith and diligence, the cure may be accomplished.'

Martha received the casket with trembling hands.

'*Tendebantque manus ripæ ulterioris amore*,' said the

wizard, with emphasis. 'Poluphloisboio thalasses. Ne plus ultra. Valete. Plaudite.'

He stalked away into the darkness, and the audience was over.

'It is working, then?' said the wizard to Juan.

The time was five weeks later, and five more consignments of enchanted wafers had been ceremoniously dispatched to the grim house on the mountain.

'It is working,' agreed Juan. 'The intelligence is returning, the body is becoming livelier and the hair is growing again.'

'Thank the Lord! It was a shot in the dark, Juan, and even now I can hardly believe that anyone in the world could think of such a devilish trick. When does Wetherall return?'

'In three weeks' time.'

'Then we had better fix our grand finale for to-day fortnight. See that the mules are ready, and go down to the town and get a message off to the yacht.'

'Yes, my lord.'

'That will give you a week to get clear with the menagerie and the baggage. And – I say, how about Martha? Is it dangerous to leave her behind, do you think?'

'I will try to persuade her to come back with us.'

'Do. I should hate anything unpleasant to happen to her. The man's a criminal lunatic. Oh, lord! I'll be glad when this is over. I want to get into a proper suit of clothes again. What Bunter would say if he saw this – '

The wizard laughed, lit a cigar and turned on the gramophone.

The last act was duly staged a fortnight later.

It had taken some trouble to persuade Martha of the necessity of bringing her mistress to the wizard's house. Indeed, that supernatural personage had been obliged to make an alarming display of wrath and declaim two whole choruses from Euripides before gaining his point. The final touch was put to the terrors of the evening by a demonstration of the ghastly effects of a sodium flame – which lends a very corpse-like aspect to the human countenance, particularly in a lonely cottage on a dark night, and accompanied by incantations and the 'Danse Macabre' of Saint-Saens.

Eventually the wizard was placated by a promise, and Martha departed, bearing with her a charm, engrossed upon parchment, which her mistress was to read and there-after hang about her neck in a white silk bag.

Considered as a magical formula, the document was perhaps a little unimpressive in its language, but its meaning was such as a child could understand. It was in English, and ran:

> '*You have been ill and in trouble, but your friends are ready to cure you and help you. Don't be afraid, but do whatever Martha tells you, and you will soon be quite well and happy again.*'

'And even if she can't understand it,' said the wizard to his man, 'it can't possibly do any harm.'

The events of that terrible night have become legend in the village. They tell by the fireside with bated breath how Martha brought the strange, foreign lady to the wizard's house, that she might be finally and for ever freed from the power of the Evil One. It was a dark night and a stormy one, with the wind howling terribly through the mountains.

The lady had become much better and brighter through the wizard's magic – though this, perhaps, was only a fresh glamour and delusion – and she had followed Martha like a little child on that strange and secret journey. They had crept out very quietly to elude the vigilance of old Tomaso, who had strict orders from the doctor never to let the lady stir one step from the house. As for that, Tomaso swore that he had been cast into an enchanted sleep – but who knows? There may have been no more to it than over-much wine. Martha was a cunning woman, and, some said, little better than a witch herself.

Be that as it might, Martha and the lady had come to the cottage, and there the wizard had spoken many things in a strange tongue, and the lady had spoken likewise. Yes – she who for so long had only grunted like a beast, had talked with the wizard and answered him. Then the wizard had drawn strange signs upon the floor round about the lady and himself. And when the lamp was extinguished, the signs glowed awfully, with a pale light of their own. The wizard also drew a circle about Martha herself, and warned her to keep inside it. Presently they heard a rushing noise, like great wings beating, and all the familiars leaped about, and the little white man with the black face ran up the curtain and swung from the pole. Then a voice cried out: 'He comes! He comes!' and the wizard opened the door of the tall cabinet with gold images upon it, that stood in the centre of the circle, and he and the lady stepped inside it and shut the doors after them.

The rushing sound grew louder and the familiar spirits screamed and chattered – and then, all of a sudden, there was a thunder-clap and a great flash of light and the cabinet was shivered into pieces and fell down. And low and behold! the wizard and the lady had vanished clean away and were never more seen or heard of.

This was Martha's story, told the next day to her neighbours. How she had escaped from the terrible house she could not remember. But when, some time after, a group of villagers summoned up courage to visit the place again, they found it bare and empty. Lady, wizard, servant, familiars, furniture, bags and baggage – all were gone, leaving not a trace behind them, except a few mysterious lines and figures traced on the floor of the cottage.

This was a wonder indeed. More awful still was the

disappearance of Martha herself, which took place three nights afterwards.

Next day, the American doctor returned, to find an empty hearth and a legend.

'Yacht ahoy!'

Langley peered anxiously over the rail of the *Abracadabra* as the boat loomed out of the blackness. When the first passenger came aboard, he ran hastily to greet him.

'Is it all right, Wimsey?'

'Absolutely all right. She's a bit bewildered, of course – but you needn't be afraid. She's like a child, but she's getting better every day. Bear up, old man – there's nothing to shock you about her.'

Langley moved hesitatingly forward as a muffled female figure was hoisted gently on board.

'Speak to her,' said Wimsey. 'She may or may not recognise you. I can't say.'

Langley summoned up his courage. 'Good evening, Mrs Wetherall,' he said, and held out his hand.

The woman pushed the cloak from her face. Her blue eyes gazed shyly at him in the lamplight – then a smile broke out upon her lips.

'Why, I know you – of course I know you. You're Mr Langley. I'm so glad to see you.'

She clasped his hand in hers.

'Well, Langley,' said Lord Peter, as he manipulated the syphon, 'a more abominable crime it has never been my fortune to discover. My religious beliefs are a little ill-defined, but I hope something really beastly happens to Wetherall in the next world. Say when!

'You know, there were one or two very queer points about that story you told me. They gave me a line on the thing from the start.

'To begin with, there was this extraordinary kind of decay or imbecility settlin' in on a girl in her twenties –

—26—

so conveniently, too, just after you'd been hangin' round the Wetherall home and showin' perhaps a trifle too much sensibility, don't you see? And then there was this tale of the conditions clearin' up regularly once a year or so – not like any ordinary brain-trouble. Looked as if it was being controlled by somebody.

'Then there was the fact that Mrs Wetherall had been under her husband's medical eye from the beginning, with no family or friends who knew anything about her to keep a check on the fellow. Then there was the determined isolation of her in a place where no doctor could see her and where, even if she had a lucid interval, there wasn't a soul who could understand or be understood by her. Queer, too, that it should be a part of the world where you, with your interests, might reasonably be expected to turn up some day and be treated to a sight of what she had turned into. Then there were Wetherall's well-known researches, and the fact that he kept in touch with a chemist in London.

'All that gave me a theory, but I had to test it before I could be sure I was right. Wetherall was going to America, and that gave me a chance; but of course he left strict orders that nobody should get into or out of his house during his absence. I had, somehow, to establish an authority greater than his over old Martha, who is a faithful soul, God bless her! Hence, exit Lord Peter Wimsey and enter the magician. The treatment was tried and proved successful – hence the elopement and the rescue.

'Well, now, listen – and don't go off the deep end. It's all over now. Alice Wetherall is one of those unfortunate people who suffer from congenital thyroid deficiency. You know the thyroid gland in your throat – the one that stokes the engine and keeps the old brain going. In some people the thing doesn't work properly, and they turn out cretinous imbeciles. Their bodies don't grow and their minds don't work. But feed 'em the stuff, and they come absolutely all right – cheery and handsome and intelligent and lively as crickets. Only, don't you see, you have to *keep* feeding it to 'em, otherwise they just go back to an imbecile condition.

'Wetherall found this girl when he was a bright young student just learning about the thyroid. Twenty years ago, very few experiments had been made in this kind of treatment, but he was a bit of a pioneer. He gets hold of the kid, works a miraculous cure, and bein' naturally bucked with himself, adopts her, gets her educated, likes the look of her, and finally marries her. You understand, don't you, that there's nothing fundamentally unsound about those thyroid deficients. Keep 'em going on the little daily dose, and they're normal in every way, fit to live an ordinary life and have ordinary healthy children.

'Nobody, naturally, knew anything about this thyroid business except the girl herself and her husband. All goes well till *you* come along. Then Wetherall gets jealous – '

'He had no cause.'

Wimsey shrugged his shoulders.

'Possibly, my lad, the lady displayed a preference – we needn't go into that. Anyhow, Wetherall did get jealous and saw a perfectly marvellous revenge in his power. He carried his wife off to the Pyrenees, isolated her from all help, and then simply sat back and starved her of her thyroid extract. No doubt he told her what he was going to do, and why. It would please him to hear her desperate appeals – to let her feel herself slipping back day by day, hour by hour, into something less than a beast – '

'Oh, God!'

'As you say. Of course, after a time, a few months, she would cease to know what was happening to her. He would still have the satisfaction of watching her – seeing her skin thicken, her body coarsen, her hair fall out, her eyes grow vacant, her speech die away into mere animal noises, her brain go to mush, her habits – '

'Stop it, Wimsey.'

'Well, you saw it all yourself. But that wouldn't be

enough for him. So, every so often, he would feed her the thyroid again and bring her back sufficiently to realise her own degradation – '

'If only I had the brute here!'

'Just as well you haven't. Well then, one day – by a stroke of luck – Mr. Langley, the amorous Mr. Langley, actually turns up. What a triumph to let him see – '

Langley stopped him again.

'Right-ho! but it was ingenious, wasn't it? So simple. The more I think of it, the more it fascinates me. But it was just that extra refinement of cruelty that defeated him. Because, when you told me the story, I couldn't help recognising the symptoms of thyroid deficiency, and I thought, 'Just supposing' – so I hunted up the chemist whose name you saw on the parcel, and, after unwinding a lot of red tape, got him to admit that he had several times sent Wetherall consignments of thyroid extract. So then I was almost sure, don't you see.

'I got a doctor's advice and a supply of gland extract, hired a tame Spanish conjurer and some performing cats and things, and barged off complete with disguise and a trick cabinet devised by the ingenious Mr. Devant. I'm a bit of a conjurer myself, and between us we didn't do so badly. The local superstitions helped, of course, and so did the gramophone records. Schubert's 'Unfinished' is first class for producing an atmosphere of gloom and mystery, so are luminous paint and the remnants of a classical education.'

'Look here, Wimsey, will she get all right again?'

'Right as ninepence, and I imagine that any American court would give her a divorce on the grounds of persistent cruelty. After that – it's up to you!'

Lord Peter's friends greeted his reappearance in London with mild surprise.

'And what have *you* been doing with yourself?' demanded the Hon. Freddy Arbuthnot.

'Eloping with another man's wife,' replied his lordship. 'But only,' he hastened to add, 'in a purely Pickwickian sense. Nothing in it for yours truly. Oh, well! Let's toddle round to the Holborn Empire, and see what George Robey can do for us.'

TAPE-MEASURE MURDER

Miss Politt took hold of the knocker and rapped politely on the cottage door. After a discreet interval she knocked again. The parcel under her left arm shifted a little as she did so, and she readjusted it. Inside the parcel was Mrs Spenlow's new green winter dress, ready for fitting. From Miss Politt's left hand dangled a bag of black silk, containing a tape measure, a pincushion, and a large, practical pair of scissors.

Miss Politt was tall and gaunt, with a sharp nose, pursed lips, and meagre iron-grey hair. She hesitated before using the knocker for the third time. Glancing down the street, she saw a figure rapidly approaching. Miss Hartnell, jolly, weather-beaten, fifty-five, shouted out in her usual loud bass voice, 'Good afternoon, Miss Politt!'

The dressmaker answered, 'Good afternoon, Miss Hartnell.' Her voice was excessively thin and genteel in its accents. She had started life as a lady's maid. 'Excuse me,' she went on, 'but do you happen to know if by any chance Mrs Spenlow isn't at home?'

'Not the least idea,' said Miss Hartnell.

'It's rather awkward, you see. I was to fit on Mrs Spenlow's new dress this afternoon. Three-thirty, she said.'

Miss Hartnell consulted her wrist watch. 'It's a little past the half-hour now.'

'Yes, I have knocked three times, but there doesn't seem to be any answer, so I was wondering if perhaps Mrs Spenlow might have gone out and forgotten. She doesn't forget appointments as a rule, and she wants the dress to wear the day after tomorrow.'

Miss Hartnell entered the gate and walked up the path to join Miss Politt outside the door of Laburnam Cottage.

'Why doesn't Gladys answer the door?' she demanded. 'Oh, no, of course, it's Thursday – Gladys's day out. I expect Mrs Spenlow has fallen asleep. I don't expect you've made enough noise with this thing.'

Seizing the knocker, she executed a deafening *rat-a-tat-tat*, and in addition thumped upon the panels of the door. She also called out in a stentorian voice, 'What ho, within there!'

There was no response.

Miss Politt murmured, 'Oh, I think Mrs Spenlow must have forgotten and gone out. I'll call round some other time.' She began edging away down the path.

'Nonsense,' said Miss Hartnell firmly. 'She can't have gone out. I'd have met her. I'll just take a look through the windows and see if I can find any signs of life.'

She laughed in her usual hearty manner, to indicate that it was a joke, and applied a perfunctory glance to the nearest window-pane – perfunctory because she knew quite well that the front room was seldom used, Mr and Mrs Spenlow preferring the small back sitting-room.

Perfunctory as it was, though, it succeeded in its object. Miss Hartnell, it is true, saw no signs of life. On the contrary, she saw, through the window, Mrs Spenlow lying on the hearthrug – dead.

'Of course,' said Miss Hartnell, telling the story afterwards, 'I managed to keep my head. That Politt creature wouldn't have had the least idea of what to do. "Got to keep our heads," I said to her. "*You* stay here, and I'll go for Constable Palk." She said something about not wanting to be left, but I paid no attention at all. One has to be firm with that sort of person. I've always found they enjoy making a fuss. So I was just going off when, at that very moment, Mr Spenlow came round the corner of the house.'

Here Miss Hartnell made a significant pause. It enabled

her audience to ask breathlessly, 'Tell me, how did he *look*?'

Miss Hartnell would then go on, 'Frankly, *I* suspected something at once! He was *far* too calm. He didn't seem surprised in the least. And you may say what you like, it isn't natural for a man to hear that his wife is dead and display no emotion whatever.'

Everybody agreed with this statement.

The police agreed with it, too. So suspicious did they consider Mr Spenlow's detachment, that they lost no time in ascertaining how that gentleman was situated as a result of his wife's death. When they discovered that Mrs Spenlow had been the monied partner, and that her money went to her husband under a will made soon after their marriage, they were more suspicious than ever.

Miss Marple, that sweet-faced – and, some said, vinegar-tongued – elderly spinster who lived in the house next to the rectory, was interviewed very early – within half an hour of the discovery of the crime. She was approached by Police Constable Palk, importantly thumbing a note-book. 'If you don't mind, ma'am, I've a few questions to ask you.'

Miss Marple said, 'In connection with the murder of Mrs Spenlow?'

Palk was startled. 'May I ask, madam, how you got to know of it?'

'The fish,' said Miss Marple.

The reply was perfectly intelligible to Constable Palk. He assumed correctly that the fishmonger's boy had brought it, together with Miss Marple's evening meal.

Miss Marple continued gently. 'Lying on the floor in the sitting-room, strangled – possibly by a very narrow belt. But whatever it was, it was taken away.'

Palk's face was wrathful. 'How that young Fred gets to know everything – '

Miss Marple cut him short adroitly. She said, 'There's a pin in your tunic.'

Constable Palk looked down, startled. He said, 'They do say, "See a pin and pick it up, all the day you'll have good luck." '

'I hope that will come true. Now what is it you want me to tell you?'

Constable Palk cleared his throat, looked important, and consulted his notebook. 'Statement was made to me by Mr Arthur Spenlow, husband of the deceased. Mr Spenlow says that at two-thirty, as far as he can say, he was rung up by Miss Marple, and asked if he would come over at a quarter past three as she was anxious to consult him about something. Now, ma'am, is that true?'

'Certainly not,' said Miss Marple.

'You did not ring up Mr Spenlow at two-thirty?'

'Neither at two-thirty nor any other time.'

'Ah,' said Constable Palk, and sucked his moustache with a good deal of satisfaction.

'What else did Mr Spenlow say?'

'Mr Spenlow's statement was that he came over here as requested, leaving his own house at ten minutes past three; that on arrival here he was informed by the maid-servant that Miss Marple was "not at 'ome".'

'That part of it is true,' said Miss Marple. 'He did come here, but I was at a meeting at the Women's Institute.'

'Ah,' said Constable Palk again.

Miss Marple exclaimed, 'Do tell me, Constable, do you suspect Mr Spenlow?'

'It's not for me to say at this stage, but it looks to me as though somebody, naming no names, had been trying to be artful.'

Miss Marple said thoughtfully, 'Mr Spenlow?'

She liked Mr Spenlow. He was a small, spare man, stiff and conventional in speech, the acme of respectability. It seemed odd that he should have come to live in the country, he had so clearly lived in towns all his life. To Miss Marple he confided the reason. He said, 'I have always intended, ever since I was a small boy, to live in the country some day and have a garden of my own. I have always been very much attached to flowers. My wife, you know, kept a flower shop. That's where I saw her first.'

A dry statement, but it opened up a vista of romance. A younger, prettier Mrs Spenlow, seen against a background of flowers.

Mr Spenlow, however, really knew nothing about flowers. He had no idea of seeds, of cuttings, of bedding out, of annuals or perennials. He had only a vision – a vision of a small cottage garden thickly planted with sweet-smelling, brightly coloured blossoms. He had asked, almost pathetically, for instruction, and had noted down Miss Marple's replies to questions in a little book.

He was a man of quiet method. It was, perhaps, because of this trait, that the police were interested in him when his wife was found murdered. With patience and perseverance they learned a good deal about the late Mrs Spenlow – and soon all St Mary Mead knew it, too.

The late Mrs Spenlow had begun life as a between-maid in a large house. She had left that position to marry the second gardener, and with him had started a flower shop in London. The shop had prospered. Not so the gardener, who before long had sickened and died.

His widow carried on the shop and enlarged it in an ambitious way. She had continued to prosper. Then she had sold the business at a handsome price and embarked upon matrimony for the second time – with Mr Spenlow, a middle-aged jeweller who had inherited a small and struggling business. Not long afterwards, they had sold the business and come down to St Mary Mead.

Mrs Spenlow was a well-to-do woman. The profits from her florist's establishment she had invested – 'under spirit guidance', as she explained to all and sundry. The spirits had advised her with unexpected acumen.

All her investments had prospered, some in quite a sensational fashion. Instead, however, of this increasing her belief in spiritualism, Mrs Spenlow basely deserted mediums and sittings, and made a brief but wholehearted plunge into an obscure religion with Indian affinities which was based on various forms of deep breathing. When, however, she arrived at St Mary Mead, she had relapsed into a period of orthodox Church-of-England beliefs. She was a good deal at the vicarage, and attended church services with assiduity. She patronized the village shops, took an interest in the local happenings, and played village bridge.

A humdrum, everyday life. And – suddenly – murder.

Colonel Melchett, the chief constable, had summoned Inspector Slack.

Slack was a positive type of man. When he had made up his mind, he was sure. He was quite sure now. 'Husband did it, sir,' he said.

'You think so?'

'Quite sure of it. You've only got to look at him. Guilty as hell. Never showed a sign of grief or emotion. He came back to the house knowing she was dead.'

'Wouldn't he at least have tried to act the part of the distracted husband?'

'Not him, sir. Too pleased with himself. Some gentlemen can't act. Too stiff.'

'Any other woman in his life?' Colonel Melchett asked.

'Haven't been able to find any trace of one. Of course, he's the artful kind. He'd cover his tracks. As I see it, he was just fed up with his wife. She'd got the money, and I should say was a trying woman to live with – always taking up with some "ism" or other. He cold-bloodedly decided to do away with her and live comfortably on his own.'

'Yes, that could be the case, I suppose.'

'Depend upon it, that was it. Made his plans careful. Pretended to get a phone call – '

Melchett interrupted him. 'No call been traced?'

'No, sir. That means either that he lied, or that the call was put through from a public telephone booth. The only two public phones in the village are at the station and the post office. Post office it certainly wasn't. Mrs Blade sees everyone who comes in. Station it might be. Train arrives at two twenty-seven and there's a bit of a bustle then. But the main thing is *he* says it was Miss Marple who called him up, and that certainly isn't true. The call didn't come from her house, and she herself was away at the Institute.'

'You're not overlooking the possibility that the husband was deliberately got out of the way – by someone who wanted to murder Mrs Spenlow?'

'You're thinking of young Ted Gerard, aren't you, sir? I've been working on him – what we're up against there is lack of motive. He doesn't stand to gain anything.'

'He's an undesirable character, though. Quite a pretty little spot of embezzlement to his credit.'

'I'm not saying he isn't a wrong 'un. Still, he did go to his boss and own up to that embezzlement. And his employers weren't wise to it.'

'An Oxford Grouper,' said Melchett.

'Yes, sir. Became a convert and went off to do the straight thing and own up to having pinched money. I'm not saying, mind you, that it mayn't have been astuteness. He may have thought he was suspected and decided to gamble on honest repentance.'

'You have a sceptical mind, Slack,' said Colonel Melchett. 'By the way, have you talked to Miss Marple at all?'

'What's *she* got to do with it, sir?'

'Oh, nothing. But she hears things, you know. Why don't you go and have a chat with her? She's a very sharp old lady.'

Slack changed the subject. 'One thing I've been meaning to ask you, sir. That domestic-service job where the deceased started her career – Sir Robert Abercrombie's place. That's where that jewel robbery was – emeralds –

worth a packet. Never got them. I've been looking it up – must have happened when the Spenlow woman was there, though she'd have been quite a girl at the time. Don't think she was mixed up in it, do you, sir? Spenlow, you know, was one of those little tuppenny-ha'penny jewellers – just the chap for a fence.'

Melchett shook his head. 'Don't think there's anything in that. She didn't even know Spenlow at the time. I remember the case. Opinion in police circles was that a son of the house was mixed up in it – Jim Abercrombie – awful young waster. Had a pile of debts, and just after the robbery they were all paid off – some rich woman, so they said, but I don't know – Old Abercrombie hedged a bit about the case – tried to call the police off.'

'It was just an idea, sir,' said Slack.

Miss Marple received Inspector Slack with gratification, especially when she heard that he had been sent by Colonel Melchett.

'Now, really, that is very kind of Colonel Melchett. I didn't know he remembered me.'

'He remembers you, all right. Told me that what you didn't know of what goes on in St Mary Mead isn't worth knowing.'

'Too kind of him, but really I don't know anything at all. About this murder, I mean.'

'You know what the talk about it is.'

'Oh, of course – but it wouldn't do, would it, to repeat just idle talk?'

Slack said, with an attempt at geniality, 'This isn't an official conversation, you know. It's in confidence, so to speak.'

'You mean you really want to know what people are saying? Whether there's any truth in it or not?'

'That's the idea.'

'Well, of course, there's been a great deal of talk and speculation. And there are really two distinct camps, if you understand me. To begin with, there are the people who think that the husband did it. A husband or a wife is, in a way, the natural person to suspect, don't you think so?'

'Maybe,' said the inspector cautiously.

'Such close quarters, you know. Then, so often, the money angle. I hear that it was Mrs Spenlow who had the money, and therefore Mr Spenlow does benefit by her death. In this wicked world I'm afraid the most uncharitable assumptions are often justified.'

'He comes into a tidy sum, all right.'

'Just so. It would seem quite plausible, wouldn't it, for him to strangle her, leave the house by the back, come across the fields to my house, ask for me and pretend he'd had a telephone call from me, then go back and find his wife murdered in his absence – hoping, of course, that the crime would be put down to some tramp or burglar.'

The inspector nodded. 'What with the money angle – and if they'd been on bad terms lately – '

But Miss Marple interrupted him. 'Oh, but they hadn't.'

'You know that for a fact?'

'Everyone would have known if they'd quarrelled! The maid, Gladys Brent – she'd have soon spread it round the village.'

The inspector said feebly, 'She mightn't have known – ' and received a pitying smile in reply.

Miss Marple went on. 'And then there's the other school of thought. Ted Gerard. A good-looking young man. I'm afraid, you know, that good looks are inclined to influence one more than they should. Our last curate but one – quite a magical effect! All the girls came to church – evening service as well as morning. And many older women became unusually active in parish work – and the slippers and scarfs that were made for him! Quite embarrassing for the poor young man.

'But let me see, where was I? Oh, yes, this young man, Ted Gerard. Of course, there has been talk about him.

He's come down to see her so often. Though Mrs Spenlow told me herself that he was a member of what I think they call the Oxford Group. A religious movement. They are quite sincere and very earnest, I believe, and Mrs Spenlow was impressed by it all.'

Miss Marple took a breath and went on. 'And I'm sure there was no reason to believe that there was anything more in it than that, but you know what people are. Quite a lot of people are convinced that Mrs Spenlow was infatuated with the young man, and that she'd lent him quite a lot of money. And it's perfectly true that he was actually seen at the station that day. In the train – the two twenty-seven down train. But of course it would be quite easy, wouldn't it, to slip out of the other side of the train and go through the cutting and over the fence and round by the hedge and never come out of the station entrance at all. So that he need not have been seen going to the cottage. And, of course, people do think that what Mrs Spenlow was wearing was rather peculiar.'

'Peculiar?'

'A kimono. Not a dress.' Miss Marple blushed. 'That sort of thing, you know, is, perhaps, rather suggestive to some people.'

'You think it was suggestive?'

'Oh, no, *I* don't think so. I think it was perfectly natural.'

'You think it was natural?'

'Under the circumstances, yes.' Miss Marple's glance was cool and reflective.

Inspector Slack said, 'It might give us another motive for the husband. Jealousy.'

'Oh, no, Mr Spenlow would never be jealous. He's not the sort of man who notices things. If his wife had gone away and left a note on the pincushion, it would be the first he'd know of anything of that kind.'

Inspector Slack was puzzled by the intent way she was looking at him. He had an idea that all her conversation

was intended to hint at something he didn't understand.
She said now, with some emphasis, 'Didn't *you* find any
clues, Inspector – on the spot?'

'People don't leave fingerprints and cigarette ash
nowadays, Miss Marple.'

'But this, I think,' she suggested, 'was an old-fashioned
crime – '

Slack said sharply, 'Now what do you mean by that?'

Miss Marple remarked slowly, 'I think, you know, that
Constable Palk could help you. He was the first person
on the – on the "scene of the crime", as they say.'

Mr Spenlow was sitting in a deck chair. He looked bewildered. He said, in his thin, precise voice, 'I may, of course,
be imagining what occurred. My hearing is not as good as
it was. But I distinctly think I heard a small boy call
after me, "Yah, who's a Crippen?" It – it conveyed the
impression to me that he was of the opinion that I had –
had killed my dear wife.'

Miss Marple, gently snipping off a dead rose head, said,
'That was the impression he meant to convey, no doubt.'

'But what could possibly have put such an idea into a
child's head?'

Miss Marple coughed. 'Listening, no doubt, to the
opinions of his elders.'

'You – you really mean that other people think that,
also?'

'Quite half the people in St Mary Mead.'

'But – my dear lady – what can possibly have given rise
to such an idea? I was sincerely attached to my wife. She
did not, alas, take to living in the country as much as I
had hoped she would do, but perfect agreement on every
subject is an impossible idea. I assure you I feel her loss
very keenly.'

'Probably. But if you will excuse my saying so, you
don't sound as though you do.'

Mr Spenlow drew his meagre frame up to its full height.

'My dear lady, many years ago I read of a certain Chinese philosopher who, when his dearly loved wife was taken from him, continued calmly to beat a gong in the street – a customary Chinese pastime, I presume – exactly as usual. The people of the city were much impressed by his fortitude.'

'But,' said Miss Marple, 'the people of St Mary Mead react rather differently. Chinese philosophy does not appeal to them.'

'But you understand?'

Miss Marple nodded. 'My Uncle Henry,' she explained, 'was a man of unusual self-control. His motto was "Never display emotion". He, too, was very fond of flowers.'

'I was thinking,' said Mr Spenlow with something like eagerness, 'that I might, perhaps, have a pergola on the west side of the cottage. Pink roses and, perhaps, wisteria. And there is a white starry flower, whose name for the moment escapes me – '

In the tone in which she spoke to her grandnephew, aged three, Miss Marple said, 'I have a very nice catalogue here, with pictures. Perhaps you would like to look through it – I have to go up to the village.'

Leaving Mr Spenlow sitting happily in the garden with his catalogue, Miss Marple went up to her room, hastily rolled up a dress in a piece of brown paper, and, leaving the house, walked briskly up to the post office. Miss Politt, the dressmaker, lived in rooms over the post office.

But Miss Marple did not at once go through the door and up the stairs. It was just two-thirty, and, a minute late, the Much Benham bus drew up outside the post office door. It was one of the events of the day in St Mary Mead. The postmistress hurried out with parcels, parcels connected with the shop side of her business, for the post office also dealt in sweets, cheap books, and children's toys.

For some four minutes Miss Marple was alone in the post office.

Not till the postmistress returned to her post did Miss Marple go upstairs and explain to Miss Politt that she wanted her old grey crêpe altered and made more fashionable if that were possible. Miss Politt promised to see what she could do.

The chief constable was rather astonished when Miss Marple's name was brought to him. She came in with many apologies. 'So sorry – so very sorry to disturb you. You are so busy, I know, but then you have always been so very kind, Colonel Melchett, and I felt I would rather come to you instead of to Inspector Slack. For one thing, you know, I should hate Constable Palk to get into any trouble. Strictly speaking, I suppose he shouldn't have touched anything at all.'

Colonel Melchett was slightly bewildered. He said, 'Palk? That's the St Mary Mead constable, isn't it? What has he been doing?'

'He picked up a pin, you know. It was in his tunic. And it occurred to me at the time that it was quite probable he had actually picked it up in Mrs Spenlow's house.'

'Quite, quite. But after all, you know, what's a pin? Matter of fact he did pick the pin up just by Mrs Spenlow's body. Came and told Slack about it yesterday – you put him up to that, I gather? Oughtn't to have touched anything, of course, but as I said, what's a pin? It was only a common pin. Sort of thing any woman might use.'

'Oh, no, Colonel Melchett, that's where you're wrong. To a man's eye, perhaps, it looked like an ordinary pin, but it wasn't. It was a special pin, a very thin pin, the kind you buy by the box, the kind used mostly by dressmakers.'

Melchett stared at her, a faint light of comprehension breaking in on him. Miss Marple nodded her head several times, eagerly.

'Yes, of course. It seems to me so obvious. She was in her kimono because she was going to try on her new dress, and she went into the front room, and Miss Politt just said something about measurements and put the tape measure round her neck – and then all she'd have to do was to cross it and pull – quite easy, so I've heard. And then, of course, she'd go outside and pull the door to and stand there knocking as though she'd just arrived. But the pin shows she'd *already been in the house.*'

'And it was Miss Politt who telephoned to Spenlow?'

'Yes. From the post office at two-thirty – just when the bus comes and the post office would be empty.'

Colonel Melchett said, 'But my dear Miss Marple, why? In heaven's name, why? You can't have a murder without a motive.'

'Well, I think, you know, Colonel Melchett, from all I've heard, that the crime dates from a long time back. It reminds me, you know of my two cousins, Antony and Gordon. Whatever Antony did always went right for him, and with poor Gordon it was just the other way about. Race horses went lame, and stocks went down, and property depreciated. As I see it, the two women were in it together.'

'In what?'

'The robbery. Long ago. Very valuable emeralds, so I've heard. The lady's maid and the tweeny. Because one thing hasn't been explained – how, when the tweeny married the gardener, did they have enough money to set up a flower shop?

'The answer is, it was her share of the – the swag, I think is the right expression. Everything she did turned out well. Money made money. But the other one, the lady's maid, must have been unlucky. She came down to being just a village dressmaker. Then they met again. Quite all right at first, I expect, until Mr Ted Gerard came on the scene.

'Mrs Spenlow, you see, was already suffering from conscience, and was inclined to be emotionally religious. This young man no doubt urged her to "face up" and to "come clean" and I dare say she was strung up to do it.

But Miss Politt didn't see it that way. All she saw was that she might go to prison for a robbery she had committed years ago. So she made up her mind to put a stop to it all. I'm afraid, you know, that she was always rather a wicked woman. I don't believe she'd have turned a hair if that nice, stupid Mr Spenlow had been hanged.'

Colonel Melchett said slowly, 'We can – er – verify your theory – up to a point. The identity of the Politt woman with the lady's maid at the Abercrombies', but – '

Miss Marple reassured him. 'It will be all quite easy. She's the kind of woman who will break down at once when she's taxed with the truth. And then, you see, I've got her tape measure. I – er – abstracted it yesterday when I was trying on. When she misses it and thinks the police have got it – well, she's quite an ignorant woman and she'll think it will prove the case against her in some way.'

She smiled at him encouragingly. 'You'll have no trouble, I can assure you.' It was the tone in which his favourite aunt had once assured him that he could not fail to pass his entrance examination into Sandhurst.

And he had passed.

THE BLACK TENT

Lord Currier's maternal uncle John was in the Cabinet and, as he was not slow to tell anyone who could be persuaded to listen, his finger was on the pulse of the world. This remarkable facility clearly did not absorb all his time or energy for, whenever he had the chance, the distinguished old gentleman was eager to quit the Olympian heights to interfere in the affairs of his more important relatives.

At eleven o'clock one evening in the library of his future mother-in-law's house in Clarges Street Lord Currier, Tommy to his closer acquaintances, was confiding his relief to his friend Albert Campion. The two were snatching a few moments respite and whisky-and-sodas whilst on the floor below them, in the rose-decorated ballroom, a ball was in progress in honour of his fiancée, the incomparable Roberta. The music of the Red Hot Cobblers came up to them. Lord Currier set down his glass and blinked at Campion.

'It was a damned near go,' he said solemnly. 'The old man's a bachelor of the worst type. I had to tell him I was in love, not buying a horse. You see, it wasn't only her grandfather who got under his skin, he's been reading the Sunday papers and got all sorts of wild ideas about women into his head – flighty, dangerous, serpents in disguise, you know the sort of thing. Of course, when I persuaded him to meet Roberta he came to his senses but it was a near thing.'

Mr Campion settled his lean form on the arm of a gigantic leather chair and adjusted his horn-rimmed spectacles.

'Uncle John is something of a power, I take it?' he murmured.

Tommy Currier's mild brown eyes opened to their widest.

'Good Lord, yes,' he said, in some surprise that the matter should have been questioned. 'Uncle John is the final and ultimate word. Uncle John pulls the strings. If I'm to have the career in the Diplomatic which my old man has set his heart on, what Uncle John says goes every time.'

'I see. And now, fortunately, Roberta goes?'

The younger man sighed ecstatically.

'She does, bless her,' he said. 'I must cut along back to the dance or she'll be looking for me. They've got a fortune-teller chap down there. She wants me to consult him and I'm in that state when I'll do anything, anything she asks. Don't you hurry. Finish your drink and come up when you feel like it.'

He trotted out of the room, his wide sleek shoulders betraying all the excitement which he kept so successfully out of his round affable face. He was so completely, not to say dementedly happy that he made his companion feel a trifle elderly.

Left to himself, Mr Campion set down his glass and reflected that Uncle John was an anachronism in an age when a grandfather who had made a fortune out of frozen meat should rightly be nothing but a valuable asset to any pretty young woman.

The music from the ballroom was not inviting and the library was cool and pleasant. True, the books in the glass-fronted cabinets did not look as though they had ever been read, and the great desk in the centre of the carpet was obviously never used, but the light was gently diffused and the atmosphere peaceful. Campion was weary. In the company of his friend, Superintendent Stanislaus Oates of the Central Criminal Branch, he had spent the best part of three nights that week in a grey office in Scotland Yard going over the documents in a particularly exasperating insurance fraud. For three days he had been out of his bed for twenty hours in every twenty-four so that now the quiet depths of the green armchair were irresistibly inviting. He slid into it gratefully. The chair enveloped and concealed him and he lay still.

A little over half an hour later he awoke quietly with every sense alert. He opened his eyes cautiously and, in the angle of the chair-arm, he glimpsed the heel of a green satin slipper on the carpet. Its owner was fighting with the bottom drawer of the bureau in the corner behind him and was doing her unsuccessful best to be as quiet about the business as was possible.

Long practice had taught Mr Campion to move soundlessly. Now he pulled himself up slowly and peered over the arm of the chair.

The girl kneeling before the bureau was forcing the catch of the bottom drawer back with a long brass paperknife. She was young, that was the first thing he noticed about her, but then he saw that her red hair hung loosely round a small and shapely head, and immediately he noticed that her green dress floated gracefully about a slender, childish figure. He watched her with polite interest and then he saw her slide the drawer open an inch or so, slip in a small hand and draw out what appeared to be a flat package. This she wrapped guiltily in a big georgette handkerchief.

Deeming that the moment had come, Mr Campion coughed apologetically.

The girl in the green dress stiffened and there was a moment of painful silence, then she turned and rose quietly to her feet. Campion found himself looking into a small, intelligent face which in a year or so would blossom inevitably into beauty. He judged her to be at the most fifteen years old. Her face was now very red and her grey-green eyes were angry and alarmed, but she was not without courage and her first remark was as bald as it was unexpected and it had in it a strong element of truth which silenced Campion.

'It's nothing to do with you,' she said, then banging the drawer shut she fled the room before Campion could stop her, leaving the paper-knife on the carpet.

Mr Campion pulled himself together and went quietly up to the ballroom.

He was mildly startled and just a little conscious of his own invidious position. He was a guest of the prospective son-in-law of the house and as such should have been doing his duty on the dance-floor and not sleeping peacefully beside a tantalus in the library. Yet he was aware that young women who open bureau drawers with paper-knives and run off with mysterious packages wrapped in georgette handkerchiefs constitute a responsibility which cannot be altogether ignored. He went to look for the girl.

The white and gilt ballroom was hot and smelt like a florist's shop. Everyone Mr Campion had ever met round a dinner table seemed to be present with her daughter, but of the little girl in the green dress there was no trace at all. Once he thought he caught a glimpse of her small heart-shaped face across the room, but on struggling through the throng towards this young woman he discovered that he was mistaken and that it was not she but Roberta Pelham herself, radiant and excited, her arm through the arm of her fiancé.

Mr Campion turned into an anteroom to find air and was thereupon astonished to be confronted by nothing less than a black velvet tent, hung with gilt fringe and topped impressively by a brass *Directoire* eagle. The tent was an incongruous contraption in this high-ceilinged Georgian room and he stood blinking at it for some seconds before it dawned on him that this must be the booth of the fortune-teller Thomas had been talking about.

Mr Campion was turning away when the tent curtain parted and old Lady Frinton, who by his reckoning should have known a great deal better at her age, came out in a flutter.

'Oh, my dear!' she exclaimed, pouncing on him happily. 'My *dear*! The creature's too astonishing! Phillida was inspired to engage him. She took my advice, of course. I told her it needs something original to make these young-people affairs faintly tolerable for adults. Come and sit down and I'll tell you everything he told me – or nearly everything – the stupid man. So amusing!'

She chuckled reminiscently, seized his arm and was leading him away when her old eyes, which were sharp and shrewd enough in all conscience, caught his interested expression and she swung round to see what had attracted him.

The floating skirt of a green dress flickered for a moment at the further end of the room and a heart-shaped face surmounted by auburn hair appeared for an instant, only to catch sight of Mr Campion and disappear again. The Dowager Lady Frinton raised her eyebrows.

'Albert!' she said. 'My dear boy! A child? Well, it's an extraordinary thing to me but I've noticed it over and over again. You clever men are absolutely devastated by immaturity, aren't you? Still, fifteen . . . dear boy, is it wise?'

'Do you know who she is?' Campion forced the enquiry in edgeways but did not for an instant dam the flow of chatter for which the old lady was justly famous.

'Who she is?' she exclaimed, her eyes crinkling. 'My dear man, you don't mean to say you haven't even met! But how touchingly romantic! I thought you young people managed these things very differently nowadays. Still, this is charming. Tell me more. You just looked at each other, I suppose? Dear me, it takes me back years.'

Campion regarded her helplessly. She was like some elderly fat white kitten, he thought suddenly, all fluff and wide smile.

'Who is she?' he repeated doggedly.

'Why, the child, of course of. . . . ' Lady Frinton was infuriating. 'Little what's-her-name – Jennifer, isn't it? My dear man, don't stand looking at me like a fish. You know perfectly well who I mean. Roberta's sister, Phillida's youngest daughter. Yes, Jennifer, that's the name. So pretty. Devonshire, isn't it?'

'A daughter?' Campion groped through this spate of scattered information. 'She lives here, then?'

'Of course she lives here. Where else should she live but with her mother? A child of fifteen living alone? Good heavens, whatever next?'

Her ladyship's eyebrows seemed in danger of disappearing altogether but she rattled on.

'She's a charming little thing, I believe, although I've never had any patience with schoolchildren myself. Still, far too young for you. Put it out of your mind, dear boy. Let me see, what was I going to tell you? Oh, about the fortune-teller, of course. Quite a remarkable man. A psychometrist. Fortunately I'm never indiscreet, but really, some of the things he told me about people I knew. . . . '

Her squeaky voice rose and fell and it occurred to Mr Campion that she must have told the seer quite as much as ever he told her. While she was talking he had leisure to wonder why Miss Jennifer Pelham had chosen the middle of a party to force open a locked drawer in the library of her own home, and why above all she should have been so infernally guilty about it.

The matter did not seem of great importance, however, and he was considering how long it would be before he could decently take his leave and go home to bed when a more or less lucid paragraph in Lady Frinton's endless recitation caught his attention.

'He took my ring and put it into an envelope. I put the envelope under the crystal and then he looked in and told me the most astonishing things about my mother. Wasn't that amazing?'

'Your ring?' enquired Mr Campion.

The old lady looked at him as though she thought he was deficient.

'I believe you're still thinking about that child,' she declared, adding spitefully, 'And at your age! I've been explaining. Cagliostro is a psychometrist. You give him something that belonged to someone dead, dead or else-where anyway, and he tells you all about them. It's remarkable, truly remarkable.'

'Cagliostro?' enquired Campion, temporarily out of his depth.

Lady Frinton threw up her tiny hands in exasperation.

'Bless the man, he's delirious,' she said, 'Cagliostro the Second is the fortune-teller. Cagliostro is the man in the tent over there. Go and see him for yourself. I can't be bothered with you if you don't use your mind at all. You young people ought to take up yoga. Come and see me and I'll put you on to a very good man.'

She trotted off happily and Campion heaved a sigh of relief, yet, having a naturally inquisitive disposition, he did not go home immediately but wandered across the room to peer into the black tent before making his way back to the ballroom.

The scene within the tent was much as he had expected. A strong overhead light shone down upon a small black velvet-covered table which supported among other things a red-satin cushion and a large crystal ball; but he was not prepared for the man who smiled at him over an unimpeachable shirt front. This Cagliostro was not the usual sleek huckster with the bright eyes and swagger which the credulous public has come to expect in its seers, but a surprisingly large man with thin fluffy hair and prominent cold light eyes. He did not speak but indicated the consultant's chair very slowly with a large fin-like hand.

Campion shook his head hastily and hurried away. It

was a trivial incident, but it left him oddly uncomfortable. He was even glad to get back to the ballroom.

He stayed for another three quarters of an hour and kept a weather eye open for the younger daughter of the house, who still interested him, but she was not in the room and he did not see her again until he was actually in the street on his way home.

It was a fine night and as he came out into the warm darkness he decided to walk the few steps from Clarges Street to his Piccadilly home. His way took him down the side of the house, which was on a corner, and as he passed a ground-floor window sprang into light and he saw Jennifer standing by the door. She remained very still for a moment, her back against the door. There was conscious drama in her pose and Campion paused on the pavement in some astonishment. As he watched she tore open a white envelope and drew out a small flat package. Immediately all trace of theatre disappeared and she became a very real girl in very real alarm.

Jennifer shook out the package and Campion saw that it was a single sheet of newspaper. For some reason the sight of it appalled the younger Miss Pelham. She held it at arms length and raised a white startled face to the blank window. And that was all.

The next moment something, presumably a sound from behind the door, caused her to start guiltily. She crumpled both newspaper and envelope into a ball and dropped it into a waste-paper basket. A second later the room was dark again.

As Mr Campion walked on down the street he blinked behind his spectacles. The unworthy notion that the younger sister of Lord Currier's prospective bride was off her little red head occurred to him, but he rejected it and for some time as he moved on he was engrossed in idle speculation.

However, by the time he reached Bottle Street he had decided that whatever the mystery might be, it was mercifully no affair of his, and he went to bed soothed by that curiously mistaken notion.

He heard no more of the Pelhams for nearly three weeks and had all but forgotten the tempestuous figure in the green dress when, one morning as he sat at his desk, a note was brought to him with a visiting-card on which was engraved simply 'Mr Waldo Allen, New York'. The note was more instructive.

> *'Dear Campion' wrote the Superintendent, 'Mr Allen has a difficult problem. While we are anxious to give him every assistance we have no information of the kind he needs. It came into my head that there is a faint chance that you may know something, so I am taking the liberty of sending him along. Yours ever, S.O.'*

Campion grinned. The good policeman's difficulty could not have been more lucidly expressed had he added a postscript: *'I cannot get rid of this chap politely, old boy. See what you can do.'*

Yet when Waldo Allen, the Wall Street financier, came into the room his personality immediately captivated his host.

Allen was a large thoughtful man with a natural dignity and an air of authority which was both unconscious and impressive. He stood, stooping a little in the doorway, peering at Campion with bright, worried eyes which were faintly shy.

'This is very kind of you', he said at last in a slow, quiet voice, and he seated himself in the armchair before the desk. He cleared his throat, hesitated, and suddenly smiled.

'I am aware that I may sound to you as though I'm crazy,' he murmured, 'but this is my problem. I'm looking for a skunk, Mr Campion, and eventually I'm going to get him. I have some influence with the authorities on the other side, and your people have been kindly and considerate. With their help I think I may be able to deal with the man I want, once I can locate him, but I've got to find him first. That's my problem. Can you help me?'

Campion sat with his head a little on one side and his pale eyes quizzical.

'A skunk?' he enquired dubiously.

The American nodded and the expression in his bright eyes was by no means amused.

'A skunk,' he said soberly. 'The lowest animal I ever hope to come across. I've never seen him but I know he exists and I have reason to believe he's in England. Have you ever been married, Mr Campion?'

The abruptness of the question was disconcerting and the visitor seemed disappointed when Mr Campion shook his head. Waldo Allen leant forward in his chair.

'I have,' he said. 'Two years ago I married one of the most charming girls in the world. She was young and very ignorant, and like a fool I took her straight away from her parents' home in South Carolina to a penthouse in New York. I gave her everything that she wanted and introduced her to my friends. Then I got on with my work and left her to settle into life in the smart city set. I can't tell you how bitterly I've reproached myself for doing just that. If I'd had any sense I'd have realised that she needed more protection than my money, and just my money, could give her. She should have had my entire attention. I should have realised that the extraordinary simplicity and childishness which I loved in her was a danger as much as it was a charm.'

He paused, and the sophisticated Mr Campion found himself unexpectedly moved by the genuine pain in that quiet, unemotional voice. Waldo Allen looked up.

'Six months ago she threw herself from the roof-garden surrounding our penthouse,' he said slowly. 'There was a lot of hush-hush business and I believe the D.A. satisfied himself that it was an accident. It was not. I wish to God it had been. That skunk had blackmailed her until she hadn't a cent or a jewel to her name and she was afraid to come to me for more.'

He rose abruptly and turned down the room.

'I won't bother you with that angle,' he said at last. 'You must take it that it was my fault. If I'd realised what a child she was then the whole tragedy would never have happened. But I didn't. I gave her money instead of understanding. What I have to tell you is what we discovered after her death. She had sold everything that was her own, Mr Campion, her bank-balance was nil. Large irregular withdrawals in cash told the story pretty clearly. I was nearly off my head. I couldn't understand it. I couldn't imagine what the child could have had to hide. But I didn't know her, you see I didn't realise her youth or her inexperience.'

Campion nodded. It was impossible not to be sorry for this big, quiet man who kept such a tight rein on his well-nigh intolerable grief.

'Did you ever discover what it was?' he enquired.

The American smiled bitterly. 'I've got a pretty shrewd idea,' he said. 'Sylvia had a personal maid, Dorothy, a coloured girl her own age. The girl had come up with her from South Carolina. After the tragedy she broke down and told all she knew. Apparently Sylvia had kept some letters. The sentimental mementoes of a boy and girl love affair which had fizzled out before I put in an appearance. Dorothy was not at all sure what had happened but she thought that someone had got hold of those letters and had convinced Sylvia that I would read a greal deal more into them than ever they had contained. To prevent me seeing them my wife ruined herself, worked herself into a state of nervous collapse and finally killed herself. I must get my hands on that man, Mr Campion. He doesn't deserve to live.'

The younger man was silent. So often in his career he

had heard similar tales that he could not now doubt this grim little story. The clever blackmailer who picks the right victim need discover very little which is truly reprehensible on which to base his threats.

Campion stirred.

'You never traced the man?'

'Never. I've spent six months on it and I've barely a clue. Sylvia went everywhere and met all the usual people, yet she was often alone. Dorothy cannot help; the girl knows no more than I do now. I've just two things to go on and they're slender enough, God knows.'

He came up to the desk as he spoke and stood looking down gravely, his big hands resting on the polished wood.

'The first clue brought me to England. Her maid says that once Sylvia burst into tears when they were alone together and said then that she wished it were July. Dorothy asked her why, and Sylvia sat staring in front of her, a terrified expression in her eyes. "He always goes to England in July", she said, but she wouldn't explain herself and, of course, the maid didn't like to press her. That's one of my clues. I know it's slender but I'm clutching at straws.'

Campion's quick smile was reassuring.

'And the other clue?' he enquired gently.

Waldo Allen straightened his back.

'Just before my wife died,' he began softly, 'she came into my study where I sat writing. I was very busy and, God forgive me, I didn't look at her. She put her arms round my neck, kissed me and whispered something. The next moment she had gone through the french windows, across the roof-garden to her death.'

His voice quivered dangerously, but he controlled himself and went on steadily enough.

'Again and again I've gone over those whispered words in my mind, but I can't get any sense out of them. I heard them distinctly. Sylvia said: "Forgive me. It's written in the ink. He must have seen it all the time". That was all.

Before I could take my mind off my work and ask her what she was talking about she'd gone.'

Campion drew a desk-pad towards him and on it wrote the strange disjointed sentences in his neat academic hand.

' "It is written in the ink" '; he read it aloud slowly. 'Are you sure of that?'

The man with the bright worried eyes nodded gravely.

'I'm certain,' he said heavily. 'Those three phrases will remain in my mind until I die. At one time I came close to persuading myself that they were evidence to the unhinged state of her brain, but now that I've seen her pitiful bank account and her empty jewel case I can't reconcile myself to any theory of that sort. My wife was not mad, Mr Campion. To all intents and purposes she was murdered. Now you understand why I've got to get my hands on that brute. Can you help me?'

Campion hesitated. From the moment when this strange, likeable personality had invaded his study to pour out a story no less tragic because it was deliberately understated, an idea had been knocking at the door of his mind. On the face of it Mr Allen's request was absurd. Even in his most self-satisfied moments Mr Campion did not presume to consider himself a magician and to undertake to look for a blackmailer who might or might not be in England and towards whose identification there was not a shred of evidence, was not the sort of quest to appeal to anyone with a reasonable opinion of his own powers.

Yet there was something very curious about the story he had just heard, and as he sat at his desk, his eyes thoughtful behind his spectacles, he suddenly realised that there was about it a startling and uncomfortable note of familiarity. The discovery rattled him. It was like hearing a tune for the second time and not being able to place the title.

The American rose.

'I fear it's too much of a tall order,' he said wearily, 'Your police were very polite, but I could see they thought it was asking for the moon. For all I know the blackguard I'm searching for may be the man who waits on me in a restaurant, the stranger who sits next to me in the theatre, or the fellow who walks past me in the street. I can't blame you if you laugh at me for bringing to you such a fatuous request.'

Campion remained staring at the pad in front of him. The ominous phrase danced before his eyes: 'It is written in the ink'. Suddenly he looked up.

'Where are you staying?'

'The Cosmopolitan. I'll be there for a week.' He hesitated, then burst out. 'If you think you can help me, for God's sake tell me.'

Campion held out his hand.

'My dear chap, how can I promise anything?'

The other man would not be dismissed.

'Something has occurred to you. You know something.'

'I don't know anything,' Campion objected. 'If I did, believe me, I'd have a great deal more to say. You must see I can't promise anything. But if it's any comfort to you, I can assure you that I shall spend the next day or so investigating a little mystery of my own which may conceivably have a bearing on your case. I can't say any more, truly, I can't say any more, can I?'

It took time to get rid of him but when at last the big man went down the staircase to the street, Campion stood by the window and watched until his visitor's long car moved quietly out of the cul-de-sac.

Some of the other man's passionate indignation had communicated itself to him and he too experienced a little of that helpless rage against the unknown. He went back to the desk and glanced once more at the pad.

' "He must have seen it all the time" ' Campion repeated the words softly. 'I wonder. . . . '

On the telephone Superintendent Oates was sympathetic but inclined to be heavily sarcastic.

'Oh yes, we'll do all your donkey work for you,' he said cheerfully, 'That's what the country pays us for. Anything you want to know, just ask the police. They like spadework. Live on it, in fact. All right, all right,' his tone became plaintive as Campion protested, 'I've said we'd do it, haven't I? Yes, we'll get out all the information you want about the party you've mentioned. But if you'd like my opinion I think you've gone off your head.'

Mr Campion thanked the Superintendent for his diagnosis and pointed out with dignity that he had not asked for it. He also presented his compliments to the Force and hoped it would get on with the job with more speed than was its custom.

As ever, when they both put down their telephones they were on the best of all possible terms.

Having put in motion the elementary machinery of an enquiry that he could but hope was not as folorn as it appeared, Mr Albert Campion set to work on his own account. His first efforts were singularly unsuccessful. Lord Currier was out of town. Both he and his fiancée were guests in a house party at Le Touquet. The date of their return was unknown.

Campion took the telephone receiver in his hand intending to call Miss Jennifer Pelham, but he thought better of it. The matter was delicate in the extreme and he shrank from the possibility of the snub direct.

Instead, in his quandary, he approached Lady Frinton.

That voluble old lady was delighted to hear his voice and said so at considerable length, but when at last he got in his request she was suddenly and uncharacteristically silent.

'The Pelham child?' she said at last, her tone dubious, 'Phillida's youngest? The one with the red hair? *That* girl?'

Mr Campion was not to be distracted.

'The youngest Miss Pelham,' he insisted patiently, 'I want an introduction.'

'Ye-es.' Lady Frinton sounded hesitant. 'You'd better come to see me,' she said after a pause. 'I hate telephones.'

At the appointed hour Mr Campion presented himself at Lady Frinton's door in Knightsbridge and braced himself for an interview which promised to be exhausting.

When he was shown in to her Lady Frinton was sitting by the open window overlooking her small paved garden, and Campion saw immediately that she was prepared to be on her guard. His anxiety increased as she overwhelmed him with a flood of small talk which bid fair to be as inexhaustible as his patience, but after half an hour on the weather, the state of the country, her many religious beliefs and her ailing pets, he cornered her. His direct question pulled her up.

'Oh yes, that Pelham girl,' she said, blinking at him. 'Well, my dear, you know I'm a great friend of her mother and you know I couldn't abuse a confidence. I shouldn't bother with the child if I were you. She's very young.'

Mr Campion leant back and folded his hands. He made a very personable figure lounging there, easily, in the needlework chair.

'I only want to meet her,' he said plaintively.

Lady Frinton's shrewd blue eyes appraised him and he was relieved to see her smile.

'My dear, you really are charming,' she said. 'So old-world, too. I only wish I could help you, but I'm afraid you must wait. Young girls have these difficult spells but, thank goodness, they get over them.'

Mr Campion's eyes flickered but his face registered nothing more intelligent than vague regret.

'What is it? The ballet or a footballer?' he enquired affably.

'Oh, nothing like that, the child's simply neurotic. I'm trying to persuade Phillida to take her to my yoga man. She has crying-fits, ungovernable tempers, morbid desires for solitude and so on and so on.'

Lady Frinton gave the information as though it had been

dragged from her and then spread out her plump hands to indicate, no doubt, that she washed them of all responsibility.

'You must wait, my dear. Phillida says the girl won't see anybody. Just before the wedding too. So unreasonable. Of course, it may be jealousy. These young people. . . .'

She shrugged her shoulders and Campion laughed. The old lady bristled.

'Believe me, I'm not making mountains out of molehills. Why, the child actually wanted to throw up her part in the Jewel Pageant after her mother positively fought for a place for her, and we're all lending her our opals. We had quite a little scene the other night and poor Phillida simply had to put her foot down. The girl's impossible, Albert. She's spoiling her looks, too, the little idiot. If I'd behaved like that when I was young my mother would have taken a hairbrush to me.'

Campion sat blinking at his hostess. He looked monumentally stupid.

'The Jewel Pageant?' he repeated. 'Would that be the show at the Babylonian?'

'Well, of course it is,' Lady Frinton gaped at him. 'Dora is getting it up for one of those eternal charities.' She spoke of her distinguished kinswoman, the Duchess of Stell, with tolerant amusement. 'A host of young females are going to parade, each representing some jewel. The Pelham girl wasn't really eligible because she's still at school, but Phillida moved heaven and earth to get her in, and now the wretched creature has turned temperamental.' She looked at her watch. 'There's a rehearsal going on now. I expect there's been trouble over that. I am sorry for Phillida. When I was fifteen I'd have given my ears to appear in public in a blaze of jewellery. Dora is lending the child her opal coronet and there's not another like it in England.'

Campion took his leave. As he passed the sunburst clock with the garden face he saw it was a quarter past five, and congratulated himself on a very instructive hour. Twenty-five minutes later he entered the ballroom of the Babylonian.

Her grace, the Duchess of Stell, her hat on the back of her head and her broad face pink with exertion, nodded to him affably.

'Frightful!' she murmured confidentially, waving her programme towards a group of forlorn young women on the platform at the far end of the room. 'Look at them. We ought to have had professional models, but of course people won't lend their jewellery then, so what can one do?' Then she shrieked. 'Come, girls, we'll go through that once more. Mary, Mary, my dear. You're diamonds, aren't you? Round the stage, come on then, all of you. Round again, slowly.'

She hurried down the room and Campion drifted towards the group of privileged onlookers, programme girls and other assistants who stood about on the polished floor.

Meanwhile, the awkward squad of granddaughters and nieces of the flower of England's nobility wriggled and did their inadequate best.

Mr Campion took up position directly behind the undieted mamas and so was able to observe the stage without much danger of being himself observed. He located Jennifer Pelham and was startled to see the change in her. She wore green still but her face was sharp and weary and her eyes hunted. As he watched he was aware that there was in her a certain conscious clumsiness. She moved with deliberate awkwardness and her mistakes were so absurd that they were entirely unconvincing. Campion was puzzled by her movements until the moment when she stumbled and collapsed. Then the explanation for her behaviour came to him with the force of a minor revelation.

For years the Duchess had approved of Mr Campion. In the next few moments he earned her undying gratitude.

No-one could have behaved with greater tact and despatch, no one could have been more helpful than Albert Campion. He swept through the chattering throng, gathered up the limp Miss Pelham and, explaining that his car was in the courtyard, declared his intention of taking her home immediately. Jennifer lay gracefully in his arms, her eyes determinedly shut. Only once did she open them, and that was when the Duchess, clucking over her like a distressed Wyandotte, murmured something about tomorrow's performance. At that moment Jennifer's heavy lids flickered wide.

'I can't,' she murmured, 'I'm so sorry. Somebody else,' then she relapsed against Mr Campion's lapel.

Her Grace sighed.

'It'll have to be the Carter girl,' she said. 'After all, opals are large and vague. It won't really matter. Still, I am sorry. Take the poor child home, Albert. Her colour's still good so it can't be anything very serious. Tell Phillida I'll phone this evening. I can't thank you enough, Albert. You are a comforting boy. Take her along.'

Mr Campion remained the soul of knight errantry until he had reached the Lagonda and packed his fainting burden into the front seat. His efficiency was remarkable. He stove off the anxious and well-meaning guests at the rehearsal and made his rescue from collapse to car in a little under seven minutes.

As he swung the grey automobile out into the traffic his manner underwent a change.

'Sit up!' he said curtly. 'Doubtless you have your own reasons for his histrionic display but there's no need to get a crick in the back of your neck. You look rather silly too.'

The fainting girl blushed, and a smile curved the corners of Campion's wide mouth as he glanced at her.

'Too difficult, my child,' he said. 'If you must dissemble, choose violent internal pain or acute rheumatism· of the knee joint. The swoon is too exacting. Duse herself couldn't fool a Boy Scout at close quarters.'

He paused abruptly. Jennifer's fiery colour had disappeared. A single tear, very large and round, squeezed beneath her left eyelid and bumped down the steep curves of her face. Mr Campion felt himself a cad and had the grace to say so.

'What's up? he enquired.

'N-n-nothing. I'm all right. Put me in a taxi if you like.' She spoke humbly.

The Lagonda was caught in a traffic-jam. He braked and sat regarding her.

'Do you remember me?' he asked.

For a moment she stared at him, then her eyes grew wide and she fumbled at the door-catch beside her. Mr Campion felt unreasonably angry.

'Look out,' he said sharply. 'At least let me put you down on the pavement. If you get out that side you'll walk into a bus.'

She turned slowly and stared at him again.

'I don't care,' she said the intensity in the young voice terrible.

At that moment the stream of traffic moved sluggishly forward and the Lagonda crawled on in the procession. Campion did not look at Jennifer and when he spoke again his tone was serious but comfortingly calm.

'Look, here,' he said, 'I don't want to butt into your affairs but I'm not quite the ape I look and I might conceivably be able to lend a useful hand. You're terrified aren't you?'

He felt her shiver at his side.

'A bit,' she admitted huskily.

'I ask you again; what's up?'

'I can't tell you.'

'You daren't; that's it, isn't it?'

'Yes – no – I don't know. Take me home, please.'

Campion nodded his regretful acquiescence.

'All right. Forgive me. We turn here, don't we?'

She sat very still and stiff until they reached Clarges Street, but as the car slid to a standstill she plucked at his sleeve, a frightened little gesture that was oddly disarming.

'Don't please tell anyone I didn't really faint,' she said, her extreme alarm counteracting the childish naïvety of the words. 'Don't tell anyone. I can't explain, but it's terribly important. You see, I just had to get out of wearing all that jewellery and yet I've got to go to the Dover House Ball the day after tomorrow. Promise, please, promise.'

He looked at her squarely.

'You can rely on me,' he said, 'but if I were you I'd risk it and tell me the whole yarn. I can usually fix these things. It's a sort of hobby of mine.'

The younger Miss Pelham caught her breath.

'I can't,' she said, 'not *you*. Not *you*, especially *not* you.'

This emphatic statement was so unexpected that Mr Campion blinked in astonishment. Jennifer, seizing her opportunity, fled into the house as if all the furies were behind her.

Mr Campion drove slowly and thoughtfully to Scotland Yard.

Superintendent Oates sat behind his square desk and regarded his visitor with a mixture of curiosity and grudging admiration.

'Where have you been all the day?' he demanded. 'I've been looking for you everywhere. How do you do it? Second sight or just plain guesswork?'

Campion raised his eyebrows.

'Turned up anything?' he enquired.

'Plenty; and Mr Allen has been in here with a cable from his American agent. There's a chance you may be right. Some people get all the luck.'

The Superintendent, a spare, grey man with the enthusiasm of a boy, rubbed his hands cheerfully.

'Well,' he said, 'we've looked up the man you suggested

and the dates are okay. He was in New York at the right time and he certainly visited the same houses as poor Mrs Allen. Of course, there's no proof but it's interesting to say the least of it. Then this cable this afternoon takes us a step further. Some of her jewellery has been traced and by sheer good luck the purchaser took the numbers of the notes with which he paid her for it. And now a goodly parcel of these notes has turned up in a Brooklyn bank. The bank officials think they may be able to furnish a description of the man who deposited the notes. It's pretty slender, but it's better than nothing. Waldo Allen is trying to persuade us to hold your man, this suspect of yours, for enquiries when we get the full dope from New York. I must say I don't like it. Better to catch a chap like him actually at work.'

Campion sat down.

'Can I talk unofficially?' he asked quietly.

Oates stared at him and, impressed by his manner, checked the flippancy which was close to his lips.

'Of course,' he said. 'Are you on to something? What's on your mind?'

Mr Campion put his cards on the table while the Super-intendent listened with his head on one side, terrier fashion.

'You say we must keep this girl out of it?' Oates said at last. 'Well, if it's blackmail that's quite possible. It's an incredible story. I don't see his game, not yet, not quite. A young married woman with her own bank account is one thing, but a fifteen-year-old could only give him chicken-feed, surely?'

Mr Campion looked lazily at the policeman.

'This fifteen-year-old was about to be entrusted with many thousand pounds' worth of opals,' he murmured. 'She was to wear them all the evening. The prospect so frightened her that she threw up her part in this pageant. It was rather an important treat to miss for a kid of that age.'

Oates was silent for a moment.

'It has been done,' he admitted at last. 'I don't like it, Campion, I don't like it at all, but still, let's keep our sense of proportion.' He had another thought. 'What could a child of that age have to hide?'

'That I can't possibly imagine.' Campion spoke gravely, his pale eyes puzzled. He could not shake from his mind Jennifer's final remark to him.

The Superintendent cut through his thoughts.

'Since you're so keen on it we might start an investigation without committing ourselves. I don't mind telling you we've had a tip from up above to do everything we can for Mr Allen. What do you suggest?'

'A word with the organisers of the Dover House Ball,' said Mr Campion promptly. 'Then a couple of your men, me, and you yourself if you feel like it – four of us in all. What do you say?'

'It's crazy,' said the Superintendent. 'You could be on to entirely the wrong man.'

'That's a possibility, but if I read aright one of Allen's two clues, then I'm not. The day after tomorrow?'

Oates sighed. 'All right. I'll get out my boiled shirt and come with you. But I warn you, if you get me into a stiff collar for nothing. . . . '

He left the threat dangling in air but Mr Campion appeared not to be listening.

There were, in fact, five of them keeping vigil in a small enclosure some forty-eight hours later, Superintendent Oates, Mr Campion, two young officers from the Mayfair squad and Waldo Allen who had insisted on accompanying them. Just outside their prison the thick black velvet curtains of a tent hung motionless. Around them the music and chatter of one of the greatest balls of the summer season eddied and swirled. The night was hot, there was scarcely enough room for the five men in the space where they hid and they were close to smothering.

Superintendent Oates stood like a rock, his keen ears strained and one hand resting restrainedly upon the sleeve of the American. From not far away they heard the sound of someone striking a match. This was the pre-arranged signal which told them that the detective on duty at the ball had seen Jennifer Pelham enter the fortune-teller's booth. The five men stiffened.

For a moment all was quiet on the other side of the curtain, then a young voice said huskily: 'I'm here.'

Cagliostro the Second did not reply immediately and Campion guessed that he had gone to the opening of the tent to see if there was anyone about. Campion knew that the room outside was deserted for he had arranged that in advance. After a pause he heard the fortune-teller's voice, slow and very cold.

'You failed.'

'I couldn't go. I was ill. Honestly, I was ill. I fainted at rehearsal and they had to send me home.'

The girl's voice was barely audible. Oates felt the American stir at his side and grasped his sleeve all the more firmly. Cagliostro spoke again.

'I am growing angry with you.' The quiet voice on the other side of the curtain had a menacing quality out of all proportion to the words.

'I gave you your opportunity. You had but to walk to a window and drop the jewellery out. In ten minutes you could have given the alarm. I asked you for nothing impossible. I was kind enough to show you a way to settle your debt. Now I shall not help you any further. You must pay me, Miss Pelham.'

'I can't, I tell you, I can't!' Jennifer was on the edge of hysteria. 'I've given you every penny I've got. Let that be enough. Give me back my letters. You got them by a trick.'

'Not at all. You gave them to me.'

'I just put them in an envelope for you to put under your crystal. I didn't know you were going to give me back a different envelope with a piece of newspaper in it. Give me the letters, please. They're not mine.'

Cagliostro laughed. 'If they were yours they'd hardly be so interesting,' he said. 'You haven't even read them, have you? If you had, my dear, I think you'd be more obliging. I shall be at the Courtney reception on the twenty-third. Get yourself invited. Come in to see me in the ordinary way and bring me something else to put in an envelope under the crystal – this time two hundred and fifty pounds in one-pound notes. It's not a large sum; I choose it because I think you can raise that much. When I see the money then I'll return the dangerous letters!'

'I can't!'

No sooner did he hear the girl's despairing exclamation than Waldo Allen charged, brushing aside the Superintendent's attempt to restrain him as if it had never been made.

It was not an edifying scene and afterwards the organisers of the ball, who had co-operated with the police against their better judgement, had a good deal to say on the subject.

Oates maintained his dignity and insisted that the commotion had been restricted to the tent and to the room which held the tent.

As ever Mr Campion had shown himself capable of calm in an emergency. He it was who realised that the first object must be to prevent murder.

Waldo Allen was at last dragged away from the gasping creature who had called himself a psychometrist.

Cagliostro was unceremoniously hustled into a waiting police-car.

Quietly, Mr Campion climbed the stairs to the room where the dismantled tent lay, a pool of inky wreckage on the parquetted floor. The detectives on duty stood woodenly by the closed doors into the ballroom.

It was some moments before Campion saw Miss Pelham curled up in the corner of a couch, her head in her arms.

He sat down beside her and solemnly proferred his

handkerchief, 'Cheer up, old lady,' he murmured. 'The worst is over. The tooth is out.'

She raised a tear-stained face to his.

'You don't understand,' she whispered. 'Now they'll find the letters.'

Campion sat up. 'Of course,' he said. 'Bless me, whose were they? Your sister's?'

She gulped and the tears dried from her eyes like a startled child's. 'How did you know?'

Realising that to confess to the gift of divination is a weakness, Mr Campion did not reply directly.

'Don't you think that it might help if you explained it all in your own words?' he suggested. 'You stole the letters in the first place; I saw you, remember. We'll skate over that. I take it you had a natural sisterly anxiety to discover the sort of man your Roberta was marrying, and you thought our unpleasant pal Cagliostro was the man to read the oracle. Is that right?'

She nodded miserably. 'I'm a sentimental, theatrical little ass,' she said with sudden frankness, adding grimly, 'I mean, I used to be. I'm also rather mad; careless and muddleheaded, you know. The idea came to me suddenly and I knew Roberta kept her private letters in that bureau. I just rushed off to get them, meaning to put them back, of course, as soon as I'd heard the reading from the fortune-teller. You startled me and I took the first package of letters that came to hand. I didn't even look at them. I just tore downstairs and then hung about until I could slip into the tent. I had some sort of idiotic idea I was looking after Roberta, don't you see, and then this went and happened.'

Mr Campion was sympathetic. 'They weren't from our Thomas?' he said. 'Whose were they? D'you know?'

The younger Miss Pelham started to weep again. 'Bobby Fellowes, I think,' she said. 'They had a sort of silly affair last year. He's frightfully young, and Roberta rather passed him on to me. He brought me here tonight, as a matter of fact. Now it will all come out, Thomas will break off his engagement and Roberta will break her heart. Bobby will be livid too. I can't bear it! I didn't know anything had happened until I opened the envelope. I thought it was the same one that I'd sealed the package in. But when I did open it I saw it wasn't. I simply thought there'd been a mistake and I went back to Cagliostro. He was frightfully serious. He said the letters showed Roberta's infidelity and he suggested I buy them back. I gave him all the money I had but it wasn't enough. You know the rest.'

Mr Campion's pleasant face was grim. 'Yes, well,' he said. 'I shouldn't worry any more. I'll get Master Fellowes' letters back for you, that I promise. Meanwhile, if it's any comfort to you let me tell you that I've known Thomas since he was four feet high, and if you think any youthful endearments from your young pal Bobby would take his mind off your sister, then, my child, you're insane.'

Jennifer breathed deeply. 'Oh, I wasn't afraid of Thomas,' she said, 'but have you heard of Uncle John?'

Mr Campion's eyes were opened. 'Heaven forgive me!' he said piously. 'I actually forgot Uncle John. You poor kid! Of course, you were alarmed. Well, look here, you go home and go to bed and I'll deliver the documents in a plain van tomorrow morning. That's a bet. Any good?'

When Miss Pelham's powers of expressing her gratitude were partially exhausted a faintly puzzled expression crept into her eyes. 'Why did *you* take so much trouble over it all!' she demanded.

Campion regarded her seriously. 'Who is Sylvia?' he said. 'I think she must have been a little girl very like you.'

Later that night the Superintendent sat in Mr Campion's Piccadilly flat and sipped a long drink to which he felt he was justly entitled.

'Yes, well, we've got him,' he said. 'The nerve of the fellow! There was nothing in those letters, Campion, nothing at all. I looked at them. Boy Scout stuff. Yet he got two hundred quid out of the kid. What I don't see is how he did it. He swapped envelopes about, that I see, but how did he hit on the right ones to keep? I mean, he could well have picked up some woman who'd simply raise Cain at the first sign of any monkey business.'

Campion leant back in his chair. 'My dear chap,' he said, 'that's where he was so clever. He picked his victims, not his evidence. Whenever a helpless-looking little girl gave him a package that felt like a bundle of love-letters he gave her back a dummy envelope and then examined what he had. If he thought they were interesting he worked his insufferable racket. If they weren't, he handed them back with an apology and some convincing story about a mistake.'

'But these letters weren't what you call interesting,' Oates objected. 'Far from it.'

'I don't know. They weren't the girl's own, you see, and they weren't from the sister's distinguished fiancé with the budding career in the Diplomatic and the irascible Uncle John. Cagliostro heard all the gossip, remember. All he had to do was to find out if Jennifer had read them. When he found she had not, all was plain sailing.'

'Skunk!' said Oates. 'Allen called him that and it suits him. We'll put him away all right, without publicity. I say, Campion, forgive a professional question, but what put you on to him?'

Campion frowned. ' "It is written in the ink" ', he quoted. 'D'you remember that?'

'Yes, I do. Mrs Allen said it before she committed suicide, didn't she? It still doesn't convey anything to me.'

'Nor me at first,' admitted Campion modestly. 'But the story of the blackmailed innocent reminded me of Jennifer, and Jennifer reminded me of that damned fortune-teller, so I put two and two together.'

'I'll buy it,' said the Superintendent.

'It's ridiculously simple. When first I looked into the

tent I saw a crystal. A fortune-teller of that kind doesn't have a crystal as a rule. He simply holds the envelope, or whatever it is, and goes into a trance. That was just a little oddity that set me thinking, and from crystals, naturally, I went on to ink. In India the fakirs look into a pool of ink instead of a crystal, you know.'

'I didn't. Still, go on.'

Campion sighed. 'You're an impossible person to have to explain thought-processes to,' he said. 'But if those last words had been "It is written in the crystal", you'd have automatically thought of fortune-tellers, wouldn't you? Well then, the ink is sometimes synonymous with the crystal, and when there's a terrified young girl in each situation, well, it sets you wondering. That's all.'

Oates laughed explosively.

'In fact, you guessed it. You picked a winning horse with a pin,' he said. 'My word, Campion, you're lucky! There was no brains in it at all.'

Mr Campion looked hurt. There are times when he feels it is his destiny to be underestimated by his friends.

McGOWNEY'S MIRACLE

When I finally found him, it was by accident. He was waiting for a cable car on Powell Street, a dignified little man about sixty, in a black topcoat and a grey fedora. He stood apart from the crowd, aloof but friendly, his hands clasped just below his chest, like a minister about to bless a batch of heathen. I knew he wasn't a minister.

A sheet of fog hung over San Francisco, blurring the lights and muffling the clang of the cable cars.

I stepped up behind McGowney and said, 'Good evening.'

There was no recognition in his eyes, no hesitation in his voice. 'Why, good evening, sir.' He turned with a little smile. 'It is kind of you to greet a stranger so pleasantly.'

For a moment, I was almost ready to believe I'd made a mistake. There are on record many cases of perfect doubles, and what's more, I hadn't seen McGowney since the beginning of July. But there was one important thing McGowney couldn't conceal: his voice still carried the throaty accents of the funeral parlour.

He tipped his hat and began walking briskly up Powell Street toward the hill, his topcoat flapping around his skinny legs like broken wings.

In the middle of the block, he turned to see if I was following him. I was. He walked on, shaking his head from side to side as if genuinely puzzled by my interest in him. At the next corner, he stopped in front of a department store and waited for me, leaning against the window, his hands in his pockets.

When I approached, he looked up at me, frowning. 'I don't know why you're following me, young man, but – '

'Why don't you ask me, McGowney?'

But he didn't ask. He just repeated his own name. 'McGowney,' in a surprised voice, as if he hadn't heard it for a long time.

I said, 'I'm Eric Meecham, Mrs Keating's lawyer. We've met before.'

'I've met a great many people. Some I recall, some I do not.'

'I'm sure you recall Mrs Keating. You conducted her funeral last July.'

'Of course, of course. A great lady, a very great lady. Her demise saddened the hearts of all who had the privilege of her acquaintance, all who tasted the sweetness of her smile – '

'Come off it, McGowney. Mrs Keating was a sharp-tongued virago without a friend in this world.'

He turned away from me, but I could see the reflection of his face in the window, strained and anxious.

'You're a long way from home, McGowney.'

'This is my home now.'

'You left Arbana very suddenly.'

'To me it was not sudden. I had been planning to leave for twenty years, and when the time came, I left. It was summer then, but all I could think of was the winter coming on and everything dying. I had had enough of death.'

'Mrs Keating was your last – client?'

'She was.'

'Her coffin was exhumed last week.'

A cable car charged up the hill like a drunken rocking horse, its sides bulging with passengers. Without warning, McGowney darted out into the street and sprinted up the hill after the car. In spite of his age, he could have made it, but the car was so crowded there wasn't a single space for him to get a handhold. He stopped running and stood motionless in the centre of the street, staring after the car as it plunged and reared up the hill. Oblivious to the honks

and shouts of motorists, he walked slowly back to the
kerb where I was waiting.

'You can't run away, McGowney.'

He glanced at me wearily, without speaking. Then he
took out a half-soiled handkerchief and wiped the moisture
from his forehead.

'The exhumation can't be much of a surprise to you,' I
said. 'You wrote me the anonymous letter suggesting it.
It was postmarked Berkeley. That's why I'm here in this
area.'

'I wrote you no letter,' he said.

'The information it contained could have come only
from you.'

'No. Somebody else knew as much about it as I did.'

'Who?'

'My – wife.'

'Your wife.' It was the most unexpected answer he could
have given me. Mrs McGowney had died, along with her
only daughter, in the flu epidemic after World War I. The
story is the kind that still goes the rounds in a town like
Arbana, even after thirty-five years. McGowney, unem-
ployed after his discharge from the army, had had no funds
to pay for the double funeral, and when the undertaker
offered him an apprenticeship to work off the debt,
McGowney accepted. It was common knowledge that after
his wife's death he never so much as looked at another
woman, except, of course, in the line of duty.

I said, 'So you've married again.'

'Yes.'

'When?'

'Six months ago.'

'Right after you left Arbana.'

'Yes.'

'You didn't lose much time starting a new life for
yourself.'

'I couldn't afford to. I'm not young.'

'Did you marry a local woman?'

'Yes.'

I didn't realise until later that he had taken 'local' to mean Arbana, not San Francisco as I had intended.

I said, 'You think your wife wrote me that anonymous letter?'

'Yes.'

The streetlights went on, and I realised it was getting late and cold. McGowney pulled up his coat collar and put on a pair of ill-fitting white cotton gloves. I had seen him wearing gloves like that before; they were as much a part of his professional equipment as his throaty voice and his vast store of sentimental aphorisms.

He caught me staring at the gloves and said, with a trace of apology, 'Money is a little tight these days. My wife is knitting me a pair of woollen gloves for my birthday.'

'You're not working?'

'No.'

'It shouldn't be hard for a man of your experience to find a job in your particular field.' I was pretty sure he hadn't even applied for one. During the past few days, I had contacted nearly every mortician within the Bay area; McGowney had not been to any of them.

'I don't want a job in my particular field,' McGowney said.

'It's the only thing you're trained for.'

'Yes. But I no longer believe in death.'

He spoke with simple earnestness, as if he had said, I no longer play blackjack, or I no longer eat salted peanuts.

Death, blackjack, or salted peanuts – I was not prepared to argue with McGowney about any of them, so I said, 'My car's in the garage at the Canterbury Hotel. We'll walk over and get it, and I'll drive you home.'

We started toward Sutter Street. The stream of shoppers had been augmented by a flow of white-collar workers, but all the people and the noise and the confusion left McGowney untouched. He moved sedately along beside me, smiling a little to himself, like a man who has developed the faculty of walking out on the world from time to time and going to live on some remote and happy island of his own. I wondered where McGowney's island was and who lived there with him. I knew only one thing for sure: on McGowney's island there was no death.

He said suddenly, 'It must have been very difficult.'

'What was?'

'The exhumation. The ground gets so hard back East in the wintertime. I presume you didn't attend, Mr Meecham?'

'You presume wrong.'

'My, that's no place for an amateur.'

For my money, it was no place for anyone. The cemetery had been white with snow that had fallen during the night. Dawn had been breaking, if you could call that meagre, grudging light a dawn. The simple granite headstone had read: ELEANOR REGINA KEATING, OCTOBER 3, 1899–JUNE 30, 1953, A BLESSED ONE FROM US IS GONE, A VOICE WE LOVED IS STILL.

The blessed one had been gone, all right. Two hours later, when the coffin was pulled up and opened, the smell that rose from it was not the smell of death, but the smell of newspapers rotted with dampness and stones grey-greened with mildew.

I said, 'You know what we found, don't you, McGowney?'

'Naturally. I directed the funeral.'

'You accept sole responsibility for burying an empty coffin?'

'Not sole responsibility, no.'

'Who was in with you? And why?'

He merely shook his head.

As we waited for a traffic light, I studied McGowney's face, trying to estimate the degree of his sanity. There seemed to be no logic behind his actions. Mrs Keating had died quite unmysteriously of a heart attack and had been buried, according to her instructions to me, in a closed coffin. The doctor who had signed the death certificate was indisputably honest. He had happened to be in Mrs Keating's house at the time, attending to her older daughter, Mary, who had had a cold. He had examined Mrs Keating, pronounced her dead, and sent for McGowney. Two days later I had escorted Mary, still sniffling (whether from grief or the same cold, I don't know) to the funeral, McGowney, as usual, said and did all the correct things.

Except one. He neglected to put Mrs Keating's body in the coffin.

Time had passed. No one had particularly mourned Mrs Keating. She had been an unhappy woman, mentally and morally superior to her husband, who had been killed during a drinking spree in New Orleans, and to her two daughters, who resembled their father. I had been Mrs Keating's lawyer for three years. I had enjoyed talking to her; she had had a quick mind and a sharp sense of humour. But as in the case of many wealthy people who have been cheated of the privilege of work and the satisfaction it brings, she had been a bored and lonely woman who carried despair on her shoulder like a pet parakeet and fed it from time to time on scraps from her bitter memories.

Right after Mrs Keating's funeral, McGowney had sold his business and left town. No one in Arbana had connected the two events until the anonymous letter arrived from Berkeley shortly before Mrs Keating's will was awaiting admission into probate. The letter, addressed to me, had suggested the exhumation and stated the will must be declared invalid since there was no proof of death. I could think of no reason why McGowney's new wife wrote the letter, unless she had tired of him and had chosen a round-about method of getting rid of him.

The traffic light changed, and McGowney and I crossed the street and waited under the hotel marquee while the doorman sent for my car. I didn't look at McGowney, but I could feel him watching me intently.

'You think I'm mad, eh, Meecham?'

It wasn't a question I was prepared to answer. I tried to look noncommital.

'I don't pretend to be entirely normal, Meecham. Do you?'

'I try.'

McGowney's hand, in its ill-fitting glove, reached over and touched my arm, and I forced myself not to slap it away. It perched on my coat sleeve like a wounded pigeon. 'But suppose you had an abnormal experience.'

'Like you?'

'Like me. It was a shock, a great shock, even though I had always had the feeling that someday it would happen. I was on the watch for it every time I had a new case. It was always in my mind. You might even say I *willed* it.'

Two trickles of sweat oozed down behind my ears into my collar. 'What did you will, McGowney?'

'I willed her to live again.'

I became aware the doorman was signalling to me. My car was at the kerb with the engine running.

I climbed in behind the wheel, and McGowney followed me into the car with obvious reluctance, as if he was already regretting what he'd told me.

'You don't believe me,' he said as we pulled away from the kerb.

'I'm a lawyer. I deal in facts.'

'A fact is what happens, isn't it?'

'Close enough.'

'Well, this happened.'

'She came back to life?'

'Yes.'

'By the power of your will alone?'

He stirred restlessly in the seat beside me. 'I gave her oxygen and adrenaline.'

'Have you done this with other clients of yours?'

—81—

'Many times, yes.'

'Is this procedure usual among members of your profession?'

'For me it was usual,' McGowney said earnestly. 'I've always wanted to be a doctor. I was in the Medical Corps during the war, and I picked up a little knowledge here and there.'

'Enough to perform miracles?'

'It was not my knowledge that brought her back to life. It was my will. She had lost the will to live, but I had enough for both of us.'

If it is true that only a thin line separates sanity and madness, McGowney crossed and recrossed that line a dozen times within an hour, jumping over it and back again, like a child skipping rope.

'You understand now, Meecham? She had lost all desire. I saw it happening to her. We never spoke – I doubt she even knew my name – but for years I watched her pass my office on her morning walk. I saw the change come over her, the dullness of her eyes and the way she walked. I knew she was going to die. One day when she was passing by, I went out to tell her, to warn her. But when she saw me, she ran. I think she realised what I was going to say.'

He was telling the truth, according to his lights. Mrs Keating had mentioned the incident to me last spring. I recalled her words. 'A funny thing occurred this morning, Meecham. As I was walking past the undertaking parlour, that odd little man rushed out and almost scared the life out of me. . . . '

In view of what subsequently happened, this was a giant among ironies. As we drove toward the Bay Bridge and Berkeley, McGowney told me his story.

It was midday at the end of June, and the little back room McGowney used as a lab was hot and humid after a morning rain.

Mrs Keating woke up as if from a long and troubled sleep. Her hands twitched, her mouth moved in distress, a pulse began to beat in her temple. Tears squeezed out from between her closed lids and slithered past the tips of her ears into the folds of her hair.

McGowney bent over her, quivering with excitement, 'Mrs Keating! Mrs Keating! You are alive!'

'Oh – God.'

'A miracle has just happened!'

'Leave me alone. I'm tired.'

'You are alive, you are *alive*!'

Slowly she opened her eyes and looked up at him. 'You officious little wretch, what have you done?'

McGowney stepped back, stunned and shaken. 'But – but you are alive. It's happened. My miracle has happened.'

'Alive, Miracle.' She mouthed the words as if they were lumps of alum. 'You meddling idiot.'

'I – But I – '

'Pour me a glass of water. My throat is parched.'

He was trembling so violently he could hardly get the water out of the cooler. This was his miracle. He had hoped and waited for it all his life, and now it had exploded in his face like an April-fool cigar.

He gave her the water and sat down heavily in a chair, watching her while she drank very slowly, as if in her short recess from life her muscles had already begun to forget their function.

'Why did you do it?' Mrs Keating crushed the paper cup in her fist as if were McGowney himself. 'Who asked you for a miracle, anyway?'

'But I – Well, the fact is – '

'The fact is, you're a blooming meddler, that's what the fact is, McGowney.'

'Yes, ma'am.'

'Now what are you going to do?'

'Well, I – I hadn't thought.'

'Then you'd better start right now.'

'Yes, ma'am.' He stared down at the floor, his head hot with misery, his limbs cold with disappointment. 'First, I had better call the doctor.'

'You'll call no one, McGowney.'

'But your family – they'll want to know right away that – '

'They are not going to know.'

'But – '

'No one is going to know, McGowney. No one at all. Is that clear?'

'Yes.'

'Now sit down and be quiet and let me think.'

He sat down and was quiet. He had no desire to move or to speak. Never had he felt so futile and depressed.

'I suppose,' Mrs Keating said grimly, 'you expect me to be grateful to you.'

McGowney shook his head.

'If you do, you must be crazy.' She paused and looked at him thoughtfully.

'You are a little crazy, aren't you, McGowney?'

'There are those who think so,' he said, with some truth. 'I don't agree.'

'You wouldn't.'

'Can't afford to, ma'am.'

The windows of the room were closed and no street sounds penetrated the heavy frosted glass, but from the corridor outside the door came the sudden tap of footsteps on tile.

McGowney bolted across the room and locked the door and stood against it.

'Mr McGowney? You in there?'

McGowney looked at Mrs Keating. Her face had turned chalky, and she had one hand clasped to her throat.

'Mr McGowney?'

'Yes, Jim.'

'You're wanted on the telephone.'

'I – can't come right now, Jim. Take a message.'

'She wants to talk to you personally. It's the Keating girl, about the time and cost of the funeral arrangements.'

'Tell her I'll call her back later.'

'All right.' There was a pause. 'You feeling okay, Mr McGowney?'

'Yes,'

'You sound kind of funny.'

'I'm fine, Jim. Absolutely first-rate.'

'Okay. Just thought I'd ask.'

The footsteps tapped back down the tile corridor.

'Mary loses no time.' McGowney spoke through dry, stiff lips. 'She wants me safely underground so she can marry her electrician. Well, your duty is clear, McGowney.'

'What is it?'

'Put me there.'

McGowney stood propped against the door like a wooden soldier. 'You mean, b-b-bury you?'

'Me, or a reasonable facsimile.'

'That I couldn't do, Mrs Keating. It wouldn't be ethical.'

'It's every bit as ethical as performing unsolicited miracles.'

'You don't understand the problems.'

'Such as?'

'For one thing, your family and friends. They'll want to see you lying in – What I mean is, it's customary to put the body on view.'

'I can handle that part of it all right.'

'How?'

'Get me a pen and some paper.'

McGowney didn't argue, because he knew he was at fault. It was his miracle; he'd have to take the consequences.

Mrs Keating predated the letter by three weeks, and wrote the following:

To whom it may concern, not that it should concern anybody except myself:

 I am giving these instructions to Mr McGowney concerning my funeral arrangements. Inasmuch as I have valued privacy during my life, I want no intrusion on it after my death. I am instructing Mr McGowney to close my coffin immediately and to see it stays closed, in spite of any mawkish pleas from my survivors.

Elinor Regina Keating

She folded the paper twice and handed it to McGowney. 'You are to show this to Mary and Joan and to Mr Meecham, my lawyer.' She paused, looking very pleased with herself. 'Well. This is getting to be quite exciting, eh, McGowney?'

'Quite,' McGowney said listlessly.

'As a matter of fact, it's given me an appetite. I don't suppose there's a kitchen connected with this place?'

'No.'

'Then you'd better get me something from the corner drugstore. A couple of tuna-salad sandwiches, on wheat, with plenty of coffee. Lunch,' she added with a satiric little smile, 'will have to be on you. I forgot my handbag.'

'Money,' McGowney said. '*Money.*'

'What about it?'

'What will happen to your money?'

'I made a will some time ago.'

'But *you*, what will you live on?'

'Perhaps,' Mrs Keating said dryly, 'you'd better perform another miracle.'

When he returned from the drugstore with her lunch, Mrs Keating ate and drank with obvious enjoyment. She offered McGowney a part of the second sandwich, but he was too disheartened to eat. His miracle, which had started out as a great golden bubble, had turned into an iron ball chained to his leg.

Somehow he got through the day. Leaving Mrs Keating in the lab with some old magazines and a bag of apples, McGowney went about his business. He talked to Mary and Joan Keating in person and to Meecham on the telephone. He gave his assistant, Jim Wagner, the rest of the afternoon off, and when Jim had gone, he filled Mrs Keating's coffin (the de luxe white-and-bronze model Mary had chosen out of the catalogue) with rocks packed in newspapers, until it was precisely the right weight.

McGowney was a small man, unaccustomed to physical exertion, and by the time he had finished, his body was throbbing with weariness.

It was at this point Mary Keating telephoned to say she and Joan had been thinking the matter over, and since Mrs Keating had always inclined toward thrift, it was decided she would never rest at ease in such an ostentatious affair as the white and bronze. The plain grey would be far more appropriate, as well as cheaper.

'You should,' McGowney said coldly, 'have let me know sooner.'

'We just decided a second ago.'

'It's too late to change now.'

'I don't see why.'

'There are – certain technicalities.'

'Well, really, Mr McGowney. If you're not willing to put yourself out a little, maybe we should take our business somewhere else.'

'No! You can't do that – I mean, it wouldn't be proper, Miss Keating.'

'It's a free country.'

'Wait a minute. Suppose I give you a special price on the white and bronze.'

'How special?'

'Say, twenty-five percent off?'

There was a whispered conference at the other end of the line and then Mary said, 'It's still a lot of money.'

'Thirty-five.'

'Well, that seems more *like* it.' Mary said, and hung up.

The door of McGowney's office opened, and Mrs Keating crossed the room, wearing a grim little smile.

McGowney looked at her helplessly. 'You shouldn't be out here, ma'am. You'd better go back and – '

'I heard the telephone ring, and I thought it might be Mary.'

'It wasn't.'

'Yes, it was, McGowney. I heard every word.'

'Well,' McGowney cleared his throat. 'Well. You shouldn't have listened.'

'Oh, I'm not surprised. Or hurt. You needn't be sorry for me. I haven't felt so good in years. You know why?'

'No, ma'am.'

'Because I don't have to go home. I'm free. Free as a bird.' She reached over and touched his coat sleeve. 'I don't have to go home, do I?'

'I guess not.'

'You'll never tell anyone?'

'No.'

'You're a very good man, McGowney.'

'I have never thought I wasn't,' McGowney said simply.

When darkness fell, McGowney got his car out of the garage and brought it around to the ambulance entrance behind his office.

'You'd better hide in the backseat,' he said, 'until we get out of town.'

'Where are we going?'

'I thought I'd drive you into Detroit, and from there you can catch a bus or a train.'

'To where?'

'To anywhere. You're free as a bird.' She got into the backseat, shivering in spite of the mildness of the night, and McGowney covered her with a blanket.

'McGowney.'

'Yes, ma'am?'

'I felt freer when I was locked in your little lab.'

'You're a bit frightened now, that's all. Freedom is a mighty big thing.'

He turned the car toward the highway. Half an hour later, when the city's lights had disappeared, he stopped the car, and Mrs Keating got into the front seat with the blanket wrapped around her shoulders, Indian style. In the gloom of oncoming headlights, her face looked a little troubled. McGowney felt duty bound to cheer her up, since he was responsible for her being there in the first place.

'There are,' he said firmly, 'wonderful places to be seen.'

'Are there?'

'California, that's the spot I'd pick. Flowers all year round, never an end to them.' He hesitated. 'I've saved a bit throughout the years. I always thought someday I'd sell the business and retire to California.'

'What's to prevent you?'

'I couldn't face the idea, of, well of being alone out there without friends or a family of some kind. Have you ever been to California?'

'I spent a couple of summers in San Francisco.'

'Did you like it?'

'Very much.'

'I'd like it, too, I'm sure of that.' He cleared his throat. 'Being alone, though, that I wouldn't like. Are you warm enough?'

'Yes, thanks.'

'Birds – well, birds don't have such a happy time of it that I can see.'

'No?'

'All that freedom and not knowing what to do with it except fly around. A life that couldn't suit a mature woman like yourself, Mrs Keating.'

'Perhaps not.'

'What I mean is – '

'I know what you mean, McGowney.'

'You – you do?'

'Of course.'

McGowney flushed. 'It's – well, it's very unexpected, isn't it?'

'Not to me.'

'But I never thought of it until half an hour ago.'

'I did. Women are more foresighted in these matters.'

McGowney was silent a moment. 'This hasn't been a very romantic proposal. I ought to say something a bit on the sentimental side.'

'Go ahead.'

He gripped the steering wheel hard. 'I think I love you, ma'am.'

'You didn't have to say that,' she replied sharply. 'I'm not a foolish young girl to be taken in by words. At my age, I don't expect love. I don't want to – '

'But you are loved,' McGowney declared.

'I don't believe it.'

'Eventually you will.'

'Is this another of your miracles, McGowney'.

'This is the important one.'

It was the first time in Mrs Keating's life she had been told she was loved. She sat beside McGowney in awed silence, her hands folded on her lap, like a little girl in Sunday school.

McGowney left her at a hotel in Detroit and went home to hold her funeral.

Two weeks later they were married by a justice of the peace in a little town outside Chicago. On the long and leisurely trip west in McGowney's car, neither of them talked much about the past or worried about the future. McGowney had sold his business, but he'd been in too much of a hurry to wait for a decent price, and so his funds were limited. But he never mentioned this to his bride.

By the time they reached San Francisco, they had gone through quite a lot of McGowney's capital. A large portion of the remainder went toward the purchase of the little house in Berkeley.

By late fall, they were almost broke, and McGowney got a job as a shoe clerk in a department store. A week later, along with his first paycheck, he received his notice of dismissal.

That night at dinner he told Eleanor about it, pretendding it was all a joke, and inventing a couple of anecdotes to make her laugh.

She listened, grave and unamused. 'So that's what you've been doing all week. Selling shoes.'

'Yes.'

'You didn't tell me we needed money that badly.'

'We'll be all right. I can easily get another job.'

'Doing what?'

'What I've always done.'

She reached across the table and touched his hand. 'You don't want to be a mortician again.'

'I don't mind.'

'You always hated it.'

'I *don't mind*, I tell you.'

She rose decisively.

'Eleanor, what are you going to do?'

'Write a letter,' she said with a sigh.

'Eleanor, don't do anything drastic.'

'We have had a lot of happiness. It couldn't last forever. Don't be greedy.'

The meaning of her words pierced McGowney's brain. 'You're going to let someone know you're alive?'

'No, I couldn't face that, not just yet. I'm merely going to show them I'm not dead so they can't divide up my estate.'

'But why?'

'As my husband, you're entitled to a share of it if anything happens to me.'

'Nothing will ever happen to you. We agreed about that, didn't we?'

'Yes, McGowney. We agreed.'

'We no longer believe in death.'

'I will address the letter to Meecham,' she said.

'So she wrote the letter,' McGowney's voice was weary. 'For my sake. You know the rest, Meecham.'

'Not quite,' I said.'

'What else do you want to know?'

'The ending.'

'The ending.' McGowney stirred in the seat beside me and let out his breath in a sigh. 'I don't believe in endings.'

I turned right at the next traffic light, as McGowney directed. A sign on the lamppost said Linden Avenue.

Three blocks south was a small green-and-white house, its eaves dripping with fog.

I parked my car in front of it and got out, pleasantly excited at the idea of seeing Mrs Keating again. McGowney sat motionless, staring straight ahead of him, until I opened the car door.

'Come on, McGowney.'

'Eh? Oh. All right. All right.'

He stepped out on the sidewalk so awkwardly he almost fell. I took his arm. 'Is anything wrong?'

'No.'

We went up the porch steps.

'There are no lights on,' McGowney said. 'Eleanor must be at the store. Or over at the neighbour's. We have some very nice neighbours.'

The front door was not locked. We went inside and McGowney turned on the lights in the hall and the sitting room to the right.

The woman I had known as Mrs Keating was sitting in a wing chair in front of the fireplace, her head bent forward as if she were in deep thought. Her knitting had fallen on the floor, and I saw it was a half-finished glove in bright colours. McGowney's birthday present.

In silence, McGowney reached down and picked up the

glove and put it on a table. Then he touched his wife gently on the forehead. I knew from the way his hand flinched that her skin was as cold as the ashes in the grate.

I said, 'I'll get a doctor.'

'No.'

'She's dead?'

He didn't bother to answer. He was looking down at his wife with a coaxing expression. 'Eleanor dear, you must wake up. We have a visitor.'

'McGowney, for God's sake – '

'I think you'd better leave now, Mr Meecham,' he said in a firm, clear voice. 'I have work to do.'

He took off his coat and rolled up his sleeves.

THE SNAIL-WATCHER

When Mr Peter Knoppert began to make a hobby of snail-watching, he had no idea that his handful of specimens would become hundreds in no time. Only two months after the original snails were carried up to the Knoppert study, some thirty glass tanks and bowls, all teeming with snails, lined the walls, rested on the desk and windowsills, and were beginning even to cover the floor. Mrs Knoppert disapproved strongly, and would no longer enter the room. It smelled, she said, and besides she had once stepped on a snail by accident, a horrible sensation she would never forget. But the more his wife and friends deplored his unusual and vaguely repellent pastime, the more pleasure Mr Knoppert seemed to find in it.

'I never cared for nature before in my life,' Mr Knoppert often remarked – he was a partner in a brokerage firm, a man who had devoted all his life to the science of finance – 'but snails have opened my eyes to the beauty of the animal world.'

If his friends commented that snails were not really animals, and their slimy habitats hardly the best example of the beauty of nature, Mr Knoppert would tell them with a superior smile that they simply didn't know all that he knew about snails.

And it was true, Mr Knoppert had witnessed an exhibition that was not described, certainly not adequately described, in any encyclopaedia or zoology book that he had been able to find. Mr Knoppert had wandered into the kitchen one evening for a bite of something before dinner, and had happened to notice that a couple of snails in the china bowl on the draining board were behaving very oddly. Standing more or less on their tails, they were weaving before each other for all the world like a pair of snakes hypnotised by a flute player. A moment later, their faces came together in a kiss of voluptuous intensity. Mr Knoppert bent closer and studied them from all angles. Something else was happening: a protuberance like an ear was appearing on the right side of the head of both snails. His instinct told him that he was watching a sexual activity of some sort.

The cook came in and said something to him, but Mr Knoppert silenced her with an impatient wave of his hand. He couldn't take his eyes from the enchanted little creatures in the bowl.

When the ear-like excrescences were precisely together rim to rim, a whitish rod like another small tentacle shot out from one ear and arched over toward the ear of the other snail. Mr Knoppert's first surmise was dashed when a tentacle sallied from the other snail, too. Most peculiar, he thought. The two tentacles withdrew, then came forth again, and as if they had found some invisible mark, remained fixed in either snail. Mr Knoppert peered intently closer. So did the cook.

'Did you ever see anything like this?' Mr Knoppert asked.

'No. They must be fighting,' the cook said indifferently and went away. That was a sample of the ignorance on the subject of snails that he was later to discover everywhere.

Mr Knoppert continued to observe the pair of snails off and on for more than an hour, until first the ears then the rods, withdrew, and the snails themselves relaxed their attitudes and paid no further attention to each other. But by that time, a different pair of snails had begun a flirtation, and were slowly rearing themselves to get into a position for kissing. Mr Knoppert told the cook that the snails were not to be served that evening. He took the bowl of them up to his study. And snails were never again served in the Knoppert household.

That night, he searched his encyclopaedias and a few general science books he happened to possess, but there was absolutely nothing on snails' breeding habits, though the oyster's dull reproductive cycle was described in detail. Perhaps it hadn't been a mating he had seen after all, Mr Knoppert decided after a day or two. His wife Edna told him either to eat the snails or get rid of them – it was at this time that she stepped upon a snail that had crawled out on to the floor – and Mr Knoppert might have, if he hadn't come across a sentence in Darwin's *Origin of Species* on a page given to gastropoda. The sentence was in French, a language Mr Knoppert did not know, but the word *sensualité* made him tense like a bloodhound that has suddenly found the scent. He was in the public library at that time, and laboriously he translated the sentence with the aid of a French-English dictionary. It was a statement of less than a hundred words, saying that snails manifested a sensuality in their mating that was not to be found elsewhere in the animal kingdom. That was all. It was from the notebooks of Henri Fabre. Obviously Darwin had decided not to translate it for the average reader, but to leave it in its original language for the scholarly few who really cared. Mr Knoppert considered himself one of the scholarly few now, and his round, pink face beamed with self-esteem.

He had learned that his snails were the freshwater type that laid their eggs in sand or earth, so he put moist earth and a little saucer of water into a big wash-bowl and transferred his snails into it. Then he waited for something to happen. Not even another mating happened. He picked up the snails one by one and looked at them, without seeing anything suggestive of pregnancy. But one snail he couldn't pick up. The shell might have been glued to the earth. Mr Knoppert suspected the snail had buried its head in the ground to die. Two more days went by, and on the morning of the third, Mr Knoppert found a spot of crumbly earth where the snail had been. Curious, he investigated the crumbles with a match stem, and to his delight discovered a pit full of shiny new eggs. Snail eggs! He hadn't been wrong. Mr Knoppert called his wife and the cook to look at them. The eggs looked very much like big caviar, only they were white instead of black or red.

'Well, naturally they have to breed some way,' was his wife's comment. Mr Knoppert couldn't understand her lack of interest. He had to go and look at the eggs every hour that he was at home. He looked at them every morning to see if any change had taken place, and the eggs were his last thought every night before he went to bed. Moreover, another snail was now digging a pit. And another pair of snails was mating! The first batch of eggs turned a greyish colour, and miniscule spirals of shells became discernible on one side of each egg. Mr Knoppert's anticipations rose to a higher pitch. At last a morning arrived – the eighteenth after laying, according to Mr Knoppert's careful count – when he looked down into the egg pit and saw the first tiny moving head, the first stubby little antennae uncertainly exploring the nest. Mr Knoppert was as happy as the father of a new child. Every one of the seventy or more eggs in the pit came miraculously to life. He had seen the entire reproductive cycle evolve to a successful conclusion. And the fact that no one, at least no one that he knew of, was acquainted with a fraction of what he knew, lent his knowledge a thrill of discovery, the piquancy of the esoteric. Mr Knoppert made notes on successive matings and egg hatchings. He narrated snail biology to fascinated, more often shocked, friends and guests, until his wife squirmed with embarrassment.

'But where is it going to stop, Peter? If they keep on reproducing at this rate, they'll take over the house!' his wife told him after fifteen or twenty pits had hatched.

'There's no stopping nature,' he replied good-humouredly. 'They've only taken over the study. There's plenty of room there.'

So more and more glass tanks and bowls were moved

in. Mr Knoppert went to the market and chose several of the more lively-looking snails, and also a pair he found mating, unobserved by the rest of the world. More and more egg pits appeared in the dirt floors of the tanks, and out of each pit crept finally from seventy to ninety baby snails, transparent as dewdrops, gliding up rather than down the strips of fresh lettuce that Mr Knoppert was quick to give all the pits as edible ladders for the climb. Mating went on so often that he no longer bothered to watch them. A mating could last twenty-four hours. But the thrill of seeing the white caviar become shells and start to move – that never diminished however often he witnessed it.

His colleagues in the brokerage office noticed a new zest for life in Peter Knoppert. He became more daring in his moves, more brilliant in his calculations, became in fact a little vicious in his schemes, but he brought money in for his company. By unanimous vote, his basic salary was raised from forty to sixty thousand dollars per year. When anyone congratulated him on his achievements, Mr Knoppert gave all the credit to his snails and the beneficial relaxation he derived from watching them.

He spent all his evenings with his snails in the room that was no longer a study but a kind of aquarium. He loved to strew the tanks with fresh lettuce and pieces of boiled potato and beet, then turn on the sprinkler system that he had installed in the tanks to simulate natural rainfall. Then all the snails would liven up and begin eating, mating, or merely gliding through the shallow water with obvious pleasure. Mr Knoppert often let a snail crawl on to his forefinger – he fancied his snails enjoyed this human contact – and he would feed it a piece of lettuce by hand, would observe the snail from all sides, finding as much aesthetic satisfaction as another man might from contemplating a Japanese print.

By now, Mr Knoppert did not allow anyone to set foot in his study. Too many snails had the habit of crawling around on the floor, of going to sleep glued to chair bottoms, and to the backs of books on the shelves. Snails spent much of their time sleeping, especially the older snails. But there were enough less indolent snails who preferred love-making. Mr Knoppert estimated that about a dozen pairs of snails must be kissing all the time. And certainly there was a multitude of baby and adolescent snails. They were impossible to count. But Mr Knoppert did count the snails sleeping and creeping on the ceiling alone, and arrived at something between eleven and twelve hundred. The tanks, the bowls, the underside of his desk and the book-shelves must surely have held fifty times that number. Mr Knoppert meant to scrape the snails off the ceiling one day soon. Some of them had been up there for weeks, and he was afraid they were not taking in enough nourishment. But of late he had been a little too busy, and too much in need of the tranquillity that he got simply from sitting in the study in his favourite chair.

During the month of June he was so busy he often worked late into the evening at his office. Reports were piling in at the end of the fiscal year. He made calculations, spotted a half-dozen possibilities of gain, and reserved the most daring, the least obvious moves for his private operations. By this time next year, he thought, he should be three or four times as well off as now. He saw his bank account multiplying as easily and rapidly as his snails. He told his wife this, and she was overjoyed. She even forgave him the ruination of the study, and the stale, fishy smell that was spreading throughout the whole upstairs.

'Still, I do wish you'd take a look just to see if anything's happening, Peter,' she said to him rather anxiously one morning. 'A tank might have overturned or something, and I wouldn't want the rug to be spoilt. You haven't been in the study for nearly a week, have you?'

Mr Knoppert hadn't been in for nearly two weeks. He didn't tell his wife that the rug was pretty much gone already. I'll go up tonight,' he said.

But it was three more days before he found time. He went in one evening just before bedtime and was surprised to find the floor quite covered with snails, with three or four layers of snails. He had difficulty closing the door without mashing any. The dense clusters of snails in the corners made the room look positively round, as if he stood inside some huge, conglomerate stone. Mr Knoppert cracked his knuckles and gazed around him in astonishment. They had not only covered every surface, but thousands of snails hung down into the room from the chandelier in a grotesque clump.

Mr Knoppert felt for the back of a chair to steady himself. He felt only a lot of shells under his hand. He had to smile a little; there were snails in the chair seat, piled up on one another, like a lumpy cushion. He really must do something about the ceiling, and immediately. He took an umbrella from the corner, brushed some of the snails off it, and cleared a place on his desk to stand. The umbrella point tore the wallpaper, and then the weight of the snails pulled down a long strip that hung almost to the floor. Mr Knoppert felt suddenly frustrated and angry. The sprinklers would make them move. He pulled the lever.

The sprinklers came on in all the tanks, and the seething activity of the entire room increased at once. Mr Knoppert slid his feet along the floor, through tumbling snails' shells that made a sound like pebbles on a beach, and directed a couple of the sprinklers at the ceiling. This was a mistake, he saw at once. The softened paper began to tear, and he dodged one slowly falling mass only to be hit by a swinging festoon of snails, really hit quite a stunning blow on the side of the head. He went down on one knee, dazed. He should open a window, he thought, the air was stifling. And there were snails crawling over his shoes and up his trouser legs. He shook his feet irritably. He was just going to the door, intending to call for one of the servants to help him, when the chandelier fell on him. Mr

Knoppert sat down heavily on the floor. He saw now that he couldn't possibly get a window open, because the snails were fastened thick and deep over the windowsills. For a moment, he felt he couldn't get up, felt as if he were suffocating. It was not only the musty smell of the room, but everywhere he looked long wallpaper strips covered with snails blocked his vision, as if he were in a prison.

'Edna!' he called, and was amazed at the muffled, ineffectual sound of his voice. The room might have been soundproof.

He crawled to the door, heedless of the sea of snails he crushed under hands and knees. He could not get the door open. There were so many snails on it, crossing and recrossing the crack of the door on all sides, they actually resisted his strength.

'Edna!' A snail crawled into his mouth. He spat it out in disgust. Mr Knoppert tried to brush the snails off his arms. But for every hundred he dislodged, four hundred seemed to slide upon him and fasten to him again, as if they deliberately sought him out as the only comparatively snail-free surface in the room. There were snails crawling over his eyes. Then just as he staggered to his feet, something else hit him – Mr Knoppert couldn't even see what. He was fainting! At any rate, he was on the floor. His arms felt like leaden weights as he tried to reach his nostrils, his eyes, to free them from the sealing, murderous snail bodies.

'Help!' He swallowed a snail. Choking, he widened his mouth for air and felt a snail crawl over his lips on to his tongue. He was in hell! He could feel them gliding over his legs like a glutinous river, pinning his legs to the floor. 'Ugh!' Mr Knoppert's breath came in feeble gasps. His vision grew black, a horrible, undulating black. He could not breathe at all, because he could not reach his nostrils, could not move his hands. Then through the slit of one eye, he saw directly in front of him, only inches away, what had been, he knew, the rubber plant that stood in its pot near the door. A pair of snails were quietly making love in it. And right beside them, tiny snails as pure as dewdrops were emerging from a pit like an infinite army into their widening world.

WOMAN TROUBLE

I never did like living in Reno. I'm a desert woman, born and raised just outside Winnemucca, Nevada. Trees and buildings, and all those crowds milling around day and night on the streets get in my way. I like to see clear and far off. Horizons, mountains. Even people stand out better in the open desert. You can see them coming, all alone and separate instead of muffled up in all that town stuff.

Have you ever smelled, real good, the sage coming in off the desert after a rain? Clean, heady, sweet. Seems to scour out the lungs and makes your brain fresh. You can remember you've got a heart, even a soul. Well, that's what I wanted for Paddy.

Paddy belongs to the desert. Wyoming country, he was born there. Up where buttes are swept by winds and you have to struggle a little to fill your lungs with oxygen, it's so high in the sky, you know. Couple of years after we were married Paddy took me back to his old home ranch. Well, it wasn't his any longer – he'd lost it fooling around in Nevada's gambling clubs. But the people who bought it from the bank are nice folks, old friends of the family, and they pretended the ranch was still Paddy's.

Paddy and I rode alongside the buttes, sometimes stopping the horses and edging them together so we could kiss. 'Paddy,' I told him, 'let's save up and buy back your ranch. Town's no good for us, we're open-country people.' Especially town's no good for Paddy, I was thinking, and he knew it.

He grinned and said, 'You're right, girl. No dice tables out here on the open range.' He patted my arm and added, 'First big killing I make, and I sure ought to be due for one soon, we'll buy us a spread. Build us a brand-new house on it with all the fixings, good as back in Reno.'

Good as! My God. A two-room-with-kitchenette apartment. A stove with an oven which baked lopsided. A dwarf-sized refrigerator. And all the gambling tables in the world, it seemed, just down the street.

'Paddy, I don't need fine things, I'm not used to them. It would be fun to camp out in a cabin, cook on a wood-stove – nothing bakes good like a wood range. It would be like when I was a kid. Homebaked bread – my mother always did her own baking and she taught me. And we could have a little garden, Paddy. You'd be outdoors a lot – indoors don't suit you, Paddy, staying in that warehouse all the time, lifting those heavy loads.'

'Lifting loads, woman?' His face took on that remote expression he always got when he decided I had gone too far interfering in men's ways. 'You mean pushing so hard on those little levers that do all the lifting? With a 180-pounds, six-one of a man to do the pushing? Well, Angie, I sure got a hard life.'

I wanted to say it was lifting the dice, shaking them, tossing them out that was too much for a 180-pounds, six-one of a man. But when he got that look Paddy scared me. No, no, I don't mean, he ever hit me or roughed me up. He never did. Why, Paddy would just spit on the ground when he heard about men who hit women. Said only feisty little men did that, who were too scared to tackle a man. But once, after that look, Paddy had walked out of our apartment and didn't come back. It took me a week to find him. Down in Vegas. And another week to beg him back.

That time I wished he had hit me instead. All the money we had in our joint savings account, $715, went that time. To the last penny. It takes a lot of standing on your feet and waiting on customers in a department store to get that much put away above what it costs to live these days.

Paddy didn't believe in savings accounts, even though I

had his name on the bank book. Said it was for men who didn't have the guts to take a chance, or for women. That's why it didn't bother him when he drew it out. Grinned, patted me on the back, and said he'd pay it back one of these days with interest.

Me, I didn't care if he ever paid it back. All I wanted back was Paddy.

Like that evening later on when I was snuggling my face against his, whispering I wouldn't trade him for the whole world tied in ribbons.

He kissed me and whispered back, 'You're a good kid.' Then he scooted me off his lap, stood up, gave me a little smack on the bottom, and said, 'Think I'll hit the clubs a while. Think I'll begin my first million tonight. So I can get you that little ranch you're always talking about. Only it'll be a big one. Maybe I'll try for two million, so's I can fence it in with those ribbons you're always talking about.'

'Oh, Paddy, please! Don't go, Paddy. I don't want to be rich. I don't even need the ranch. Paddy, you know it's just you I need. And you've been away so much lately. Every night, Paddy, the last few weeks.'

'Maybe there'll be a few more nights, too,' he said easily. 'Stick with it, one of these nights I'll strike it rich.'

'I'll go with you, Paddy.'

His face set. 'No. You bug me at the tables.'

No use arguing with Paddy. Unless I wanted to set out on another search all over Nevada.

I remember it rained that night in Reno. A good steady rain. Once I thought, I'll just go along Virginia Street, down the alley by the clubs, find out which one Paddy's in, say it was raining hard and that I'd brought him an umbrella. But it scared me to think of the way his face would look – *I'm a man, Angie, don't wet-nurse me. You bug me at the tables, Angie.* Or maybe he wouldn't say anything. Just never come home.

I'd rather he hit me every day, honest I would.

I woke up in the morning and felt for him next to me.

The sheet was cool, untouched. All around me, all through the apartment, was the sweet sage smell that rises off the desert after a rain. But it wouldn't make the ache in my head go away. I perked some coffee, waited a while to eat, and hoped he would show up before he had to go to work. And I said to myself, *Damn the gambling and the gamblers, damn Reno to hell.*

Reno could have been a nice place, you know. A sweet hometown with the Truckee River running through, willows all along it. Over to the west, Mount Rose with snow still on it in summer. Old brown fat Peavine Mountain squatting toward the north. And the clean lovely desert spread to the east. My God, it could have been nice to live in with the man you love. Only it wasn't.

I left a place set at the table in case he showed up. Then I went down on Virginia Street, making like I was window shopping. At 6:30 in the morning, yet! Hoping I'd see him, but that he wouldn't see me: *Angie, you trying to make a woman out of me? I thought you married me because I was a man.* At 6:30 he could be grabbing a bite to eat at one of the club lunch counters, because he had to be at work by seven.

Then I saw him. Coming out of a club with a tall red-blonde holding onto his arm, almost head-high with him. Laughing, throwing her head back, tossing her long shiny hair. She had on a long black dress and it fit her like she was the model on which all women ought to be patterned. I noticed that especially because I'm short and stocky-built. Not fat or anything, just short and stocky-built, the strong kind. I used to help my Dad chop wood – Mother and Dad never had any boys.

I wanted to walk over and sock the girl in the nose. But I always have a sense to be fair about things. It was Paddy who needed the sock in the nose. How would the girl know Paddy belonged to me if he didn't tell her?

I speeded up and came even with them just as she leaned toward him and kissed his cheek. Paddy had his arm up hailing a taxi, I said, 'Hi, Paddy, won't you be late for work?'

Paddy was a gambler. His faced stayed cool and easy, and it was like hoods dropped over his eyes so I couldn't see into them. 'Hi, Angie,' he said with his mouth. But I could feel the inside of him saying, *Get the hell out of here*. That wasn't fair. He was the one on the spot, not me. Besides, this was woman trouble. I'd never had woman trouble with Paddy before. Far as I knew. A wife can't buckle under when it's woman trouble.

'I laid out your breakfast on the table – you shouldn't go to work on an empty stomach. Paddy, I don't think I've met your friend.'

I was talking to Paddy, but I was looking square at this woman. Woman she was, somewhere between 25 and 30, not much younger than me. She had the skin and the looks of an 18-year-old, only young kids don't get that confident look on them. This woman looked strong and sure of herself, like maybe she'd fought her way up.

She was beautiful, I'll say that. Her eyes were so blue their colour almost hurt you to look at. Big, too. Only thing, they stared at me bold as brass, shrewd too. Had me figured first look, and it was striking her funny. She took on a little half-smile like she was holding back a laugh.

She knew how to put on makeup, just enough to turn her skin to honey and rose. Or maybe the Lord shot the works on her, maybe she was born that way. Makeup on her eyes, though, and lashes that almost brushed her cheeks. And like a halo, all that red-blonde hair.

'Is this your wife?' she asked Paddy.

He nodded and said, easy, 'Sure is. Angie, meet Molly.'

She looked him level in the eye, laughed, and said, 'You're a cool one, I'll say that for you.' She turned to me. 'Chin up, lady, so he can take a poke at it for good measure.' She laughed again, climbed in the taxi and drove off.

What she said shook Paddy. He whipped his face away from the taxi like he'd been slapped, and he didn't give me that goodbye look like he had just before he'd hopped off for Vegas. He said, 'I'm sorry, Angie. But you shouldn't have come looking for me. And I'm not going to lie to you, tell you I was just coming out to put her in the taxi. I was going with her.'

Well, I couldn't hardly jump on him after that. I mean, he'd come square with me. So I said, 'I'm sorry too, Paddy. See you tonight. I've fixed up a good roast for dinner.' *Last night while you made up to this Molly with her bold, laughing, beautiful face, I was home cooking for you. I'm not ugly, Paddy. I got big brown eyes, nice features – you told me it's brown eyes you like, not blue like yours. You said brown eyes always got you.*

He let a deep breath sigh out and said, 'Okay. See you tonight.'

'You've never hit me, Paddy. Not once. She shouldn't have said that.'

Kind of like it hurt as the words came out he said. 'She's seen 'em hit.' Then he turned and walked off.

What do you do when you love a man and as far as you know he's never two-timed you before, and then you find out he did – or was going to? And you begin thinking maybe all those gambling nights and the money gone, that $715 out of the savings account – maybe it wasn't all for gambling?

You brood on it, if you're like me.

All day long while I was selling girdles, pantyhose and things, I couldn't stop thinking about that tall bold Molly. The way she laughed and told off Paddy, and him standing there looking like he could eat her. And the contempt she'd had for his little dumb wife.

Paddy was there when I got home. He didn't say anything, just pulled me down on his lap and kissed my forehead and my eyes. 'You got nice eyes, Angie,' he said.

'They never did see nothing bad about me. You got nice lovin' eyes.'

That's all. What I wanted to say was such a big lump in me that I was afraid to let it out. So I just kissed him.

But after dinner I said, 'Paddy, let's pull out and go on up to Wyoming. We could save for our own place up there as well – maybe better – as here in Reno. I could find a job and maybe you could get us a little house on a ranch where you'd work. There's an old cabin on your home place, maybe they'd rent it to us and we could fix it up. Get our roots in.'

'One of these days,' he said. 'Maybe.'

He helped me with the dishes that night – usually he didn't do that, said he felt silly lifting teacups with a rag in his hand. But that night he helped me. And he kissed me sweet. Tender, it was. Never once mentioned going to the clubs. It was wonderful.

But sometime in the night – well, it was two o'clock when I turned on the light – I found myself alone in the bed. Paddy was nowhere in the apartment.

Molly, her name was, *Angie, meet Molly*. That's all, no last name. How do you find a Molly in a place as big as Reno?

You get up and dress and go down to the gambling clubs and start looking for Paddy. Or Molly.

But I didn't go. Paddy needed some kind of honour, even if it was the kind I made up myself.

Around four o'clock I laid out some potatoes, ready to fry the way Paddy likes them. Set the table pretty. Listened for the creak of the elevator which meant somebody was coming up. Went to the bathroom to do what I could about my face. Bluish circles under my eyes smudged the upper part of my face. Face puffy from worry and lack of sleep – or like a puff adder getting mad, ready to strike. I was only in my early thirties, but this morning I looked 40 or more. Little dumpy woman. Why wouldn't Paddy, eyes blue as heaven, six-one of muscle, a sidewise grin, why wouldn't –

'Stop it!' I told myself in the mirror. 'Stop it!'

Paddy loved me. He told me so lots of times. And Paddy never lied, no matter what else he did.

I put the potatoes away in the refrigerator, drank a cup of coffee and walked to work. It wasn't far, and besides we didn't have a car any more. Used to, but Paddy hit a winning streak a year or so back and wanted to raise his bets. So I signed the car over – it was in my name – and Paddy sold it. Oh, well, it costs money for gas.

It's tough to stand on your feet all day, straightening up counters that customers are always messing up the minute you've folded things. It's tough smiling, when you ache all over from wondering where Paddy's gone to. I thought once I'd call him at work. But if he was there he'd be mad. And if he wasn't there his boss would be mad knowing Paddy's wife was hunting for him again.

I tried to eat a sandwich at lunch, but it just wouldn't go down. So I asked my boss could I go home, I didn't feel good. He was real nice, told me not to come back till I felt completely okay. They like me at work. Steady, always on time. Just a dumb, steady, day-after-day sales-clerk that redheaded Molly wouldn't be caught dead being.

I went home and took a couple of aspirins. Tried to lie down and relax. Got up and mopped the kitchen and bathroom. Took a shower. Put on my new coral pants suit. Took it off. Broad as a barn door from the rear. Put on a long straight jersey dress. Looked like a Japanese wrestler in a nightgown. Finally put back on the dark dress I had worn to work. And it was past five o'clock and no Paddy.

Well, Reno's free and open – anybody can go in the clubs and play a few nickels and dimes in the slot machines. That's what I'd tell Paddy if I saw him. But maybe he wouldn't see me. I could hide behind the machines, leave once I knew where – no. Not if he was with Molly.

I walked my legs off that night. Tried to eat a hamburger. Couldn't make it. Got to bed around three in the morning. Alone.

Next morning I called at work and said I was still sick. It was no lie. I was sick. The boss was nice, said to take care of myself. So I was ashamed to walk the streets, running in and out of clubs. I stayed in the apartment. Which was good because Paddy's boss telephoned and asked what happened to him the last two days. 'We're sick,' I said. What kind of sick? 'We must have eaten something funny. Sick to our stomachs.'

'Yeah,' his boss said. 'Not down in Vegas again, is he, Angie, and you packing to go find him?'

'Listen, Pete, you got no right to say that – my God, can't a man have a stomach ache without – '

'Okay, okay, Angie, cool it. Take care of yourselves. Tell Paddy to forget about tomorrow, it's Saturday, he might as well get a good start on Monday.'

'Thanks, Pete, I'll tell him.'

If Paddy was in the clubs he was like a ghost slipping in and out, because I hit them all. And that wasn't Paddy's style. Even losing, he'd stick at one table, waiting for the odds to break his way. And Paddy hadn't left for Vegas, he was still in Reno. My insides told me so.

They kept telling me something else. Paddy was with Molly.

So I concentrated on how I could find Molly.

You ever looked over the list of attorneys in the phone-book yellow pages? In Reno? You wonder how they all eat, except Reno's built on divorce as well as gambling – some fine recommendation for your hometown, huh? I started calling attorney's offices and ran smack into, 'Molly? The last name, please? You say you saw this lady drop her purse in one of the clubs and there's no identification in it, so how do you know the name is Molly? Oh. One of the dealers. Well, my suggestion would be to ask that dealer about her, or turn over the purse to the cashier or the police.' A long pause. 'May I ask why you didn't just give it to the lady?' Or, 'I'm sorry but we never give out clients' names. Why don't you try the police?'

Well, it was a dumb try anyway.

I thought, why not go down to that club where I first saw Paddy with her and ask around?

Down to the clubs. Jangling, brassy sound of slot machines, busy, busy. Everybody pulling handles like it was a job doing some good, like cleaning up the world or something every time a coin dropped in. Most of the time nothing was coming out, no loaf of bread or can of beans, nothing. Once in a while a little money to be stuffed back into the machine.

'Say, do you know a pretty redhead named Molly? Tall girl, dressed good. She was here the other night. I – I've got something I think may belong to her. I got to find her.'

The dealer at the blackjack table grinned sidewise and said, 'Honey, I hope it's something nice you got for her. If it is, you might try the office. Something different, you better take it home. No, I don't know any tall redhead named Molly.'

I tried a couple of other dealers. Then the lunch counter. A waitress there said, 'Say, aren't you Paddy Finley's wife?'

I nodded and she said, 'I thought so. See, I used to live in your same apartment house, couple of floors below, but I used to see you come in together.'

'I've got something may be this Molly's,' I said again. 'The other day down here I saw her with – something like it. But I don't know where to find her. I just thought someone here might know her.'

She gave me a quirky smile. 'I don't know her, honey, but I do know Paddy, he's here a lot. Hard to miss Paddy, looks like kids used to think cowboy heroes ought to look. Eastern divorcees still think that. You know what I'd do,

—112—

Mrs Finley – I'd go home, take two-three aspirins, and have yourself a nice rest. Then when Paddy came home you'd be in shape to flatten him. Wanta cup of coffee. I'll throw in the aspirin?'

It's peculiar, how when your mind's upset it's the middle of your stomach that hurts. Like a knot tied in it. But all the time the real hurt is in your mind where you can't touch it.

Out on the street, up a way, I got this queer feeling. Like I wanted to shake all over but was too frozen to do it. I felt something either pulling on me or breathing on me. I mean, it was screwy, like I was a Geiger counter and had run into what I was looking for. I turned.

Across Second Street, headed towards the alley that leads into the clubs, was Molly. Wearing a long bright-green skirt and a white turtleneck sweater. With all that pretty reddish hair in a big topknot, like she was deliberately making herself taller than she already was. Conspicuous, you know?

Paddy wasn't with her.

I was so relieved I felt like I ought to walk over and apologise to her. Instead I went close to the store windows, turned, and watched her swing along the street. Like she'd owned Reno so long she'd even forgotten it belonged to her.

Then I saw him, Paddy, walking fast behind her, his long legs giving at the knee in that little bend that cowpunchers never quite lose. He came up to her, grabbed her arm, flung her face to face with him. She wasn't surprised. Just took on a strong bold look. Said something. Laughed. He grabbed her throat and shook her back and forth. Her long legs kicked at him, her fingers raked his cheeks. Her knee came up hard. Paddy staggered back, bent over. Even from across the street I could see he was pale, sick.

Molly turned away, cool as you please, not even touching her throat though it was bound to be hurting. Bold as brass. Still owning the town, she was.

I cut across the traffic to Paddy. He was leaning against a building, while people clustered around staring, eyes thrilled like they were watching a movie being shot.

'Paddy, let's go home.'

Somebody snickered.

Flames shot through me. Like a chimney long unused and then too much paper is put in the firepot and the soot blazes and sets the house on fire. I plunged into the ring of gawkers, punching, slapping, screaming for them to mind their own business, to leave my Paddy alone.

I felt hands on my shoulders. Paddy's hands. 'Angie, that's enough. Let's get out of here.'

The crowd parted and we walked through it, turned towards the river. Paddy hailed a taxi and we got in it. Paddy wasn't walking too good.

'That Molly – that Molly, why did you – ' I began after we shut the door of our apartment.

'I don't want to talk about it,' Paddy said, his face white and drawn. He went in the bathroom and closed the door.

I made some coffee, then stood by the stove wondering whether he'd rather have steak or soup. Or if either of us ever wanted to eat again.

It's hard for a wife of twelve years not to ask her man why he chokes a girl he's just met. If he just met her. Especially with Paddy always spitting on the ground at the mention of men who hit women. Said they ought to take out their mad on wrangling horses or find a man their size or bigger. Now he was choking Molly. Like she had set him crazy.

And then she bested him, right in the middle of Reno with his wife and a crowd watching. *Damn you, Paddy, how'd that look in the papers if a cop had been around and taken you both to the station and me, too? The papers saying your girl friend beat you up and your wife beat up the crowd for snickering. Like you were some ragdoll for women to toss around. Damn you, Paddy, how'd you like that?*

Paddy was a long time in the bathroom. I heard the bath water running. When he came out he was shaved and had on clean underthings I kept in a bureau for him in the bathroom. 'I got soup hot and steak ready to broil,' I said as he went through the living room to the bedroom, that's the screwy way our apartment was.

'I don't want anything.'

I heard him moving around the bedroom. Pretty soon he came out, dressed up, and his suitcase in his hand. 'So long, Angie,' he said.

'You can't go like this, Paddy. It's not right, it's not fair to me. We got to talk. Listen, Paddy, I can overlook what happened. Just tell me why, then we won't talk about it any more.'

'This time don't come looking for me,' he said, staring straight ahead at the outside door.

'Paddy, you don't want her after what she done – she don't want you, you don't want a woman don't want you. But I want you.'

'So long, Angie.'

'Paddy, let's pack up and head for Wyoming, get out of this damn state with its no-good life, gambling, and loose women like – '

He wheeled on me, his eyes blue fire. 'Don't say her name!'

He opened the door and went out. I just followed him, like a puppy dog that's been kicked but won't stay home. Down the hall after him. He took the stairs instead of the elevator, his long legs going fast. I kept up. Outside on the side-walk, down to the corner, me with no purse or anything.

He turned and said, 'Angie, I don't want you no more.' He started walking again, with me right behind.

He began running. I'm stubby-built, but I've got lasting power. I ran behind him, down almost to Virginia Street. Paddy stopped and I stood beside him.

'You want to go along and hear me tell her I love her before I kill her?'

'You're not going to kill anybody.'

'Okay, just keep hanging onto my tail.' He started walking, and I did too. We crossed the Truckee Bridge, over by the old Post Office, past the Holiday Hotel. Turned back again, the opposite direction, with him trying to lose me, up the hill above the river, then we turned again.

'You got no pride, Angie,' he said over his shoulder.

What's pride? It don't fill emptiness. I kept walking.

Finally he stopped in front of a fine old house above the river, not far from downtown, that was split into apartments. 'She lives here,' Paddy said. 'I'm going in. And if she's not there I'll wait for her. Because she's mine, she's not going to change her mind just because she's got her divorce and is tired of playing around. Angie, you go get you a divorce. I'm taking Molly. One way or another.'

He went up the porch steps, through the entrance, up the stairs. Me back of him. At the top of the stairs he turned and said, 'You're asking for it, Angie,' and hauled back his arm. I stood, waiting for it. If he hit me, maybe he'd think of me the way he did Molly. But his hand dropped.

He knocked on a door, with a number 3 on it. Inside were footsteps and a woman asked. 'Who is it?' Molly.

'You know who,' Paddy said.

She laughed. 'You want to get messed up again?' She slid a bolt on the other side and walked away.

Paddy stepped back and kicked the door. Ordinarily a kick that hard would have gone on through. But this was an old-fashioned house with heavy oak doors. Nothing happened except a big deep scar on the finish.

Paddy kicked again. Then he went crazy. Kept kicking that door like a bronco with a cactus under its saddle, his face a sick-grey and his eyes blazing. I pulled at him. He shook me off and kept kicking. Nobody came out of the apartment across the hall – the folks must have been gone. Downstairs a woman was yelling. The landlady, it turned out, who went back inside and called the police.

Suddenly the cops were there, no sirens or anything, and they were manhandling Paddy. It took the two of them to handcuff him and drag him downstairs. I stood there, frozen. One cop came back, knocked on Molly's door, asked her to open up and tell him what the trouble was. 'No trouble of mine,' she said through the door. 'I didn't call you. Nobody came in my apartment. Just some stupid idiot kicking my door. Go talk to the one who called you.'

'It's the police. We need information.'

She didn't answer. He turned to me, 'You in on this lady? You trying to get inside, too?'

I shook my head. 'I'm his wife. I never touched the door. He just wanted to talk to her. She wouldn't talk to him and he got mad. There wasn't any more to it than that, he just lost his temper.'

'Some temper the way the door's beat up. You better come down to the station and tell the Chief about it.'

'I'm his wife. I've got no complaint. And if I did, you can't make me say anything against Paddy. I'm his wife. I've got no complaint.'

'Well I have!' the landlady yelled behind us. 'Breaking up my door, disturbing my tenants, you bet I'll complain, I'll follow you down to the station in my car.'

'I'll pay for all the damage,' I said. 'You tell the Chief that.'

The policeman and the landlady left and I sat down on the top stairstep, shaking like a Washoe Zephyr had struck me. After a bit the bolt slid on Molly's door and the door slowly opened.

She saw me. 'Oh,' she said.

I didn't say anything.

'You're his wife, aren't you?' I nodded.

'Listen, I'll be straight with you. When I first hit this

town I bumped into Paddy. In one of the clubs. I was just getting my bearings, had no place to go or anyone to see. And Paddy – well, he has a way with him. Anyway, I didn't know he was married, so we played around. Then you showed up, talking about breakfast. So I split. But he looked me up after that and said he'd left you. Kept hanging around. But frankly, lady, I run on a different track than Paddy. With bosses, not hired help. So I said bye-bye and he wouldn't listen. So he tried muscling me around.' She laughed, high and hard. 'Shows how stupid a good-looking guy can be. I was trained by pros, and he's an amateur.'

'Paddy never once raised his hand to me.'

She looked at me wise, and a little sad. 'Maybe it would have worked out better if he had: Honest to God. Women!' She went back inside and closed the door.

I'd been trying to hate her. But I couldn't. I couldn't even hate Paddy. I felt nothing but sick, sitting there in a strange place like a cast-off ragdoll with its stuffing out.

I got up and went outdoors.

Like I said, it was an old-fashioned house turned into apartments. Whoever had changed it had made kind of a thing out of it being old-fashioned. They'd kept the old veranda, shaped like an L, and put up an old-time hanging porch swing around the corner from the house front. I felt so done in that I went and rested in the swing.

After a while a car drove up. It was the landlady looking like she'd bit into a chunk of iron. She stomped inside, never saw me. It got dark, but I just kept sitting there.

Maybe I had a hunch what would happen.

Molly came out of the house. She went down the steps to the sidewalk, her hair shimmering under the porch light and her long black dress swirled with embroidery that matched the colour of her hair. When she reached the sidewalk, she turned towards town.

I heard footsteps, running from a clump of trees across the street. I stood up, my heart feeling like it filled my whole chest. Molly stopped, tall and defiant, turning towards the man who rushed at her. Paddy. I knew it would be Paddy. She laughed, never a flinch out of her. 'Did that poor fool woman bail you out?'

'They didn't hold me. I paid for the door.'

'Well, scram! You can't pay for me. The price is too high.'

He called her a name. Then pleading like, his hands reaching out almost as if he was trying to climb up some slick and muddy riverbank. 'Please, Molly. Please! I'm begging, Molly. I never felt this way before about anybody. I've got to have you, Molly!'

'Go to hell,' she said. 'I'm no horse you can break. So lay off the big he-man Wild West stuff with me.'

Paddy swung. She dodged but the blow glanced her head. She staggered back. He came at her again, both his hands grabbing.

She must have reached in her purse. I couldn't see. I only heard a sharp crack, the sound reverberating in my ears until it made me dizzy. Paddy was on the ground, crawling around like he was trying to find something.

I floated down the steps, no feet, out to the sidewalk. Then Molly was on the pavement and I was pounding her head onto the concrete.

.

See Paddy out there? Gentlest man in the world. Sweet and quiet, just rocking on the porch. Hums to himself and rocks. Oh, now and again he walks to the little corral I built and pets the mare i bought after I moved us up here to Wyoming. But Paddy just stays gentle and quiet, that's his real nature. That Molly had no right to stir him up, make fun of him. Then try to kill him. She turned him crazy, her face and her bigtime ways.

Right after the trial I brought Paddy back to Wyoming.

Yes, the trial scared me. Not so much for myself as for Paddy. Because if I got sent to the penitentiary, who'd look after him? That shot of Molly's addled him. Struck his head. Made him like a child. Sometimes he cries at night, gets on the floor and crawls around. Just like he did that night. Like he's looking for something he'll never find.

Molly didn't die right away. Not for almost two weeks after that night. But that didn't get me off. Manslaughter it was. In the heat of passion. And my lawyer brought out that I was protecting my husband. So they gave me a suspended sentence. On probation for three years. I have to check in every month.

So I rent this little house on Paddy's old home place from the folks who own it now. Family friends. They keep an eye on Paddy while I'm at work. Except for some nights Paddy's happy. Thinks the mare is a whole string of horses, calls her a lot of different names.

Me?

Well, I'm kind of happy, too. Kind of. No more worry about Paddy running off to the clubs. And by now I'm used to it.

Used to what?

Oh, like with the mare, Paddy calls me by a different name. Just one. Molly. So it hurts a little, but I just figure it's me who answers. Me, Angie.

MR WRONG

Everybody – that is to say the two or three people she knew in London – told Meg that she had been very lucky indeed to find a car barely three years old, in such good condition and at such a price. She believed them gladly, because actually buying the car had been the most nerve-racking experience. Of course she had been told – and many times by her father – that all car dealers were liars and thieves. Indeed, to listen to old Dr Crosbie, you would think that nobody could *ever* buy a second-hand car, possibly even any *new* car, without its brakes or steering giving way the moment you were out of sight of the garage. But her father had always been of a nervous disposition: and as he intensely disliked going anywhere, and had now reached an age where he could fully indulge this disapprobation, it was not necessary to take much notice of him. For at least fifteen of her twenty-seven years Meg silently put up with his saying that there was no place like home, until, certain that she had exhausted all the possibilities of the small market town near where they lived, she had exclaimed, 'That's just it, Father! That's why I want to see somewhere else – *not* like it.'

Her mother, who had all the prosaic anxiety about her only child finding 'a really nice young man, Mr Right' that kind, anxious mothers tend to have – especially if their daughter can be admitted in the small hours to be 'not exactly a beauty' – smiled encouragingly at Meg and said, 'But Humphrey, dear, she will always be coming back to stay. She *knows* this is her home, but all young girls need a change.' (The young part of this had become emphasised as Meg plodded steadily through her twenties with not a romance in sight.)

So Meg had come to London, got a job in an antique shop in the New King's Road, and shared a two-room flat with two other girls in Fulham. One of them was a secretary, and the other a model: both were younger than Meg and ten times as self-assured; kind to her in an off-hand manner, but never becoming friends, nothing more than people she knew – like Mr Whitehorn, who ran the shop that she worked in. It was her mother who had given Meg three hundred pounds towards a car, as the train fares and subsequent taxis were proving beyond her means. She spent very little in London: she had bought one dress at Laura Ashley, but had no parties to go to in it, and lacked the insouciance to wear it to work. She lived off eggs done in various ways, and quantities of instant coffee – in the shop and in the flat. Her rent was comfortingly modest by present-day standards, she walked to work, smoked very occasionally, and set her own hair. Her father had given her a hundred pounds when she was twenty-one: all of this had been invested, and to it she now added savings from her meagre salary and finally went off to one of London's northern suburbs to answer an advertisement about a second-hand MG.

The car dealer, whom she had imagined as some kind of tiger in a loud checked suit with whisky on his breath, had proved to be more of a wolf in a sheepskin car-coat – particularly when he smiled, which displayed a frightening number of teeth that seemed to stretch back in his raspberry mouth and down his throat with vulpine largesse. He smiled often, and Meg took to not looking at him whenever he began to do it. He took her out on a test drive: at first he drove, explaining all the advantages of the car while he did so, and then he suggested that she take over. This she did, driving very badly, with clashing of gears and stalling the engine in the most embarrassing places. 'I can see you've got the hang of it, Mr Taunton said. 'It's always difficult driving a completely new car. But you'll find that she's most reliable: will start in all weather, economical on fuel, and needs the minimum of servicing.'

When Meg asked whether the car had ever had an accident, he began to smile, so she did not see his face when he replied that it hadn't been an accident, just a slight brush. 'The respray, which I expect you've noticed, was largely because the panel-work involved, and mind you, it *was* only panel-work, made us feel that it could do with a more cheerful colour. I always think aqua-blue is a nice colour for a ladies' car. And this is definitely a ladies' car.'

She felt his smile receding when she asked how many previous owners the car had had. He replied that it had been for a short time the property of some small firm that had since gone out of business. 'Only driven by one of the directors and his secretary.'

That sounded all right, thought Meg: but she was also thinking that for the price this was easily the best car she could hope for, and somehow, she felt, he knew that she knew she was going to buy it. His last words were: 'I hope you have many miles of motoring before you, madam.' The elongated grin began, and as it was for the last time, she watched him – trying to smile back – as the pointed teeth became steadily more exposed down his cavernous throat. She noticed then that his pale grey eyes very nearly met, but were narrowly saved from this by the bridge of his nose, which was long and thrusting, and almost made up for his having a mouth that had clearly been eaten away by his awful quantity of teeth. They had nothing going for each other beyond her buying and his selling a car.

Back in the showroom office, he sank into his huge moquette chair and said: 'Bring us a coffee, duck. I've earned it.' And a moony-faced blonde in a mini-skirt with huge legs that seemed tortured by her tights, smiled and went.

Meg drove the MG – her *car* – back to London in the first state of elation she had ever known since she had won the bending competition in a local gymkhana. She had a car! Neither Samantha nor Val were in such a position. She really drove quite well, as she had had a temporary job working for a doctor near home who had lost his licence for two years. Away from Mr Taunton (*Clive* Taunton he had repeatedly said), she felt able and assured. The car was easy to drive, and responded, as MGs do, with a kind of husky excitement to speed.

When she reached the flat, Samantha and Val were so impressed that they actually took her out to a Chinese meal with their two boy-friends. Meg got into her Laura Ashley dress and enjoyed every sweet and sour moment of it. Everybody was impressed by her, and this made her prettier. She got slightly drunk on rice wine and lager and went to work the next day, in her car, feeling much more like the sort of person she had expected to feel like in London. Her head ached, but she had something to show for it: one of the men had talked to her several times – asking where she lived and what her job was, and so forth.

Her first drive north was the following Friday. It was cold, a wet and dark night – in January she never finished at the shop in time even to start the journey in the light – and by the time she was out of the rush, through London and on Hendon Way, it was raining hard. She found the turn off to the M1 with no difficulty: only three hours of driving on that and then about twenty minutes home. It was nothing, really; it just seemed rather a long way at this point. She had drunk a cup of strong black instant at Mr Whitehorn's, who had kindly admired the car and also showed her the perfect place to park it every day, and she knew that her mother would be keeping something hot and home-made for her whatever time she got home. (Her father never ate anything after eight o'clock in the evening for fear of indigestion, something from which he had never in his life suffered and attributed entirely to this precaution.)

Traffic was fairly heavy, but it seemed to be more lorries than anything else, and Meg kept on the whole to the middle lane. She soon found, as motorists new to a motorway do, that the lanes, the headlights coming towards her, and the road glistening with rain had a hypnotic effect, as though she and the car had become minute, and she was being spun down some enormous, endless striped ribbon. 'I mustn't go to sleep,' she thought. Ordinary roads had too much going on in them for one to feel like that. About half her time up the motorway, she felt so tired with trying not to feel sleepy that she decided to stop in the next park, open the windows and have a cigarette. It was too wet to get out, but even stopping the windscreen-wipers for a few minutes would make a change. She stopped the engine, opened her window, and before she had time to think about smoking again, fell asleep.

She awoke very suddenly with a feeling of extreme fear. It was not from a dream; she was sitting in the driver's seat, cramped, and with rain blowing in through the open window, but something else was very wrong. A sound – or noises, alarming in themselves, but, in her circumstances, frighteningly out of place. She shut her window except for an inch at the top. This made things worse. What sounded like heavy, laboured, stertorous, even painful breathing was coming, she quickly realized, from the *back* of the car. The moment she switched on the car light and turned round, there was utter silence, as sudden as the noise stopping in the middle of a breath. There was nobody in the back of the car, but the doors were not locked, and her large carrier bag – her luggage – had fallen to the floor. She locked both doors, switched off the car light and the sounds began again, exactly where they had left off – in the middle of a breath. She put both the car light and her headlights on, and looked again in the back. Silence, and it was still empty. She considered making sure that there was nobody parked behind her, but somehow she didn't want to do that. She switched on the engine and started it. Her main feeling was to get away from the place as quickly as possible. But even when she had started to do this and found herself trying to turn the sounds she had heard into something else and accountable, they wouldn't. They remained in her mind, and she could all too clearly recall them, as the heavy breaths of someone either mortally ill, or in pain, or both, coming quite distinctly from the back of the car. She drove home as fast as she could, counting the minutes and the miles to keep her mind quiet.

She reached home – a stone and slate-roofed cottage – at a quarter past nine, and her mother's first exclamation when she saw her daughter was that she looked dreadfully tired. Instantly, Meg began to feel better; it was what her mother had always said if Meg ever did anything for very long away from home. Her father had gone to bed: so she sat eating her supper with surprising hunger, in the kitchen, and telling her mother the week's news about her job and the two girls she shared with and the Chinese-meal party. 'And is the car nice, darling?' her mother asked at length. Meg started to speak, checked herself, and began again. 'Very nice. It was so kind of you to give me all that money for it,' she said.

The week-end passed with almost comforting dullness, and Meg did not begin to dread returning until after lunch on Sunday. She began to say that she ought to pack; her mother said she must have tea before she left, and her father said that he didn't think that *anyone* should drive in the dark. Or, indeed, at all, he overrode them as they both started saying that it was dark by four anyway. Meg eventually decided to have a short sleep after lunch, drink a cup of tea and then start the journey. 'If I eat one of Mummy's teas, I'll pass out in the car,' she said, and as she said 'pass out', she felt an instant, very small, ripple of fear.

Her mother woke her from a dreamless, refreshing sleep at four with a cup of dark, strong Indian tea and two Bourbon biscuits.

'I'm going to pack for you,' she said firmly. She had also unpacked, while Meg was finishing her supper on Friday night. 'I've never known such a hopeless packer. All your clothes were cramped up and crushed together as though someone had been stamping on them. Carrier bags,' she scolded, enjoying every minute; 'I'm lending you this nice little case that Auntie Phil left me.'

Meg lay warmly under the eiderdown in her own room watching her mother, who quite quickly switched from packing to why didn't Meg drink her tea while it was hot. 'I know your father won't drink anything until it's lukewarm, but thank goodness, you don't take after him. In that respect,' she ended loyally, but Meg knew that her mother missed her, and got tired and bored dealing with her father's ever-increasing regime of what was good or bad for him.

'Can I come next week-end?' she asked. Her mother rushed across the room and enfolded her.

'I should be most upset if you didn't, she said, trying to make it sound like a joke.

When Meg left, and not until she was out of sight of home, she began to worry about what had happened on the journey up. Perhaps it could have been some kind of freak wind, with the car window open, she thought. Being able even to think that encouraged her. It was only raining in fits and starts on the way back, and the journey passed without incident of any kind. By the time Meg had parked, and slipped quietly into the flat that turned out to be empty – both girls were out – she really began to imagine that she had imagined it. She ate a boiled egg, watched a short feature on Samantha's television about Martinique, and went to bed.

The following weekend was also wet, but foggy as well. At one moment during a tedious day in the shop (where there was either absolutely nothing to do, or an endless chore, like packing china and glass to go abroad), Meg thought of putting off going to her parents but they were not on the telephone, and that meant that they would have to endure a telegram. She thought of her father, and decided against that. He would talk about it for six months, stressing it as an instance of youthful extravagance, reiterating the war that it had made upon his nerves, and the proof it was that she should never have gone to London at all. No – telegrams were out, except in an emergency. She would just have to go – whatever the weather, or anything else.

Friday passed tediously: her job was that of packing up the separate pieces of a pair of giant chandeliers in pieces of old newspaper and listing what she packed. Sometimes she got so bored by this that she even read bits from the old, yellowing newsprint. There were pages in one paper of pictures of a Miss World competition: every girl was in a bathing-dress and high-heeled shoes, smiling that extraordinary smile of glazed triumph. They must have an awfully difficult time, Meg thought – fighting off admirers. She wondered just how difficult that would turn out to be. It would probably get easier with practice.

At half past four, Mr Whitehorn let her go early: he was the kind of man who operated in bursts of absentminded kindness, and he said that in view of her journey, the sooner she started the better. Meg drank her last cup of instant coffee, and set off.

Her progress through London was slow, but eventually she reached Hendon Way. Here, too, there were long hold-ups as cars queued at signal lights. There were also straggling lines of people trying to get lifts. She drove past a good many of these, feeling her familiar feelings about them, so mixed that they cancelled one another out, and she never, in fact, did anything about the hitchers. Meg

was naturally a kind person: this part of her made her feel
sorry for the wretched creatures, cold, wet, and probably
tired; wondering whether they would *ever* get to where
they wanted to be. But her father had always told her
never to give lifts, hinting darkly at the gothic horrors that
lay in wait for anyone who ever did that. It was not that
Meg ever consciously agreed with her father; rather that
in all the years of varying warnings, some of his anxiety
had brushed off on her – making her shy, unsure of what
to do about things, and feeling ashamed of feeling like
that. No, she was certainly not going to give anyone a lift.

She drove steadily on through the driving sleet,
pretending that the back of her car was full of pieces of
priceless chandeliers, and this served her very well until
she came to the enevitable hold-up before she reached
Hendon, when a strange thing happened.

After moving a few yards forwards between each set of
green lights, she finally found herself just having missed
yet another lot, but head of the queue in the right-hand
lane. There, standing under one of the tall, yellow lights,
on an island in the streaming rain, was a girl. There was
nothing in the least remarkable about her appearance at
first glance: she was short, rather dumpy, wearing what
looked like a very thin mackintosh and unsuitable shoes;
her head was bare; she wore glasses. She looked wet
through, cold and exhausted, but above all there was an
air of extreme desolation about her, as though she was
hopelessly lost and solitary. Meg found, without having
thought at all about it, that she was opening her window
and beckoning the girl towards the car. The girl responded
– she was only a few yards away – and as she came nearer,
Meg noticed two other things about her. The first was that
she was astonishingly pale – despite the fact that she had
dark, reddish hair and was obviously frozen: her face was
actually livid, and when she extended a tentative hand in
a gesture that was either seeking reassurance about help,
or anticipating the opening of the car door, the collar of

her mackintosh moved, and Meg saw that, at the bottom of her white throat, the girl had what looked like the most unfortunate purple birth mark.

'Please get in,' Meg said, and leaned over to open the seat beside her. Then two things happened at once. The girl simply got into the back of the car – Meg heard her open the door and shut it gently, and a man, wearing a large, check overcoat, tinted glasses and a soft black hat tilted over his forehead slid into the seat beside her.

'How kind,' he said, in a reedy, pedagogic voice (almost as though he was practising to be someone else, Meg thought); 'we were wondering whether anyone at all would come to our aid, and it proves that charming young women like yourself behave as they appear. The good Samaritan is invariably feminine these days.'

Meg, who had taken the most instant dislike to him of anyone she had ever met in life, said nothing at all. Then, beginning to feel bad about this, at least from the silent girl's point of view, she asked:

'How far are you going?'

'Ah, now that will surprise you. My secretary and I broke down this morning on our way up, or down to Town, he sniggered; 'and it is imperative that we present ourselves in the right place at the right time this evening. I only wish to go so far as to pick up our car, which should now be ready.' His breath smelled horribly of stale smoke and peppermints.

'At a garage?' The whole thing sounded to Meg like the most preposterous story.

'Between Northampton and Leicester. I shall easily be able to point the turning out to you.'

Again, Meg said nothing, hoping that this would put a stop to his irritating voice. 'What a bore,' she thought: 'I *would* be lumbered with this lot.' She began to consider the social hazards of giving people lifts. Either they sat in total silence – like the girl in the back – or they talked. At this point he began again.

'It is most courageous of you to have stopped. There are so many hooligans about, that I always say it is most unjust to the older and more respectable people. But it is true that an old friend of mine once gave a lift to a *young man*, and the next thing she knew, the poor dear was in a ditch; no car, a dreadful headache, and no idea where she was. It's perfectly ghastly what some people will do to some people. Have you noticed it? But I imagine you are too young: you are probably in search of *adventure – romance* – or whatever lies behind those euphemisms. Am I right?'

Meg, feeling desperately that *anything* would be better than this talking all the ime, said over her shoulder to her obstinately silent passenger in the back: 'Are you warm enough?'

But before anyone else could have said anything, the horrible man said at once: 'Perfectly, thank you. Physically speaking, I am not subject to great sensitivity about temperature.' When he turned to her, as he always seemed to do, at the end of any passage or remark, the smell of his breath seemed to fill the car. It was not simply smoke and peppermints – underneath that was a smell like rotting mushrooms. 'She must be asleep,' Meg thought, almost resentfully – after all there was no escape for *her* – *she* could not sleep, was forced to drive and drive and listen to this revolting front-seat passenger.

'Plastic,' he continued ruminatively (as though she had even *mentioned* the stuff), 'the only real use that plastic has been to society was when the remains, but unmistakable – unlike the unfortunate lady – when the remains of Mrs Durand Deacon's red plastic handbag were discovered in the tank full of acid. Poor Haigh must have thought he was perfectly safe with acid, but of course, he had not reckoned on the durable properties of some plastics. That was the end of *him*. Are you familiar with the case at all?'

'I'm not very interested in murder, I'm afraid.'

'Ah – but fear and murder go hand in hand,' he said at

once, and, she felt, deliberately misunderstanding her. She had made the mistake of apologising for her lack of interest –

'. . . in fact, it would be difficult to think of any murder where there had not been a modicum, and sometimes, let's face it, a very great deal of fear.' Glancing at him, she saw that his face, an unhealthy colour, or perhaps that was the headlights of oncoming cars, was sweating. It could not still be rain: the car heater was on: it was sweat.

She stuck it out until they were well on the way up the M1. His conversation was both nasty and repetitive, or rather, given that he was determined to talk about fear and murder, he displayed a startling knowledge of different and horrible cases. Eventually, he asked suddenly whether she would stop for him, 'a need of nature', he was sure she would understand what he meant. Just there a lorry was parked on the shoulder, and he protested that he would rather go on – he was easily embarrassed and preferred complete privacy. Grimly, Meg parked.

'That will do perfectly well,' she said as firmly as she could, but her voice came out trembling with strain.

The man slid out of the car with the same reptilian action she had noticed when he got in. He did not reply. The moment that he was out, Meg said to the girl: 'Look here, if he's hitching lifts with you, I do think you might help a bit with the conversation.'

There was no reply. Meg, turning to the back, began almost angrily: 'I don't care if you are asleep – ' but then she had to stop because a small scream seemed to have risen in her thoat to check her.

The back seat was empty.

Meg immediately looked to see whether the girl could have fallen off the back seat on to the floor. She hadn't. Meg switched on the car light; the empty black mock-leather seat glistened with emptiness. For a split second, Meg thought she might be going mad. Her first sight of the girl, standing under a lamp on the island at Hendon,

recurred sharply. The pale, thin mac, the pallor, the feeling
that she was so desolate that Meg had *had* to stop for her.
But she had *got into* the car – of course she had! Then she
must have got out, when the man got out. But he hadn't
shut his door, and there had been no noise from the back.
She looked at the back doors. They were both unlocked.
She put out her hand to touch the seat: it was perfectly
dry, and that poor girl had been so soaked when she had
got in – *had got in* – she was certain of it, that if she had
just got out, the seat would have been at least damp. Meg
could hear her heart thudding now, and for a moment,
until he returned, she was almost glad that even that man
was some sort of company in this situation.

He seemed to take his time about getting back into the
car: she saw him – as she put it – slithering out of the dark
towards her, but then he seemed to hesitate; he disappeared from sight, and it was only when she saw him by
the light of her right-hand side light that she realized he
had been walking round the car. *Strolling* about, as though
she was simply a chauffeur to him! She called through the
window to him to hurry up, and almost before he had got
into the car, she said, 'What on earth's become of your
secretary?'

There was a slight pause, then he turned to her: 'My
*sec*retary?' His face was impassive to the point of offensive-
ness, but she noticed that he was sweating again.

'You know,' she said impatiently; she had started the
engine and was pulling away from the shoulder. 'The girl
you said you'd had a breakdown with on your way to
London.'

'Ah yes: poor little Muriel. I had quite forgotten her. I
imagine her stuffing herself with family high tea and, I
don't doubt, boy-friend – some provincial hairdresser who
looks like a pop star, or perhaps some footballer who
looks like a hairdresser.'

'What *do* you mean?'

He sniggered. 'I am not given to oversight into the

affairs of any employee I may indulge in. I do not like prolonged relationships of any kind. I like them sudden – short – and sweet. In fact, I – '

'No – *listen!* You know perfectly well what I'm talking about.'

She felt him stiffen, become still with wariness then quite unexpectedly, he asked: 'How long have you had this car?'

'Oh – a week or so. Don't make things up about your secretary. It was her I really stopped for. I didn't even see you.'

It must be his sweat that was making the car smell so much worse. 'Of course, I noticed at once that it was an MG,' he said.

'The girl in the back,' Meg said desperately: he seemed to be deliberately stupid as well as nasty. 'She was standing on the island, under a lamp. She wore a mac, but she was obviously soaked to the skin, I beckoned to her, and she came up and got into the back without a word. At the same time as you. So come off it, inventing nasty, sneering lies about your secretary. Don't pretend *you* didn't know she was there. You probably used her as a decoy – to get a lift at all.'

There was a short, very unpleasant silence. Meg was just beginning to be frightened, when he said, 'What did your friend look like?'

It was no use quibbling with him about not being the girl's friend. Meg said: 'I told you . . .' and instantly realized that she had done nothing of the kind. Perhaps the girl really hadn't been his secretary. . . .

'All you have done is allege that you picked up my secretary with me.'

'All right. Well, she was short – she wore a pale mac – I told you that – and, and glasses – her hair was a dark reddish colour – I suppose darker because she was wet through, and she had some silly shoes on and she looked *ill*, she was so white – a sort of livid white, and when she – '

'Never heard of her – never heard of anyone like her.'

'No, but you *saw* her, didn't you? I'm sorry if I thought she was your secretary – the point is you saw her, didn't you? *Didn't* you?'

He began fumbling in his overcoat pocket, from which he eventually drew out a battered packet of sweets, the kind where each sweet is separately wrapped. He was so long getting a sweet out of the packet and then starting to peel off the sticky paper that she couldn't wait.

'Another thing. When she put out her arm to open the door, I saw her throat – '

His fingers stopped unwrapping the paper. She glanced at them: he had huge, ugly hands that looked the wrong scale beside the small sweet –

'She had a large sort of birth mark at the bottom of her throat, poor thing.'

He dropped the sweet: bent forward in the car to find it. When, at last, he had done so, he put it straight into his mouth without attempting to get any more paper off. Briefly, the smell of peppermint dominated the other, less pleasant odours. Meg said, 'Of course, I don't suppose for a moment you could have seen *that*.'

Finally, he said: 'I cannot imagine who, or what, you are talking about. I didn't see any *girl* in the back of *your* car.'

'But there couldn't be someone in the back of my car without my knowing!'

There seemed to Meg to be something wrong about his behaviour. Not just that it was unpleasant; wrong in a different way; she felt that he knew perfectly well about the girl, but wouldn't admit it – to frighten her, she supposed.

'Do you mind if I smoke?'

He seemed to be very bad at lighting it. Two matches

wavered out in his shaky hands before he got an evil-smelling fag going.

Meg, because she still felt a mixture of terror and confusion about what had or had not happened, decided to try being very reasonable with him.

'When you got into the car,' she began carefully, 'you kept saying "we" and talking about your secretary. *That's* why I thought she must be.'

'Must be what?'

A mechanical response; sort of playing-for-time stuff, Meg thought.

'You must excuse me, but I really don't know what you are talking about.'

'Well, I think you *do*. And before you can say "do what?" I mean *do* know what you are talking about.'

She felt, rather than saw him glance sharply at her, but she kept her eyes on the road.

Then he seemed to make up his mind. 'I have a suggestion to make. Supposing we stop at the next service area and you tell me all about everything? You have clearly got a great deal on your mind; in fact, you show distinct symptoms of being upset. Perhaps if we – '

'No thank you.' The idea of his being the slightest use to talk to was both nauseating and absurd. She heard him suck in his breath through his teeth with a small hissing sound: once more she found him reminding her of a snake. Meg hated snakes.

Then he began to fumble about again, to produce a torch and to ask for a map. After some ruminating aloud as to where they were, and indeed where his garage was likely to be, he suggested stopping again 'to give my, I fear, sadly weakened eyes an opportunity to discover my garage'.

Something woke up in Meg, an early warning or premonition of more, and different trouble. Garages were not marked on her map. She increased their speed, stayed in the middle lane until a service station that she had noticed marked earlier at half a mile away loomed and glittered in the wet darkness. She drove straight in and said:

'I don't like you very much. I'd rather you got out now.' Again she heard him suck his breath through his teeth. The attendant had seen the car, and was slowly getting into his anorak to come out to them.

'How cruel!' he said, but she sensed his anger. 'What a pity! What a chance lost!'

'Please get out at once, or I'll get the man to turn you out.'

With his usual agility, he opened the door at once, and slithered out.

'I'm sorry,' Meg said weakly: 'I'm sure you did know about the girl. I just don't trust you.'

He poked his head in through the window. 'I'm far from sure that *I* trust *you*.' There were little bits of scum at the ends of his mouth. 'I really feel that you oughtn't to drive alone if you are subject to such extreme hallucinations.'

There was no mistaking the malice in his voice, and just as Meg was going to have one last go at his admitting that he *had* seen the girl, the petrol attendant finally reached her and began unscrewing her petrol cap. He went, then. Simply withdrew his head, as though there were not more of him than that, and disappeared.

'How many?'

'Just two, please.'

When the man went off slowly to get change, Meg wanted to cry. Instead, she locked all the doors and wound up the passenger window. She had an unreasonable fear that he would come back and that the attendant might not help her to oust him. She even forgot the change, and wound up her own window, so that nobody could get into the car. This made the attendant tap on her window; she started violently, which set her shivering.

'Did you – did you see where the man who was in the front of my car went? He got out just now.'

'I didn't see anyone. Anyone at all.'

'Oh thank you.'

'Night.' He went thankfully back to his brightly lit and doubtless scorching booth.

Before she drove off, Meg looked once more at the back seat. There was no one there. The whole experience had been so prolonged, as well as unnerving, that apart from feeling frightened she felt confused. She wanted badly to get away as fast as possible, and she wanted to keep quite still and try to sort things out. He *had* known that the girl had been in the car. He had enjoyed – her fear. Why else would he have said 'we' so much? This made her more frightened, and her mind suddenly changed sides.

The girl *could not* have got out of the back without opening and shutting – however quietly – the door. There had been no sound or sounds like that. In fact, from the moment the girl had got into the car she had made no sound at all. Perhaps she, too, had been frightened by the horrible man. Perhaps she had *pretended* to get in, and at the last moment, slipped out again.

She opened her window wide to get rid of the smells in the car. As she did so, a possible implication of what the petrol attendant had said occurred. He hadn't seen *anyone*; he hadn't emphasised it like that, but he had repeated 'anyone at all'. Had he just meant that he hadn't looked? Or had he looked, and seen nobody? Ghosts don't talk, she reminded herself, and at once was back to the utterly silent girl.

Her first journey north in the car, and the awful breathing sounds coming from its back, could no longer be pushed out of her mind. The moment that she realized this, both journeys pounced forward into incomprehensible close-ups of disconnected pictures and sounds, recurring more and more rapidly, but in different sequences, as though, through their speed and volume, they were trying to force her to understand them. In the end, she actually cried out: 'All *right*! The car is haunted. Of course, I see that!'

A sudden calm descended upon her, and in order to further it, or at least stop it as suddenly stopping, she added: 'I'll think about it when I get home,' and drove mindlessly the rest of the way. If any spasm about what had recently happened attempted to invade her essential blankness, she concentrated upon seeing her mother's face, smelling the dinner in the kitchen, and hearing her father call out who was there.

'. . . thought he might be getting a severe cold, so he's off to bed. He's had his arrowroot with a spot of whisky in it and asked us to be extra quiet in *case* he gets a wink of sleep.'

Meg hugged her without replying: it was no good trying to be conspiratorial with her mother about her father; there could never be a wink or a smile. Her mother's loyalty had stiffened over the years, until now she could relate the most absurd details of her father's imaginary fears and ailments with a good-natured but completely impassive air. 'Have we got anything to drink?' she asked.

'Darling – I'm sure we have somewhere. But it's so unlike you to want a drink that I didn't put it out. It'll be in the corner cupboard in the sitting-room.'

Meg knew this, knew also that she would find the untouched half-bottles of gin and Bristol Milk that were kept in case anyone 'popped in'. But the very few people who did always came for cups of tea or coffee at the appropriate times of day. Her parents could not really afford drink – except for her father's medicinal whisky.

When she brought the bottles into the kitchen, she said, 'You have one too. I shall feel depraved drinking all by myself.'

'Well dear, then I'll be depraved with you. Just a drop of sherry. We needn't tell Father. It might start him worrying about your London Life. Been meeting anyone interesting lately?'

Meg had offered her mother a cigarette with her sherry, and her mother, delighted, had nearly burned her wispy fringe bending over the match to light it, and was now blowing out frantic streams of smoke from her nose before it got too far. It was all right to smoke if you didn't inhale. On a social occasion, that was. Like it being all right to drink a glass of sherry at those times.

'This *is* nice,' her mother said, and then added, 'Have you been *meeting* anyone nice, dear? At all your parties and things?'

It was then that Meg realized that she could not possibly – ever – pour out all her anxieties to her mother. Her mother simply would not be able to understand them. 'Not this week,' she said. Her mother sighed, but Meg was not meant to hear, and said that she supposed it took time in a place like London to know people.

Meg had a second, strong gin, and then said that she would pay her mother back, but she was tired, and needed a couple of drinks. She also smoked four cigarettes before dinner, and felt so revived that she was able to eat the delicious steak-and-kidney pie followed by baked apples with raisins in them. Her mother had been making Meg Viyella nightgowns with white lace ruffles, and wanted to show them to her. They were brought into the kitchen, which was used for almost everything in winter as it saved fuel. 'I've been quite excited about them,' her mother said, when she laid out the nightgowns. 'Not quite finished, but such fun doing each one in a different colour.'

She listened avidly when Meg told her things about Mr Whitehorn and the shop: she even liked being told about the *things* in the shop. She laughed at Meg's descriptions when they were meant to be in the least amusing, and looked extremely earnest and anxious when Meg told her about the fragility and value of the chandeliers. When it was time to go to bed, and she had filled their two hot-water bottles, she accompanied Meg to the door of her bedroom. They kissed, and her mother said: 'Bless you, dearie. I don't know what I'd do without you. Although, of course, one of these days I shall have to when Mr Right comes along.'

Meg cleaned her teeth in the ferociously cold bathroom and went back to her – nearly as cold – bedroom. Hot-water bottles were essential: Viyella nightdresses would be an extra comfort. From years of practice, she undressed fast and ingeniously, so that at no time was she ever naked. Whenever her mother mentioned Mr Right she had a vision of a man with moustaches and wearing a bowler hat mowing a lawn. She said her prayers kneeling beside her high, rather uncomfortable bed, and the hot-water bottle was like a reward.

In the night she awoke once, her body tense and crowded with fears: 'I could *sell* the car, and get another,' she said, and almost at once relaxed, the fears receded until they fell through some blank slot at the back of her mind and she was again asleep.

This decision, combined with a week-end of comfortingly the same ordered, dull events made her able to set aside, almost to shut up, the things – as she called them – that had happened, or seemed to have happened, in the car. On Sunday morning she found her mother packing the back with some everlasing flowers 'for your flat', a huge, dark old tartan car-rug 'in case you haven't enough on your bed', and a pottery jar full of home-made marmalade 'to share with your friends at breakfast'.

'There's plenty of room for the things on the floor, as you're so small, really, that you have your driving seat pushed right forward.'

When she said good-bye and set off, it was with the expectation of the journey to London being uneventful, and it was.

The trouble, she discovered, after trying in her spare time

for a week, was that she *could not* sell the car. She had started with the original dealer who had sold it to her, but he had said, with a bland lack of regret, that he was extremely sorry, but this was not the time of year to sell second-hand cars and that the best he could offer was to take it back for a hundred pounds less than she had paid for it. As this would completely rule out having any other car excepting a smashed-up or clapped-out Mini that would land her with all kinds of garage bills (and, like most car-owners, Meg was not mechanically minded), she had to give up that idea from the start.

She advertised in her local newspaper shop (cheap, and it would be easy for people to try out the car) but this only got her one reply: a middle-aged lady with a middle-aged poodle who came round one evening. At first it seemed hopeful; the lady said it was a nice colour and looked in good condition, but when she got into the driver's seat with Meg beside her to drive it round the block, her dog absolutely refused to get into the back as he was told to do. His owner tried coaxing, and he whimpered and scrabbled out of the still-open door; she tried a very unconvincing authority: 'Cherry! Do as you are told at once,' and his whimpering turned to a series of squealing yelps. 'He *loves* going in cars. I don't know what's come over him!'

Out in the street again, all three of them, he growled and tried to snap at Meg. 'I'm sorry dear, but I can't possibly buy a car that Cherry won't go in. He's all I've got. Naughty Cherry. He's usually such a mild, sweet dog. Don't you dare bite at Mummy's friends.'

And that was that. She asked Mr Whitehorn and her flatmates, and finally, their friends, but nobody seemed to want to buy her car, or even wanted to help her get rid of it. By Friday, Meg was in a panic at the prospect of driving north again in it. She had promised herself that she wasn't going to, and as long as the promise had seemed to hold (surely she could find *someone* who would want it) she had been able not to think about the alternative. By Friday morning she was so terrified that she did actually send a telegram to her mother, saying that she had 'flu and couldn't drive home.

After she had sent it, she felt guilty and relieved in about equal proportions. The only way she could justify such behaviour was to make sure of selling the car that weekend. Samantha told her to put in an ad in the *Standard* for the next day. 'You're bound to make the last edition anyway,' she said. So Meg rang them, having spent an arduous half-hour trying to phrase the advertisement. 'Pale blue MG – ' was how it finally began.

Then she had to go to work. Mr Whitehorn was in one of his states. It was not rude to think this, since he frequently referred to them. There was a huge order to be sent to New York that would require, he thought, at least a week's packing. He had got hold of tea chests, only to be told that he had to have proper packing cases. There was plenty of newspaper and straw in the basement. He was afraid that that was where Meg would have to spend her day.

The basement was whitewashed and usually contained only inferior pieces, or things that needed repair. While working, Meg was allowed to have an oil stove, but it was considered too dangerous to leave it on by itself. Her first job was a huge breakfast, lunch, tea and coffee service bought by Mr Whitehorn in a particularly successful summer sale in Suffolk. It had to be packed and listed, all two hundred and thirty-six pieces of it. It was lying on an old billiard table with a cut cloth, and Meg found that the most comfortable way to pack it was to bring each piece to a chaise-longue whose stuffing was bristling out at every point, and put the heap of newspapers on the floor beside her. Thus she could sit and pack, and after each section of the set she could put things back on the table in separate clutches with their appropriate labels. She was feeling much better than when she had woken up. Not having to face the drive: having put an advertisement into a serious paper almost made her feel that she had sold the car already: Val had said that she might go to a film with her on Sunday afternoon if her friend didn't turn up and she didn't think he would, so that was something to look forward to, and packing china wasn't really too bad if you took it methodically and didn't expect ever to finish.

In the middle of the morning, Mr Whitehorn went out in his van to fetch the packing cases. He would be back in about an hour, he said. Meg, who had run up to the shop to hear what he said – the basement was incredibly muffled and quiet – made herself a mug of coffee and went back to work. There was a bell under the door-rug, so that she could hear it if customers came.

She was just finishing the breakfast cups when she saw it. The newspaper had gone yellow at the edges, but inside, where all the print and pictures were, it was almost as good as new. For a second, she did not pick up the page, simply stared at a large photograph of head and shoulders, and MI MYSTERY in bold type above it.

The picture was of the girl she had picked up in Hendon. She knew that it was, before she picked it up, but she still had to do that. She *might* be wrong, but she knew she wasn't. The glasses, the hair, the rather high forehead . . . but she was smiling faintly in the picture . . .

' . . . petite, auburn-haired Mary Carmichael was found wrapped in her raincoat in a ditch in a lane not one hundred yards from the M1 north of Towcester. She had been assaulted and strangled with a lime green silk scarf that she was seen wearing when she left her office . . . Mr Turner was discovered in the boot of the car – a black MG that police found abandoned in a car-park. The car belonged to Mr Turner, who had been stabbed a number of times and is thought to have died earlier than Miss Carmichael . . . '

She realized then that she was reading a story continued from page one. Page one of the newspaper was missing.

She would never know what Mr Turner looked like. She looked again at the picture of the girl. 'Taken on holiday the previous year.' Even though she was smiling, or trying to smile, Mary Carmichael looked timid and vulnerable.

' . . . Mr Turner, a travelling salesman and owner of the car, is thought to have given a lift or lifts to Mary Carmichael and some other person, probably a man, not yet identified. The police are making extensive inquiries along the entire length of the route that Mr Turner regularly travelled. Mr Turner was married, with three children. Miss Carmichael's parents, Mr and Mrs Gerald Carmichael of Manchester, described their only daughter as very quiet and shy and without a boy-friend.'

The paper was dated March of the previous spring.

Meg found that her eyes were full of tears. Poor, poor Mary. Last year she had been an ordinary timid, not very attractive girl who had been given a lift, and then been horribly murdered. How frightened she must have been before she died – with being – assaulted – and all that. And now, she was simply a desolate ghost, bound to go on trying to get lifts, or to be helped, or perhaps even to *warn* people . . . 'I'll pray for you,' she said to the picture, which now was so blurred through her tears that the smile, or attempt at one, seemed to have vanished.

She did not know how long it was before the implications, both practical and sinister, crept into her mind. But they did, and she realized that they had, because she began to shiver violently – in spite of feeling quite warm – and fright was prickling her spine up to the back of her neck.

Mystery Murders. If Mr Turner was not the murderer of Mary, then only one other person could be responsible. The horrible man. The way he had talked of almost nothing but awful murders . . . She must go to the police immediately. She could describe him down to the last detail: his clothes, his voice, his tinted spectacles, his frightful smell . . . He had been furious with her when

she had put him down at the service station . . . but, one
minute, before that, before *then*, when she had let him
out on the shoulder where the lorry was, he had taken
ages to come back into the car – had walked right round
it, and then, when he got in, and she had questioned him
about the girl, and described her, he had become all
sweaty, and taken ages to reply to anything she said. He
must have *recognised* the car! She was beginning to feel
confused: there was too much to think about at once. This
was where being clever would be such a help, she thought.

She began to try to think quietly, logically: absolutely
nothing but lurid fragments came to mind: 'a modicum,
and sometimes, let's face it, a very great deal of fear'; the
girl's face as she stood under the light on the island. Meg
looked back at the paper, but there was really no doubt
at all. The girl in the paper *was* the same girl. So – at last
she had begun to sort things out – the girl *was* a ghost:
the car, therefore, must be haunted. He certainly knew,
or realised, something about all this: his final words – 'I'm
far from sure that *I* trust *you*' – that was because she had
said that she didn't trust him. So – perhaps he thought she
knew what had happened. Perhaps he had thought she was
trying to trap him, or something like that. If he *really*
thought that, and he was actually guilty, he surely
wouldn't leave it at that, would he? He'd be afraid of her
going to the police, of what, in fact, she was shortly going
to do. He couldn't *know* that she hadn't seen the girl
before, in the newspaper. But if he couldn't know, how
could the police?

At this point, the door-bell rang sharply, and Meg
jumped. Before she could do more than leap to her feet,
Mr Whitehorn's faded, kindly voice called down. 'I'm
back, my dear girl. Any customers while I've been away?'

'No.' Meg ran up the stairs with relief that it was he.
'Would you like some coffee?'

'Splendid notion.' He was taking off his teddy-bear

overcoat and rubbing his dry, white hands before the fan heater.

Later, when they were both nursing steaming mugs, she asked: 'Mr Whitehorn, do you remember a mystery murder case on the M1 last spring? Well, two murders, really? The man was found in the boot of the car, and the girl – '

'In a ditch somewhere? Yes, indeed. All over the papers. The real trouble is, that although I adore reading detective stories, *real* detective stories, I mean, I always find real-life crime just dull. Nasty, and dull.'

'I expect you're right.'

'They caught the chap though, didn't they? I expect he's sitting in some tremendously kind prison for about eighteen months. Be out next year, I shouldn't wonder. The law seems to regard property as far more important than murder, in my opinion.'

'Who did they catch?'

'The murderer, dear, the murderer. Can't remember his name. Something like Arkwright or James. Something like that. But there's no doubt at all that they caught him. The trial was all over the papers, as well. How have you been getting on with your marathon?'

Meg found herself blushing: she explained that she had been rather idle for the last half hour or so, and suggested that she make up the time by staying later. No, no, said Mr Whitehorn, such honesty should be rewarded. But, he added, before she had time to thank him, if she *did* have an hour to spend tomorrow, Saturday morning, he would be most grateful. Meg had to agree to this, but arranged to come early and leave early, because of her advertisement.

The worst of having had that apparently comforting talk with Mr Whitehorn was that if they *had* already caught the man, then there couldn't be any point in going to the police. She had no proof that she hadn't seen a picture of poor Mary Carmichael; in fact, she realised that she might easily have done so, and simply not remembered because she didn't read murder cases. Going to the police and saying that you had seen a ghost, given a ghost a *lift* in your car, and *then* seen a picture in a newspaper that identified them, would just sound hysterical or mad. And there would be no point in describing the horrible man, if, in fact, he was just horrible but not a murderer. But at least she didn't have to worry about him: his behaviour had simply seemed odd and then sinister, *before* Mr Whitehorn had said that they had caught the murderer. There was nothing she needed to do about any of it. Except get rid of a haunted car.

After her scrambled eggs and Mars bar, she did some washing, including her hair and her hair-brush, and went to bed early. Just before she went to sleep, the thought occurred to her that her mother always thought that people – all people – were really better than they seemed, and her father was certain that they were worse. Possibly, they were just *what* they seemed – no more and no less.

In the morning, second post, she got a letter from her mother full of anxiety and advice. The letter, after many kind and impractical admonitions, ended: 'and you are not to think of getting up or trying to drive all this way unless you are feeling completely recovered. I do wish I could come down and look after you, but your father thinks he may be getting this wretched bug. He has read in the paper that it is all over the place, and is usually the first to get anything, as you know. Much love, darling, and take *care* of yourself.'

This made Meg feel awful about going to Mr Whitehorn's but she had promised him, and letting down one person gave one no excuse whatsoever for letting down another. Samantha had promised to sit on the telephone while Meg was out, as she was waiting for one of her friends to call.

When she got back to the flat, Samantha was on the telephone, and Val was obviously cross with her. 'She's been *ages* talking to Bruce and she is going out with him in a minute, and I said I'd do the shopping, but she won't even say what she wants. She's a drag.'

Samantha said: 'Hold on a minute – six grapefruit and two rump steaks – that's all,' and went on listening, laughing and talking to Bruce. Meg gazed at her in dismay. How on earth were people who had read her advertisement and were *longing* to ring her up about it to get through? The trouble about Samantha was that she was so *very* marvellous to look at that it was awfully difficult to get her to do anything she didn't want to do.

Val turned kindly to Meg and said loudly: 'And your ad's in, isn't it? Samantha – you really are the limit. Meg, what would you like me to shop for you?'

Meg felt that this was terribly kind of Val, who was also pretty stunning, but in a less romantic way. Neither of the girls had ever shopped for her before; perhaps Val was going to become her friend. When she had made her list of cheese, apples, milk, eggs and Nescafe, Val said, 'Look, why don't we share a small chicken? I'll buy most of it, if you'll do the cooking. For Sunday,' she added, and Meg felt that Val was almost her friend already.

Val went, and at once, Samantha said to the telephone: 'All *right*: meet you in half an hour. Bye.' In one graceful movement she was off the battered sofa and stood running her hands through her long, black hair and saying: 'I haven't got a *thing* to wear!'

'Did anyone ring for me?'

'What? Oh – yes, one person – no, two, as a matter of fact. I told them you'd be in by lunch-time.'

'Did they sound interested in the car?'

'One did. Kept asking awful technical questions I couldn't answer. The other one just wanted to know if the car could be seen at this address and the name of the owner.' She was pulling off a threadbare kimono, looking at her face in a small, magnifying mirror she seemed always to have with her. 'Another one. . . ! They keep bobbing up like corks! I've gone on to this diet not a moment too soon.'

An hour went slowly by: nobody rang up about the car. Samantha finally appeared in fantastically expensive-looking clothes as though she was about to be photographed. She borrowed 50p off Meg for a taxi and went, leaving an aura of chestnut bath-stuff all over the flat.

The weekend was a fearful anti-climax. On Saturday, three people rang up – none of them people who had called before; one said that he thought it was a drop-head, seemed, indeed, almost to accuse her of it not being, although she had distinctly said saloon in her ad. Two said they would come and look at the car: one of these actually arrived, but he only offered her a hundred pounds less than she was asking, and that was that. On Sunday morning Meg cooked for ages, the chicken and all the bits, like bread sauce and gravy, that were to live up to it. At twelve-thirty Val got a call from one of her friends, and said she was frightfully sorry, but that she had to be out to lunch after all.

'Oh dear! Shall I keep it till the evening? The chicken will be cold, but the other – '

Val interrupted her by saying with slight embarrassment that she wouldn't be back to dinner, either. '*You* eat it,' she ended, with guilty generosity.

When she had gone, the flat seemed very empty. Meg tried to comfort herself with the thought that anyway, she *couldn't* have gone to the cinema with Val, as she would have to stay in the flat in case the telephone rang. But she had been looking forward to lunch. If a person sat down to a table with you and had a meal, you stood a much better chance of getting to know them. Sundays only seemed quieter in London than they were in the country, because of the contrast of London during the week. As she sat down to her leg of chicken with bread sauce, gravy and potatoes done as her mother did them at home, she wondered whether coming to London was really much good after all. She did not seem to be making much headway: it wasn't turning out at all how she had imagined it might, and at this moment she felt rather homesick. Whatever happened, she'd go home next weekend, and talk to her mother about the whole thing. Not – the car – thing, but Careers and Life.

Two more people rang during the afternoon. One was for Samantha, but the other was about the car. They asked her whether she would drive it to Richmond for them to see it, but when she explained why she couldn't they lost interest. She kept telling herself that it was too long a chance to risk losing other possible buyers by going out for such a long time, but as the grey afternoon settled drearily to the darker grey evening, she wondered whether she had been wrong.

She wrote a long letter to her mother, describing Samantha's clothes and Val's kindness, and saying that she was already feeling better (another lie, but how could she help it?): then she read last month's *Vogue* magazine and wondered what all the people in it, who wore rich carcoats and gave fabulous, unsimple dinner-parties and shooting lunches and seemed to know at least eight ways of doing their hair, were doing now. On the whole, they all seemed in her mind to be lying on velvet or leather sofas with one of their children in a party dress sitting quietly reading, and pots of azaleas and cyclamen round them in a room where you could only see one corner of a family portrait and a large white or honey-coloured dog at their feet on an old French carpet. She read her horoscope: it said, you will encounter some interesting people, but do not go more than half-way to meet them, and watch finances – last month's horoscope anyway, so that somehow whether it had been right or not hardly counted. When she thought it must be too late for any more people to ring up, she had a long, hot bath, and tried to do her hair at least one other way. But her hair was too short, too fine, and altogether too unused to any outlandish intention, and obstinately slipped or fell back into its ordinary state. It was also the kind of uninteresting colour that people never even bothered to describe in books. She yawned, a tear came out of one eye, and she decided that she had better get on with improving her mind, to which end she settled down to a vast and heavy book on Morocco that Val said people were talking about . . .

All week she packed and packed: china, glass, silver and bits of lamps and chandeliers. On Wednesday, someone rang up for her at the shop while she was out buying sausage rolls and apples for Mr Whitehorn's and her lunches. Mr Whitehorn seemed very vague about them: it hadn't seemed to be about the car, but something about her weekend plans, he thought. He *thought*, he reiterated, as though this made the whole thing more doubtful. Meg could not think who it could be – unless it was the very shy young man with red hair and a stammer who had once come in to buy a painting on glass about Nelson's death. He had been very nice, she thought, and he had stayed for quite a long time after he had bought the picture and told her about his collection of what she had learned to call Nelsoniana. That was about the only person it could be, and she hoped he'd ring again, but he didn't.

By Wednesday, she had long given up hope of anyone buying the car as a result of the advertisement. Val and Samantha told her that Bruce and Alan both said it was the wrong time of the year to sell second-hand cars, and she decided that she had better try to sell it in the north, nearer home.

On Wednesday evening she had a sudden, irrational attack of fear. However much she reasoned with herself, she simply did not *want* to drive up the M1 alone in the car that she was now certain was haunted. She couldn't stand the thought of hearing the sounds she had heard, of seeing the girl again in the same place (possibly, why not?

– ghosts were well known for repeating themselves): and when Samantha and Val came in earlier than usual and together, she had a – possibly not hopeless – idea. Would either or both of them like to come home for the weekend with her?

Their faces turned at once to each other; it was easy to see the identical appalled blankness with which they received the proposal. Before they could *say* that they wouldn't come, Meg intercepted them. 'It's lovely country, and my mother's a marvellous cook. We could go for drives in the car – ' but she knew it was no good. They couldn't possibly come, they both said almost at once: they had dates, plans, it was awfully kind of her, and perhaps in the summer they might – yes, in the summer, it might be marvellous *if* there was a free weekend . . .

Afterwards, Meg sat on her bed in the very small room that she had to herself, and cried. They weren't enough her friends for her to plead with them, and if she told them why she was frightened, they would be more put off than ever.

Next morning she asked Mr Whitehorn if he had ever been up north to sales and auctions and things like that.

Yes, he went from time to time.

'I suppose you wouldn't like to come up this weekend to stay? I could drive you to any places you wanted to go.'

Mr Whitehorn looked at her with his usual tired face, but also with what she could see was utter amazement.

'My dear child,' he said, when he had had time to think of it, 'I couldn't possibly do anything, *anything* at all like that at such short notice. It would throw out all my plans, you see. I always make plans for the weekend. Perhaps you have not realised it,' he went on, 'but I am a homosexual, you see. I thought you would know; running this shop and the states I get into. But I *always* plan my free time. I am lunching with a very dear friend in Ascot, and sometimes, not always, I stay the night there.' The confidence turned him pink. 'I had absolutely no intention of *misleading* you.'

Meg said of course not, and then they both apologised to each other and said it didn't matter in the least.

On Thursday evening both girls were out, and Meg, who had not slept at all well for the last two nights, decided that she was too tired to go on her own to the cinema, although it was *A Man for All Seasons* that she had missed and always wanted to see. She ate a poached egg and half a grapefruit that Samantha said was left over from her diet, and suddenly she had a brain-wave. What she was frightened of, she told herself, was the idea that the poor girl would be waiting for her again at Hendon. If, therefore, she *avoided* Hendon, and got on to the M1 further north, she would be free of this anxiety. There might still be those awful sounds again, like she had heard the first time, but she would just have to face that, drive steadily home, and when she got there, she decided, she would jolly well tell her mother about the whole thing. The idea, and the decision to tell her mother, cheered her so much that she felt less tired, and went down to the car to fetch the map. There, the car rug that her mother had given her in case she did not have enough on her bed pricked her conscience. She had managed to toil up the stairs with the flowers and marmalade and her case, but she had completely forgotten the rug; this was probably because her mother had put it in the car herself, and it now lay on the floor in the back. She would take it home, as she really didn't need it, and usually her father used it to protect his legs from draughts when he sat in or out of doors.

She found a good way on the map. She simply did not go left on to Hendon Way, but used the A1000 through Barnet and turned left on the St Albans road. She could get on to the M1 on the way to Watford. It was easy. That evening she packed her party dress so that her mother could see it. She always packed the night before, so that she didn't rush too much in the mornings, got to work on time, and parked her car, as usual, round the corner from the shop. Mr Whitehorn had simply chalked 'No Parking' on the brick wall, and so far it had always worked.

On Friday morning, she and Mr Whitehorn met each other elaborately, as though far more had occurred between them than had actually happened: the first half hour was heavy with off-handed good will, and they seemed to get in each other's way far more often than usual. They used the weather as a kind of demilitarised zone of conversation. Mr Whitehorn said that he heard on the wireless that there was going to be fog again, and Meg, who had heard it too, said oh dear and thanked him for telling her. Later in the morning, when things had eased between them, Mr Whitehorn asked her whether she had been successful in selling her car. Trains were so much easier in this weather, he added. They were, indeed. But she could hardly tell him that as she lived seventeen miles from the station, and her parents didn't drive, and the last bus had left by the time the train she would be able to catch had arrived, and her salary certainly couldn't afford a taxi . . . she couldn't tell him any of that: it would look like asking, begging for more money – she would never do it . . .

But the train became a recurrent temptation throughout the long cold and, by the afternoon, foggy day. She banished the idea in the end by reminding herself that, with the cost of the advertisement, she simply did not have the money for the train fare: the train was out of the question.

Mr Whitehorn, who had spent the morning typing lists for the Customs (he typed with three fingers in erratic, irritable bursts), said that he would buy their lunch, as he needed the exercise.

When he had gone, Meg, who had been addressing labels to be stuck on to the packing cases, felt so cold that she fetched the other paraffin heater from the basement and lit it upstairs. She did not like to get another cardigan from her case in the car, as in spite of its being so near, it was out of sight from the shop, and Mr Whitehorn hated the shop to be left empty for a moment. This made her worry, stupidly, whether she had locked the car. It was the kind of worry that one had like wondering if one had actually posted a letter *into* the letter-box: of course, one would have, but once any idea to the contrary set in, it would not go. So the moment he came back with hot sausages and Smith's crisps from the pub, she rushed out to the car. She had, in fact, left one back door open: she could have sworn that she hadn't, but there it was. She got herself another cardigan out of her case in the boot, and returned to her lunch. It was horrible out; almost dark, or at any rate opaque, with the fog, and the bitter, acrid air that seemed to accompany fogs in towns. At home, it would be a thick white mist – well, nearly white, but certainly not smelling as this fog smelled. The shop, in contrast, seemed quite cosy. One or two people came to 'look around' while they ate; but there was never very much to see. Mr Whitehorn put all the rubbish that got included in lots he had bid for on to trays with a mark saying that anything on the tray cost 50p, or £1. Their serious stuff nearly always seemed to go abroad, or to another dealer. Mr Whitehorn always made weak but kindly little jokes about his rubbish collectors, as he called the ones who bought old photograph albums, moulded glass vases, or hair-combs made of tortoiseshell and bits of broken paste.

While she was making their coffee, Meg wondered whether perhaps Mr Whitehorn would be a good person to talk about the haunted car to. Obviously, asking him to stay had been a silly mistake. But he might be just the person to understand what was worrying her; to believe her and to let her talk about it. That was what she most wanted, she realised. Someone, almost anyone, to *talk* to her about it: to sort out what was honestly frightening, and what she had imagined or invented as fright.

But immediately after lunch, he set about his typing again, and got more and more peevish, crumpling up bits of paper and throwing them just outside the waste-paper basket, until she hardly liked to ask him, at five, whether she might go.

However, she did ask, and he said it would be all right.

He could not know how difficult she found it to leave: she said good night to him twice by mistake, started to put her old tweed coat on, and then decided that with the second cardigan she wouldn't need it, took ages tying on her blue silk head-square, and nearly forgot her bag. She took out her car keys while she could find them easily in the light, shut the shop door behind her and, after one more look at him, angrily crouched over his typewriter, went to the car.

Once she got into the car, her courage and common sense returned. It was only, at the worst, a four-hour journey: she would be home then, and everything would be all right. She flung her overcoat into the back – it was far easier to drive without it hanging around the gear lever – had one final look at her map before she shut the car door, and set off.

It was more interesting going a different way out of London, even though it seemed to be slower, but the traffic, the fog, and making sure all the time that she was on the right road, occupied her mind, almost to the exclusion of anything else. She found her way on to the M1 quite easily; the signs posting it were more frequent and bigger than any other sign.

She drove for over an hour on the motorway, and there was no sound in the car, no agonised, laboured breathing - nothing. It was getting rather hot, but the heater cleared the windscreen and she couldn't do without it for long. The fog was better, too, although patchy, and in the clearer bits she could see the fine misty rain that was falling all the time. She was sticking to the left-hand lane, because although it meant that lorries passed her from time to time, she felt safer in the fog than if she had been in the middle, and possibly unable to see either side of the road. She opened a crack of window because the car seemed to be getting impossibly hot and full of stale air. Another two hours, she thought, and decided that she might as well stop to take off her thick cardigan – she could use the hard shoulder just for that – and perhaps she had made far too much of her nerves and anxiety about the whole journey. She drew up carefully, and then saw a service area ahead – safer in one of those. 'At least I didn't give in,' she thought, and thought also how ashamed of herself she would have been if she had.

As she drew up in the car-park, she was just about to get out of her cardigan, when a huge hand reached out in front of her and twitched the driving mirror so that she could see him. He was smiling, his eyes full of triumph and malice. His breath reeked over her shoulder as she gave a convulsive gasp of pure shock. 'You must be a ghost!' She heard herself repeating this in a high voice utterly unlike her own. 'You must be a ghost: you *must* be!'

'Only had to pick the car lock twice. You shouldn't have locked it *again* in the middle of the day.'

She knew she should start the car and drive back out on to the road, but she couldn't see behind her, and nearly lost all control when she felt something hard and pointed sticking into the back of her neck.

'They caught Mr Wrong, you see. But you seemed to know *so much*, and as you were driving the same car, I simply had to catch up with you somehow. Two birds with one stone, as it were.'

She made an attempt to get the brake off, but a hand clamped over her wrist with such sudden force that she cried out.

'Ever since you turned me out in that unkind manner,

I have been trying to track you down. That is all I have done, but your advertisement was a great help.' She saw him watching her face in the mirror and licking the scum off his lips. She made a last effort.

'I shall turn you out again – any minute – I shall!'

He sucked in his breath, but he was still smiling.

'Oh no, you won't. This time, it will all be done my way.'

She thought she screamed once, in that single second of astonished disbelief and denial before she felt the knife jab smoothly through the skin on her neck when speechless terror overwhelmed her and she became nothing but fear – heart thudding, risen in her throat as though it would burst from her: she put one hand to the wound and felt no knife – only her own blood – there, as he said:

'Don't worry *too* much: just stick to fear. The fate worse than death tends to occur after it. I've always liked them warm.'

GREAT-AUNT ALLIE'S FLYPAPERS

'You see my dear Adam,' explained the Canon gently as he walked with Chief Superintendent Dalgliesh under the Vicarage elms: 'Useful as the legacy would be to us I wouldn't feel happy in accepting it if Great Aunt Allie came by her money in the first place by wrongful means.'

What the Canon meant was that he and his wife wouldn't be happy to inherit Great Aunt Allie's fifty thousand pounds if, sixty seven years earlier, she had poisoned her elderly husband with arsenic in order to get it. As Great Aunt Allie had been accused and acquitted of just that charge in a 1902 trial which, for her Hampshire neighbours, had rivalled the Coronation as a public spectacle the Canon's scruples were not altogether irrelevant. Admittedly, thought Dalgliesh, most people faced with the prospect of fifty thousand pounds would be happy to subscribe to the commonly held convention that once an English Court has pronounced its verdict the final truth of the matter has been established once and for all. There may possibly be a higher judicature in the next world but hardly in this. And so Hubert Boxdale might normally be happy to believe. But, faced with the prospect of an unexpected fortune, his scrupulous conscience was troubled. The gentle but obstinate voice went on:

'Apart from the moral principle of accepting tainted money, it wouldn't bring us happiness. I often think of that poor woman, driven restlessly around Europe in her search for peace, of that lonely life and unhappy death.'

Dalgliesh recalled that Great Aunt Allie had moved in a predictable progress with her retinue of servants, current lover and general hangers-on from one luxury Riviera hotel to the next with stays in Paris or Rome as the mood suited her. He was not sure that this orderly programme of comfort and entertainment could be described as being restlessly driven around Europe or that the old lady had been primarily in search of peace. She had died, he recalled, by falling overboard from a millionaire's yacht during a rather wild party given by him to celebrate her eighty-eighth birthday. It was perhaps not an edifying death by the Canon's standards but he doubted whether she had, in fact, been unhappy at the time. Great Aunt Allie (it was impossible to think of her by any other name) if she had been capable of coherent thought, would probably have pronounced it a very good way to go. But this was hardly a point of view he could put to his companion.

Canon Hubert Boxdale was Superintendent Adam Dalgliesh's godfather. Dalgliesh's father had been his Oxford contemporary and life-long friend. He had been an admirable godfather, affectionate, uncensorious, genuinely concerned. In Dalgliesh's childhood he had been mindful of birthdays and imaginative about a small boy's pre-occupations and desires. Dalgliesh was very fond of him and privately thought him one of the few really good men he had known. It was only surprising that the Canon had managed to live to seventy-one in a carnivorous world in which gentleness, humility and unworldliness are hardly conducive to survival let alone success. But his goodness had in some sense protected him. Faced with such manifest innocence even those who exploited him, and they were not a few, extended some of the protection and compassion they might show to the slightly subnormal.

'Poor old darling', his daily woman would say, pocketing pay for six hours when she had worked five and helping herself to a couple of eggs from his refrigerator. 'He's really not fit to be let out alone.' It had surprised the then young and slightly priggish detective constable

Dalgliesh to realise that the Canon knew perfectly well about the hours and the eggs but thought that Mrs Copthorne with five children and an indolent husband needed both more than he did. He also knew that, if he started paying for five hours she would promptly work only four and extract another two eggs and that this small and only dishonesty was somehow necessary to her self-esteem. He was good. But he was not a fool.

He and his wife were, of course, poor. But they were not unhappy; indeed it was a word impossible to associate with the Canon. The death of his two sons in the 1939 war had saddened but not destroyed him. But he had anxieties. His wife was suffering from disseminated sclerosis and was finding it increasingly hard to manage. There were comforts and appliances which she would need. He was now, belatedly, about to retire and his pension would be small. A legacy of fifty thousand pounds would enable them both to live in comfort for the rest of their lives and would also, Dalgliesh had no doubt, give them the pleasure of doing more for their various lame dogs. Really, he thought, the Canon was an almost embarrassingly deserving candidate for a modest fortune. Why couldn't the dear silly old noodle take the cash and stop worrying? He said cunningly:

'She was found not guilty you know by an English jury. And it all happened nearly seventy years ago. Couldn't you bring yourself to accept their verdict?'

But the Canon's scrupulous mind was impervious to such sly innuendos. Dalgliesh told himself that he should have remembered what, as a small boy, he had discovered about Uncle Hubert's conscience; that it operated as a warning bell and that, unlike most people, he never pretended that it hadn't sounded or that he hadn't heard it or that, having heard it, something must be wrong with the mechanism.

'Oh, I did, while she was alive. We never met you know. I didn't wish to force myself on her. After all she was a wealthy woman. My grandfather made a new Will on his marriage and left her all he possessed. Our ways of life were very different. But I usually wrote briefly at Christmas and she sent a card in reply. I wanted to keep some contact in case, one day, she might want someone to turn to and would remember that I am a priest.'

And why should she want that? thought Dalgliesh. To clear her conscience? Was that what the dear old boy had in mind? So he must have had doubts from the beginning. But of course he had! Dalgliesh knew something of the story and the general feeling of the family and friends was that Great Aunt Allie had been extremely luck to escape the gallows. His own father's view, expressed with reticence, reluctance and compassion had not in essentials differed from that given by a local reporter at the time.

'How on earth did she expect to get away with it? Damn lucky to escape topping if you ask me.'

'The news of the legacy came as a complete surprise?' asked Dalgliesh.

'Indeed yes. I only saw her once at that first and only Christmas six weeks after her marriage when my grandfather died. We always talk of her as Great Aunt Allie but in fact, as you know, she married my grandfather. But it seemed impossible to think of her as a step-grandmother. There was the usual family gathering at Colebrook Croft at the time and I was there with my parents and my twin sisters. I was barely four and the twins were just eight months old. I can remember nothing of my grandfather or of his wife. After the murder – if one has to use that dreadful word my mother returned home with us children leaving my father to cope with the police, the solicitors and the news-men. It was a terrible time for him. I don't think I was even told that grandfather was dead until about a year later. My old nurse, who had been given Christmas as a holiday to visit her own family, told me that, soon after my return home, I asked her if grandfather was now young and beautiful for always. She, poor woman, took it as a sign of infant prognostication and piety. Poor Nellie was sadly superstitious and sentimental I'm afraid. But I knew nothing of grandfather's death at the time and certainly can recall nothing of that Christmas visit or of my new step-grandmother. Mercifully, I was little more than a baby when the murder was done.'

'She was a music hall artiste wasn't she?' asked Dalgliesh.

'Yes and a very talented one. My grandfather met her when she was working with a partner in a hall in Cannes. He had gone to the south of France with a manservant for his health. I understand that she extracted a gold watch from his chain and when he claimed it, told him that he was English, had recently suffered from a stomach ailment, had two sons and a daughter and was about to have a wonderful surprise. It was all correct except that his only daughter had died in childbirth leaving him a grand-daughter, Marguerite Goddard.'

'And all easily guessable from his voice and appearance', said Dalgliesh. 'I suppose the surprise was the marriage?'

'It was certainly a surprise, and a most unpleasant one for the family. It is easy to deplore the snobbishness and the conventions of another age and indeed there was much in Edwardian England to deplore. But it was not a propitious marriage. I think of the difference in back-ground, education and way of life, the lack of common interest. And there was this great disparity of age. My grandfather had married a girl just three months younger than his own granddaughter. I cannot wonder that the family were concerned; that they felt that the union could not, in the end, contribute to the contentment or happiness of either party.'

'And that was putting it charitably,' thought Dalgliesh. The marriage certainly hadn't contributed to their happi-ness. From the point of view of the family it had been a disaster. He recalled hearing of an incident when the local vicar and his wife, a couple who had actually dined at

Colebrook Croft on the night of the murder, first called on the bride. Apparently old Augustus Boxdale had introduced her by saying:

'Meet the prettiest little variety artiste in the business. Took a gold watch and notecase off me without any trouble. Would have had the elastic out of my pants if I hadn't watched out. Anyway she stole my heart, didn't you sweetheart?' All this accompanied by a hearty slap on the rump and a squeal of delight from the lady who had promptly demonstrated her skill by extracting the Reverend Arthur Venable's bunch of keys from his left ear.

Dalgliesh thought it tactful not to remind the Canon of this story.

'What do you wish me to do Sir?' he enquired.

'It's asking a great deal I know when you're so busy. But if I had your assurance that you believed in Aunt Allie's innocence I should feel happy about accepting the bequest. I wondered if it would be possible for you to see the records of the trial. Perhaps it would give you a clue. You're so clever at this sort of thing.'

He spoke without flattery but with an innocent wonder at the strange avocations of men. Dalgliesh was, indeed, very clever at this sort of thing. A dozen or so men at present occupying security wings in H.M. prisons could testify to Chief Superintendent Dalgliesh's cleverness as, indeed, could a handful of others walking free whose defending Counsel had been in their own way as clever as Chief Superintendent Dalgliesh. But to re-examine a case over sixty years old seemed to require clairvoyance rather than cleverness. The trial judge and both learned Counsel had been dead for over fifty years. Two world wars had taken their toll. Four reigns had passed. It was highly probable that, of those who had slept under the roof of Colebrook Croft on that fateful Boxing Day night of 1901, only the Canon still survived. But the old man was troubled and had sought his help and Dalgliesh, with a day or two's leave due to him, had the time to give it.

'I'll do what I can' he promised.

The transcript of a trial which had taken place 67 years ago took time and trouble to obtain even for a Chief Superintendent of the Metropolitan Police. It provided little potential comfort for the Canon. Mr Justice Bellows had summed up with that avuncular simplicity with which he was wont to address juries, regarding them apparently as a panel of well-intentioned but cretinous children. And the facts could have been comprehended by any intelligent child. Part of the summing up set them out with admirable lucidity:

'And so gentlemen of the jury, we come to the night of December 26th. Mr Augustus Boxdale, who had perhaps indulged a little unwisely on Christmas Day, had retired to bed in his dressing room after luncheon suffering from a recurrence of the slight indigestive trouble which had afflicted him for most of his life. You have heard that he had taken luncheon with the members of his family and ate nothing which they too did not eat. You may feel you can acquit luncheon of anything worse than overrichness.

Dinner was served at eight p.m. promptly as was the custom at Colebrook Croft. There were present at that meal, Mrs Augustus Boxdale the deceased's bride; his elder son Captain Maurice Boxdale with his wife; his younger son the Reverend Henry Boxdale with his wife, his granddaughter Miss Marguerite Goddard and two neighbours, the Reverend and Mrs Arthur Venables.

You have heard how the accused took only the first course at dinner which was ragout of beef and then, at about eight twenty, left the dining room to sit with her husband.

Shortly after nine o'clock she rang for the parlour maid, Mary Huddy, and ordered a basin of gruel to be brought up to Mr Boxdale. You have heard that the deceased was fond of gruel, and indeed as prepared by Mrs Muncie the cook it sounds a most nourishing and comforting dish for an elderly gentleman of weak digestion.

You have heard Mrs Muncie describe how she prepared the gruel according to Mrs Beaton's admirable recipe and in the presence of Mary Huddy in case, as she said 'The master should take a fancy to it when I'm not at hand and you have to make it.' After the gruel had been prepared Mrs Muncie tasted it with a spoon and Mary Huddy carried it upstairs to the main bedroom together with a jug of water to thin the gruel if it were too strong. As she reached the door Mrs Boxdale came out, her hands full of stockings and underclothes. She has told you that she was on her way to the bathroom to wash them through. She asked the girl to put the basin of gruel on the wash-stand by the window and Mary Huddy did so in her presence. Miss Huddy has told you that, at the time, she noticed the bowl of fly papers soaking in water and she knew that this solution was one used by Mrs Boxdale as a cosmetic wash. Indeed, all the women who spent that evening in the house, with the exception of Mrs Venables, have told you that they knew that it was Mrs Boxdale's practice to prepare this solution of fly papers.

Mary Huddy and the accused left the bedroom together and you have heard the evidence of Mrs Muncie that Miss Huddy returned to the kitchen after an absence of only a few minutes. Shortly after nine o'clock the ladies left the dining room and entered the drawing room to take coffee. At nine fifteen p.m. Miss Goddard excused herself to the company and said that she would go to see if her grandfather needed anything. The time is established precisely because the clock struck the quarter hour as she left and Mrs Venables commented on the sweetness of its chime. You have also heard Mrs Venables' evidence and the evidence of Mrs Maurice Boxdale and Mrs Henry Boxdale that none of the ladies left the drawing room during the evening and Mr Venables had testified that the three gentlemen remained together until Miss Goddard appeared about three quarters of an hour later to inform them that her grandfather had become very ill and to request that the doctor be sent for immediately.

Miss Goddard has told you that, when she entered her grandfather's room, he was just finishing his gruel and was grumbling about its taste. She got the impression that this was merely a protest at being deprived of his dinner rather than that he genuinely considered that there was something wrong with the gruel. At any rate, he finished most of it and appeared to enjoy it despite his grumbles.

You have heard Miss Goddard describe how, after her grandfather had had as much as he wanted of the gruel, she took the bowl next door and left it on the washstand. She then returned to her grandfather's bedroom and Mr Boxdale, his wife and his granddaughter played three-handed whist for about three-quarters of an hour.

At ten o'clock Mr Augustus Boxdale complained of feeling very ill. He suffered from griping pains in the stomach, from sickness, and from looseness of the bowel. As soon as the symptoms began Miss Goddard went downstairs to let her uncles know that her grandfather was worse and to ask that Doctor Eversley should be sent for urgently. Doctor Eversley has given you his evidence. He arrived at Colebrook Croft at ten thirty p.m. when he found his patient very distressed and weak. He treated the symptoms and gave what relief he could but Mr Augustus Boxdale died shortly before midnight.

Gentlemen of the Jury, you have heard Marguerite Goddard describe how, as her grandfather's paroxysms increased in intensity, she remembered the gruel and wondered whether it could have disagreed with him in some way. She mentioned this possibility to her elder uncle, Captain Maurice Boxdale. Captain Boxdale has told you how he at once handed the bowl with its residue of gruel to Doctor Eversley with the request that the Doctor should lock it in a cupboard in the library, seal the lock, and himself keep the key. You have heard how the contents of the bowl were later analysed and with what result.'

An extraordinary precaution for the gallant Captain to have taken, thought Dalgliesh and a most perspicacious young woman. Was it by chance or by design that the bowl hadn't been taken down to be washed up as soon as the old man had finished with it? Why was it, he wondered that Marguerite Goddard hadn't rung for the parlour maid and requested her to remove it? Miss Goddard appeared the only other suspect. He wished he knew more about her.

But, except for the main protagonists, the characters in the drama did not emerge very clearly from the trial report. Why, indeed, should they? The British accusatorial system of trial is designed to answer one question, is the accused guilty beyond reasonable doubt of the crime charged? Exploration of the nuances of personality, speculation and gossip have no place in the witness box. The two Boxdale brothers came out as very dull fellows indeed. They and their estimable, respectable sloping-bosomed wives had sat at dinner in full view of each other from eight until after nine o'clock (a substantial meal that dinner) and had said so in the witness box more or less in identical words. The ladies' bosoms might have been heaving with far from estimable emotions of dislike, envy, embarrassment, or resentment of the interloper. If so they didn't tell the Court.

But the two brothers and their wives were clearly innocent, even if a detective of that time could have conceived of the guilt of a gentlefolk so well respected so eminently respectable. Even their impeccable alibis had a nice touch of social and sexual distinction. The Rev. Arthur Venables had vouched for the gentlemen, his good wife for the ladies. Besides, what motive had they? They could no longer gain financially by the old man's death. If anything, it was in their interest to keep him alive in the hope that disillusion with his marriage or a return to sanity might occur to cause him to change his Will. So far Dalgliesh had learned nothing that could cause him to give the Canon the assurance for which he hoped.

It was then that he remembered Aubrey Glatt. Glatt was a wealthy amateur criminologist who had made a study of all the notable Victorian and Edwardian poison cases. He was not interested in anything earlier or later being as obsessively wedded to his period as any serious historian, which indeed he had some claim to call himself. He lived in a Georgian house in Winchester – his affection for the Victorian and Edwardian age did not extend to its architecture – and was only three miles from Colebrook Croft. A visit to the London Library disclosed that he hadn't written a book on the case but it was improbable that he had totally neglected a crime so close at hand and so in period. Dalgliesh had occasionally helped him with technical details of police procedure. Glatt, in response to a telephone call, was happy to return the favour with the offer of afternoon tea and information.

Tea was served in his elegant drawing room by a parlour maid in gophered cap with streamers. Dalgliesh wondered what wage Glatt paid her to persuade her to wear it. She looked as if she could have played a role in any of his favourite Victorian dramas and Dalgliesh had an uncomfortable thought that arsenic might be dispensed with the cucumber sandwiches.

Glatt nibbled away and was expansive.

'It's interesting that you should have taken this sudden and, if I may say so, somewhat inexplicable interest in the Boxdale murder. I got out my notebook on the case only yesterday. Colebrook Croft is being demolished to make way for a new housing estate and I thought I would visit it for the last time. The family, of course, haven't lived there since the 1914-18 war. Architecturally it's completely undistinguished but one grieves to see it go. We might drive over after tea if you are agreeable.

'I never wrote my book on the case you know. I planned

a work entitled *The Colebrook Croft Mystery* or *Who Killed Augustus Boxdale?* But the answer was all too obvious.'

'No real mystery?' suggested Dalgliesh.

'Who else could it have been but Allegra Boxdale? She was born Allegra Porter you know. Do you think her mother could have been thinking of Byron? I imagine not. There's a picture of her on page two of the notebook by the way, taken by a photographer in Cannes on her wedding day. I call it beauty and the beast.'

The photograph had scarcely faded and Great Aunt Allie smiled plainly at Dalgliesh across nearly seventy years. Her broad face with its wide mouth and rather snub nose was framed by two wings of dark hair swept high and topped in the fashion of the day by an immense flowered hat. The features were too coarse for real beauty but the eyes were magnificent, deep set and well spaced and the chin round and determined. Beside this vital young Amazon poor Augustus Boxdale, smiling fatuously at the camera and clutching his bride as if for support, was but a frail and undersized beast. Their pose was unfortunate. She looked as if she were about to fling him over her shoulder.

Glatt shrugged. 'The face of a murderess? I've known less likely ones. Her Counsel suggested of course that the old man had poisoned his own gruel during the short time she left it on the wash-stand to cool while she visited the bathroom. But why should he? All the evidence suggests that he was in a state of post nuptial euphoria, poor senile old booby. Our Augustus was in no hurry to leave this world particularly by such an agonising means. Besides, I doubt whether he even knew the gruel was there. He was in bed next door in his dressing room remember.'

Dalgliesh asked: 'What about Marguerite Goddard? There's no evidence about the exact time when she entered the bedroom.'

'I thought you'd get on to that. She could have arrived

while her step-grandmother was in the bathroom, poisoned the gruel, hidden herself either in the main bedroom or elsewhere until it had been taken in to Augustus, then joined her grandfather and his bride as if she had just come upstairs. It's possible I admit. But is it likely? She was less inconvenienced than any of the family by her grandfather's second marriage. Her mother was Augustus Boxdale's eldest child and married, very young, a wealthy patent medicine manufacturer. She died in childbirth and her husband only survived her by a year. Marguerite Goddard was an heiress. She was also most advantageously engaged to Captain the Honorable John Brize-Lacey. It was quite a catch for a Boxdale – or a Goddard. Marguerite Goddard young, beautiful, secure in the possession of the Goddard fortune not to mention the Goddard emeralds and the eldest son of a Lord was hardly a serious suspect. In my view Defence Counsel, that was Roland Gort Lloyd, remember, was wise to leave her strictly alone.'

'It was a memorable defence I believe.'

'Magnificent. There's no doubt Allegra Boxdale owed her life to Gort Lloyd. I know that concluding speech by heart.'

'Gentlemen of the Jury, I beseech you in the sacred name of Justice to consider what you are at. It is your responsibility and yours alone to decide the fate of this young woman. She stands before you now, young, vibrant, glowing with health, the years stretching before her with their promise and their hopes. It is in your power to cut off all this as you might top a nettle with one swish of your cane. To condemn her to the slow torture of those last waiting weeks; to that last dreadful walk; to heap calumny on her name; to desecrate those few happy weeks of marriage with the man who loved her so greatly; to cast her into the final darkness of an ignominious grave.'

Pause for dramatic effect. Then the crescendo in that magnificent voice. 'And on what evidence gentlemen? I ask you.' Another pause. Then the thunder. 'On what evidence?'

'A powerful defence,' said Dalgliesh. 'But I wonder how it would go down with a modern Judge and Jury.'

'Well it went down very effectively with that 1902 Jury. Of course the abolition of capital punishment has rather cramped the more histrionic style. I'm not sure that the reference to topping nettles was in the best of taste. But the Jury got the message. They decided that, on the whole, they preferred not to have the responsibility of sending the accused to the gallows. They were out six hours reaching their verdict and it was greeted with some applause. If any of those worthy citizens had been asked to wager five pounds of their own good money on her innocence I suspect that it would have been a different matter. Allegra Boxdale had helped him, of course. The Criminal Evidence Act, passed three years earlier enabled him to put her in the witness box. She wasn't an actress of a kind for nothing. Somehow she managed to persuade the Jury that she had genuinely loved the old man.'

'Perhaps she had,' suggested Dalgliesh. 'I don't suppose there had been much kindness in her life. And he was kind.'

'No doubt. No doubt. But love!' Glatt was impatient. 'My dear Dalgliesh! He was a singularly ugly old man of sixty-nine. She was an attractive girl of twenty-one!'

Dalgliesh doubted whether love, that iconoclastic passion was susceptible to this kind of simple arithmetic but he didn't argue. Glatt went on:

'And the prosecution couldn't suggest any other romantic attachment. The police got in touch with her previous partner of course. He was discovered to be a bald, undersized little man, sharp as a weasel, with a buxom uxorious wife and five children. He had moved down the coast after the partnership broke up and was now working with a new girl. He said regretfully that she was coming along nicely thank you gentlemen but would never be a patch on Allie and that, if Allie got her neck out of the noose and ever wanted a job, she knew where to come. It was obvious even to the most suspicious policeman that his interest was purely professional. As he said: 'What was a grain or two of arsenic between friends?'

'The Boxdales had no luck after the trial. Captain Maurice Boxdale was killed in 1916 leaving no children and the Reverend Edward lost his wife and their twin daughters in the 1918 influenza epidemic. He survived until 1932. The boy Hubert may still be alive, but I doubt it. That family were a sickly lot.

'My greatest achievement, incidentally, was in tracing Marguerite Goddard. I hadn't realised that she was still alive. She never married Brize-Lacey or, indeed, anyone else. He distinguished himself in the 1914–18 war, came successfully through, and eventually married an eminently suitable young woman, the sister of a brother officer. He inherited the title in 1925 and died in 1953. But Marguerite Goddard may be alive now for all I know. She may even be living in the same modest Bournemouth hotel where I found her. Not that my efforts in tracing her were rewarded. She absolutely refused to see me. That's the note that she sent out to me by the way.'

It was meticulously pasted into the notebook in its chronological order and carefully annotated. Aubrey Glatt was a natural researcher; Dalgliesh couldn't help wondering whether this passion for accuracy might not have been more rewardingly spent than in the careful documentation of murder.

The note was written in an elegant upright hand, the strokes black and very thin but unwavering.

'Miss Goddard presents her compliments to Mr Aubrey Glatt. She did not murder her grandfather and has neither the time nor inclination to gratify his curiosity by discussing the person who did.'

Aubrey Glatt said: 'After that extremely disobliging note I felt there was really no point in going on with the book.'

Glatt's passion for Edwardian England extended to more than its murders and they drove to Colebrook Croft high above the green Hampshire lanes in an elegant 1910 Daimler. Aubrey wore a thin tweed coat and deerstalker hat and looked, Dalgliesh thought, rather like a Sherlock Holmes with himself as attendant Watson.

'We are only just in time my dear Dalgliesh', he said when they arrived. 'The engines of destruction are assembled. That ball on a chain looks like the eyeball of God, ready to strike. Let us make our number with the attendant artisans. You as a guardian of the law will have no wish to trespass.'

The work of demolition had not yet begun but the inside of the house had been stripped and plundered, the great rooms echoed to their footsteps like gaunt and deserted barracks after the final retreat. They moved from room to room, Glatt mourning the forgotten glories of an age he had been born thirty years too late to enjoy; Dalgliesh with his mind on more immediate and practical concerns.

The design of the house was simple and formalised. The first floor, on which were most of the main bedrooms, had a long corridor running the whole length of the facade. The master bedroom was at the southern end with two large windows giving a distant view of Winchester Cathedral tower. A communicating door led to a small dressing room.

The main corridor had a row of four identical large windows. The brass curtain rods and wooden rings had been removed (they were collectors' items now) but the ornate carved pelmets were still in place. Here must have hung pairs of heavy curtains giving cover to anyone who wished to slip out of view. And Dalgliesh noted with interest that one of the windows was exactly opposite the door of the main bedroom. By the time they had left

Colebrook Croft and Glatt had dropped him at Winchester Station, Dalgliesh was beginning to formulate a theory.

His next move was to trace Marguerite Goddard if she were still alive. It took him nearly a week of weary searching, a frustrating trail along the south coast from hotel to hotel. Almost everywhere his enquiries were met with defensive hostility. It was the usual story of a very old lady who had become more demanding, arrogant and eccentric as her health and fortune waned; an unwelcome embarrassment to manager and fellow guests alike. The hotels were all modest, a few almost sordid. What, he wondered, had become of the Goddard fortune?

From the last landlady he learned that Miss Goddard had become ill, really very sick indeed, and had been removed six months previously to the local district general hospital. And it was there that he found her.

The Ward Sister was surprisingly young, a petite, dark haired girl with a tired face and challenging eyes.

'Miss Goddard is very ill. We've put her in one of the side wards. Are you a relative? If so, you're the first one who has bothered to call and you're lucky to be in time. When she is delirious she seems to expect a Captain Brize-Lacey to call. You're not he by any chance?'

'Captain Brize-Lacey will not be calling. No, I'm not a relative. She doesn't even know me. But I would like to visit her if she's well enough and is willing to see me. Could you please give her this note.'

He couldn't force himself on a defenceless and dying woman. She still had the right to say no. He was afraid she would refuse him. And if she did, he might never learn the truth. He thought for a second and then wrote four words on the back page of his diary, signed them, tore out the page, folded it and handed it to the Sister.

She was back very shortly.

'She'll see you. She's weak of course and very old but she's perfectly lucid now. Only please don't tire her.'

'I'll try not to stay too long.'

The girl laughed:

'Don't worry. She'll throw you out soon enough if she gets bored. The Chaplain and the Red Cross librarian have a terrible time with her. Third door on the left. There's a stool to sit on under the bed. We ring a bell at the end of visiting time.'

She bustled off, leaving him to find his own way. The corridor was very quiet. At the far end he could glimpse through the open door of the main ward the regimented rows of beds, each with its pale blue coverlet; the bright glow of flowers on the over-bed tables and the laden visitors making their way in pairs to each bedside. There was a faint buzz of welcome, a hum of conversation. But no one was visiting the side wards. Here in the silence of the aseptic corridor Dalgliesh could smell death.

The woman propped high against the pillows in the third room on the left no longer looked human. She lay rigidly, her long arms disposed like sticks on the coverlet. This was a skeleton clothed with a thin membrane of flesh beneath whose yellow transparency the tendons and veins were plainly visible as if in an anatomist's model. She was nearly bald and the high domed skull under its spare down of hair was as brittle and vulnerable as a child's. Only the eyes still held life, burning in their deep sockets with an animal vitality. But when she spoke her voice was distinctive and unwavering, evoking as her appearance never could the memory of imperious youth.

She took up his note and read aloud four words:

' " It was the child". You are right, of course. The four-year-old Hubert Boxdale killed his grandfather. You signed this note Adam Dalgliesh. There was no Dalgliesh connected with the case.'

'I am a detective of the Metropolitan Police. But I'm not here in any official capacity. I have known about this case for a number of years from a dear friend. I have a natural curiosity to learn the truth. And I have formed a theory.'

'And now, like that poseur Aubrey Glatt, you want to write a book?'

'No. I shall tell no one. You have my promise.'

Her voice was ironic.

'Thank you. I am a dying woman Mr Dalgliesh. I tell you that, not to invite your sympathy which it would be an impertinence for you to offer and which I neither want nor require but to explain why it no longer matters to me what you say or do. But I too have a natural curiosity. Your note, cleverly, was intended to provoke it. I should like to know how you discovered the truth.'

Dalgliesh drew the visitors' stool from under the bed and sat down beside her. She did not look at him. The skeleton hands still holding his note did not move.

'Everyone in Colebrook Croft who could have killed Augustus Boxdale was accounted for, except the one person whom nobody considered, the small boy. He was an intelligent, articulate and lonely child. He was almost certainly left to his own devices. His nurse did not accompany the family to Colebrook Croft and the servants who were there had the extra work of Christmas and the care of the delicate twin girls. The boy probably spent much time with his grandfather and the new bride. She too was lonely and disregarded. He could have trotted around with her as she went about her various activities. He could have watched her making her arsenical face wash and, when he asked as a child will what it was for, could have been told "to make me young and beautiful". He loved his grandfather but he must have known that the old man was neither young nor beautiful. Suppose he woke up on that Boxing Day night overfed and excited after the Christmas festivities. Suppose he went to Allegra Boxdale's room in search of comfort and companionship and saw there the basin of gruel and the arsenical mixture together on the washstand. Suppose he decided that here was something he could do for his grandfather.'

The voice from the bed said quietly:

'And suppose someone stood unnoticed in the doorway and watched him.'

'So you were behind the window curtains on the landing looking through the open door?'

'Of course. He knelt on the chair, two chubby hands clasping the bowl of poison, pouring it with infinite care into his grandfather's gruel. I watched while he replaced the linen cloth over the basin, got down from his chair, replaced it with careful art against the wall and trotted out into the corridor and back to the nursery. About three seconds later Allegra came out of the bathroom and I watched while she carried the gruel into my grandfather. A second later I went into the main bedroom. The bowl of poison had been a little heavy for Hubert's small hands to manage and I saw that a small pool had been spilt on the polished top of the washstand. I mopped it up with my handkerchief. Then I poured some of the water from the jug into the poison bowl to bring up the level. It only took a couple of seconds and I was ready to join Allegra and my grandfather in the bedroom and sit with him while he ate his gruel. I watched him die without pity and without remorse. I think I hated them both equally. The grandfather who had adored, petted and indulged me all through my childhood had deteriorated into this disgusting old lecher, unable to keep his hands off his woman even when I was in the room. He had rejected me and his family, jeopardised my engagement, made our name a laughing stock in the County, and for a woman my grandmother wouldn't have employed as a kitchen maid. I wanted them both dead. And they were both going to die. But it would be by other hands than mine. I could deceive myself that it wasn't my doing.'

Dalgliesh asked: 'When did she find out?'

'She knew that evening. When my grandfather's agony began she went outside for the jug of water. She wanted a cool cloth for his head. It was then that she noticed that the level of water in the jug had fallen and that a small pool of liquid on the washstand had been mopped up. I should have realised that she would have seen that pool. She had been trained to register every detail; it was almost subconscious with her. She thought at the time that Mary Huddy had spilt some of the water when she set down the tray and the gruel. But who but I could have mopped it up? And why?'

'And when did she face you with the truth?'

'Not until after the trial. Allegra had magnificent courage. She knew what was at stake. but she also knew what she stood to gain. She gambled with her life for a fortune.'

And then Dalgliesh understood what had happened to the Goddard inheritance.

'So she made you pay?'

'Of course. Every penny. The Goddard fortune, the Goddard emeralds. She lived in luxury for sixty-seven years on my money. She ate and dressed on my money. When she moved with her lovers from hotel to hotel it was on my money. She paid them with my money. And if she has left anything, which I doubt, it is my money. My grandfather left very little. He had been senile and had let money run through his fingers like sand.'

'And your engagement?'

'It was broken, you could say by mutual consent. A marriage, Mr Dalgliesh, is like any other legal contract. It is most successful when both parties are convinced they have a bargain. Captain Brize-Lacey was sufficiently discouraged by the scandal of a murder in the family. He was a proud and highly conventional man. But that alone might have been accepted with the Goddard fortune and the Goddard emeralds to deodorise the bad smell. But the marriage couldn't have succeeded if he had discovered that he had married socially beneath him, into a family with a major scandal and no compensating fortune.'

Dalgliesh said: 'Once you had begun to pay you had no choice but to go on. I see that. But why did you pay? She could hardly have told her story. It would have meant involving the child.'

'Oh no! That wasn't her plan at all. She never meant to involve the child. She was a sentimental woman and she was fond of Hubert. No, she intended to accuse me of murder outright. Then, if I decided to tell the truth, how would it help me? How could I admit that I had watched Hubert, actually watched a child barely four years old preparing an agonising death for his grandfather without speaking a word to stop him? I could hardly claim that I hadn't understood the implication of what I had seen. After all, I wiped up the spilled liquid, I topped up the bowl. She had nothing to lose remember, neither life nor reputation. They couldn't try her twice. That's why she waited until after the trial. It made her secure for ever. But what of me? In the circles in which I moved reputation was everything. She needed only to breathe the story in the ears of a few servants and I was finished. The truth can be remarkably tenacious. But it wasn't only reputation. I paid in the shadow of the gallows.'

Dalgliesh asked, 'But could she ever prove it?'

Suddenly she looked at him and gave an eery screech of laughter. It tore at her throat until he thought the taut tendons would snap.

'Of course she could! You fool! Don't you understand? She took my handkerchief, the one I used to mop up the arsenic mixture. That was her profession remember. Some time during that evening, perhaps when we were all crowding around the bed, two soft plump fingers insinuated themselves between the satin of my evening dress and my flesh and extracted that stained and damning piece of linen.'

She stretched out feebly towards the bedside locker. Dalgliesh saw what she wanted and pulled open the drawer. There on the top was a small square of very fine linen with a border of hand-stitched lace. He took it up. In the corner was her monogram delicately embroidered.

And half of the handkerchief was still stiff and stained with brown.

She said: 'She left instructions with her solicitors that this was to be returned to me after her death. She always knew where I was. She made it her business to know. You see, it could be said that she had a life interest in me. But now she's dead. And I shall soon follow. You may have the handkerchief Mr Dalgliesh. It can be of no further use to either of us now.'

Dalgliesh put it in his pocket without speaking. As soon as possible he would see that it was burnt. But there was something else he had to say. 'Is there anything you would wish me to do? Is there anyone you want told, or to tell? Would you care to see a priest?'

Again there was that uncanny screech of laughter but it was softer now:

'There's nothing I can say to a priest. I only regret what I did because it wasn't successful. That is hardly the proper frame of mind for a good confession. But I bear her no ill will. No envy, malice or uncharitableness. She won; I lost. One should be a good loser. But I don't want any priest telling me about penance. I've paid, Mr Dalgliesh. For sixty-seven years I've paid. And in this world, young man, the rich only pay once.'

She lay back as if suddenly exhausted. There was silence for a moment. Then she said with sudden vigour.

'I believe your visit has done me good. I would be obliged if you would make it convenient to return each afternoon for the next three days. I shan't trouble you after that.'

Dalgliesh extended his leave with some difficulty and stayed at a local inn. He saw her each afternoon. They never spoke again of the murder. And when he came punctually at two p.m. on the fourth day it was to be told that Miss Goddard had died peacefully in the night with apparently no trouble to anyone. She was, as she had said, a good loser.

A week later Dalgliesh reported to the Canon.

'I was able to see a man who has made a detailed study of the case. He had already done most of the work for me. I have read the transcript of the trial and visited Colebrook Croft. And I have seen one other person, closely connected with the case but who is now dead. I know you will want me to respect confidences and to say no more than I need.'

It sounded pompous and minatory but he couldn't help that. The Canon murmured his quiet assurance. Thank God he wasn't a man to question. Where he trusted, he trusted absolutely. If Dalgliesh gave his word there would be no more questioning. But he was anxious. Suspense hung around them. Dalgliesh went on quickly:

'As a result I can give you my word that the verdict was a just verdict and that not one penny of your grandfather's fortune is coming to you through anyone's wrong doing.'

He turned his face away and gazed out of the vicarage window at the sweet green coolness of the summer's day so that he did not have to watch the Canon's happiness and relief. There was a silence. The old man was probably giving thanks in his own way. Then he was aware that his godfather was speaking. Something was being said about gratitude, about the time he had given up to the investigation.

'Please don't misunderstand me Adam. But when the formalities have been completed I should like to donate something to a charity named by you, one close to your heart.'

Dalgliesh smiled. His contributions to charity were impersonal; a quarterly obligation discharged by banker's order. The Canon obviously regarded charities as so many old clothes; all were friends but some fitted better and were more affectionately regarded than others.

But inspiration came:

'It's good of you to think of it, Sir. I rather liked what I learned about Great Aunt Allie. It would be pleasant to give something in her name. Isn't there a society for the assistance of retired and indigent variety artistes, conjurors and so on?'

The Canon, predictably, knew that there was and could name it.

Dalgliesh said: 'Then I think Canon that Great Aunt Allie would agree that a donation in her name would be entirely appropriate.'

INSTRUMENT OF JUSTICE

When Frances Liley read in the obituary column of *The Times* of the death of Oliver Darnell, beloved husband of Julia, suddenly at his home, she folded her arms on the table before her, put her head down on them and burst into violent tears. Anyone who had seen her then would have assumed that she was weeping at the loss of a dear friend. In fact, they were tears of relief, healing and wonderful. At last she was free. No threat hung over her any more. Or so she thought until she had had time to do a little thinking.

As soon as she had she sat back abruptly, dried her eyes roughly and sat staring before her, a dark, angularly handsome woman of forty, possessed by a new horror. For when a person died his solicitor or his executors or someone would have to go through his papers and somewhere they would find those terrible photographs. And God knew what would happen then. At least with Oliver, Frances had known where she was. Two thousand a year to him, which it had not been too difficult for her to find, and she had been relatively safe. But if someone else found the photographs and felt inclined to send them to Mark, her husband, he would immediately go ahead with the divorce that he wanted and would certainly get custody of their two children. That would be intolerable. She must think and think fast.

Luckily she had always had a quick brain. After only a few minutes she knew what to do, or at least what was worth trying. Telephoning Julia Darnell, she said, 'It's Frances, Julia. I've just seen the news about Oliver. I'm so terribly sorry. I can hardly believe it. It was his heart, was it? There was always something the matter with it, wasn't there? Listen, my dear, please be quite honest with me, but would you like me to come down? I mean, if you're alone now and I can help in any way. But don't say you'd like me to come if you'd sooner I didn't. Of course I'll come to the funeral, but I could come straight away and stay on for a few days, unless you've some other friend with you.'

Julia was tearfully grateful. She had no relations of her own and had never liked Oliver's, and though the neighbours, she said, had been very kind, she was virtually alone. And she and Frances were such very old friends, she could think of no one who could help so much to break the dreadful new loneliness of bereavement. Of course Julia had never known of her husband's brief adultery with Frances, or that he had supplemented his not very large income as a painter of very abstract pictures with a sideline in blackmail, and her affection for Frances was uncomplicated and sincere. Promising to arrive that afternoon, Frances telephoned Mark in his office to tell him what had happened and that she would probably be away for a few days. The children were no problem, because they were away at their boarding school. Packing a suitcase, she set off for the Darnells' cottage in Dorset.

By that time she had a plan of sorts in her mind. On the morning of the funeral she intended to wake up with what she would claim was a virus and say that she was feeling too ill to go out. Then, during the one time when she could be certain the cottage would be empty, she would make a swift search of it for the photographs. The probability was that they were somewhere in Oliver's studio, a very private place in which Julia had never been allowed to touch anything, even to do a little cautious dusting. If they were not there, of course, if, for instance, Oliver had kept them in the bank, then there was nothing for Frances to do but go home and wait for the worst to happen, but with luck, she thought, she would find them.

Unfortunately her plan was wrecked by the fact that on the morning of the funeral it was Julia who woke up with a virus. She had a temperature of a hundred and two, complained of a sore throat and could only speak in a husky whisper. Frances called the doctor who gave Julia some antibiotics and said that she must certainly stay in bed and not go out into the chill of the February morning, even to attend her husband's funeral. Julia, with bright spots of fever on her plump, naturally pale cheeks, cried bitterly and said, 'But all those people coming back here to lunch, Frances – what *am* I to do about them? I can't possibly put them off now.'

For Julia had insisted that Oliver's relations, who were coming from a distance, and such neighbours as were kind enough to come to the funeral, must be given lunch in her house after it, and she and Frances had spent most of the day before assembling cold meats, salads, cheeses and a supply of rather inferior white wine for what Frances felt would be a gruesome little party, but the thought of which seemed to comfort Julia.

Again thinking fast, Frances said, 'Don't worry, I'll look after them for you. I'll go to the service, but I won't go on to the cemetery, I'll come straight back from the church and have everything ready for your friends when they arrive. Now just stay quiet and I'll look after everything.'

She gave Julia the pills that the doctor had left for her and also brought her a mug of hot milk into which she had emptied two capsules of sodium amytal which she had found in the bathroom cabinet. They would almost certainly ensure that Julia would be asleep by the time that Frances returned from the church, and though she would not have as long for her search as she had hoped, she might still be fortunate.

There were not many people in the church. A man sitting next to Frances, who started a low-voiced conversation with her before the coffin had been brought in or the vicar appeared, introduced himself as Major Sowerby and said that his wife was desperately sorry not to be able to attend, but she was in bed with a virus.

'There's a terrible lot of it around in the village,' he said. 'Is it true poor Mrs Darnell's laid up with it too?'

'I'm afraid so,' Frances said.

'Tragic for her. Most upsetting. She and Oliver were so devoted to one another. Of course I didn't understand his painting, but Isobel, my wife, who knows a lot more about that sort of thing than I do, says he deserved much more recognition than he ever had. Great dedication, she says, and such integrity.'

'Oh, complete,' Frances agreed with a sweet, sad smile, and thought that in its way it was true. Oliver had been dedicated to exploiting any woman who had been fool enough to be charmed by his astonishing good looks and to trust him. As soon as the service was over she hurried out of the church, leaving the other mourners to go on to the cemetery, and made her way along the lane that led to the Darnells' cottage.

As she entered it, she stood still, listening. All was quiet. So it looked as if the sodium amytal had done its work and Julia was asleep. But just to make sure, Frances went to the foot of the stairs and called softly, 'Julia!'

There was no reply. She waited a moment, then wrenched off her coat, dropped it on a chair and went swiftly along the passage to Oliver's studio. Presently she would have to attend to the setting out of the lunch for Julia's guests, but the search much come first. Opening the door of the studio, she went in and only then understood the reason for the quiet in the house. Julia, in her dressing-gown, was lying in the middle of the floor with her head a terrible mass of blood and with a heavy hammer on the floor beside her.

Frances was not an entirely hard-hearted person. Also, she was by nature law-abiding. Her first impulse, as she stared at the battered thing on the floor, was to call the police. But then a habit that she had of having second thoughts asserted itself. It was still of desperate importance to her to find the photographs and once the police were in the house she would have no further chance of searching for them. That made the situation exceedingly complex. For one thing, how were the police to know that it had not been Frances whom Julia, drugged and half-asleep, had heard downstairs in her husband's studio, and coming downstairs to investigate, been killed by her for it? If Frances called the police now, she thought, she might find herself in deep trouble.

But if she did not and searched for the photographs first, she would presently find herself with a cooling body on her hands and sooner or later would have to explain why she had failed to report it a few hours earlier. It did not help that she was almost certain that she knew who the murderer was. A virus can be a very convenient thing, and Mrs Sowerby, who had not attended the church, would not have found out that Julia was ill and would have assumed that the house was empty. Looking round the studio, where drawers had been pulled out and papers, letters, sketches, notebooks, spilled on the floor, Frances wondered if the woman had found the photographs or letters that Oliver had presumably been holding over her before she committed murder, or if she was still in terror that someone else would find them. But even if she were, she was unlikely to come back for the present, knowing that a dozen guests would shortly be arriving. Taking the key out of the door, locking it on the outside and putting the key into the pocket of the suit that she was wearing, Frances went out to the kitchen to go on with preparing the lunch.

She took all the things that she and Julia had made the day before out of the refrigerator, spooned the various salads, the prawns with rice and peppers, the cucumbers in sour cream, the coleslaw and the rest, into cut glass bowls, arranged the slices of cold turkey, meat loaf and ham on dishes, and set them out on the table in the dining-room. She put silver and wine glasses on the table and drew the corks of several of the bottles of wine. The meal was only just ready when the first guests arrived.

They were the vicar, Arthur Craddock, and his wife. He was a slender, quiet-looking man whose voice, as he recited the psalms that Julia had chosen and described Oliver's improbable virtues, had seemed unexpectedly vibrant and authoritative. But any authority that he might achieve when he was performing his professional duties was sadly diminished, in a mere social setting, by his wife, a large, hearty woman who looked kindly, but accustomed to domination and who upset Frances at once by saying that she would just pop upstairs to have a few words with poor Julia, tell her how splendidly everything had gone off and how much she had been missed.

'But the infection,' Frances stammered. 'I believe it's all round the village and I know she wouldn't want you to be exposed to it here.'

'I'm never ill,' Mrs Craddock replied. 'Ask my husband. We were in India for a time, you know, and I've nursed patients through bubonic plague and never a whit the worse. I'm sure I could give Julia a little comfort.'

'Well, later, perhaps,' Frances said, recovering her presence of mind. 'I went up to see her myself a few minutes ago and found her asleep. The doctor gave her a sedative. He said rest was what she needed, and I'm sure he's right. I know she hasn't slept properly for days. But she's looking very peaceful now, so I don't think we should disturb her.'

'Ah no, of course not,' Mrs Craddock agreed. 'Was that Dr Bolling? Excellent man. The best type of good, old-fashioned family doctor whom you can really trust.'

She let herself and her husband be shepherded into the dining room and they had each just accepted a glass of wine when the doorbell rang again and Frances left them to admit the next guests.

They were a brother and a cousin of Oliver's, both of whom, he had once told Frances, he knew disliked him. The next to arrive was Major Sowerby and gradually the dining room filled, the hushed tones in which everyone spoke on first arriving rising by degrees until the noise in the room resembled that of any ordinary cocktail party. The food on the table was eaten with appetite, the wine was drunk, and the atmosphere became one of what seemed to Frances a faintly gruesome hilarity, quelled only now and again by guilt when someone was tactless enough to remind the others that these were funeral baked meats that they were consuming.

Slightly flushed, Oliver's brother remarked, 'Julia was always a jolly good cook. Pity she can't be with us now.'

'She must have taken a great deal of trouble over this,' Mrs Craddock said, 'but I expect it was good for her, taking her mind off her sorrow. I'd like to take a little of it up to her and tell her how we've all been thinking of her, because with all the noise we've been making I'm sure she must be awake by now. I'll just pop up with a plateful, shall I, and perhaps a glass of wine?'

'That's the ticket,' Major Sowerby said, 'though whisky might do her more good. I took a good strong whisky up to my wife before I left for the church, and a sandwich. She said a sandwich was all she could face. Actually I had to insist on her staying in bed, she was so upset at not being able to make it to the funeral, but obviously she wasn't fit to go out. The fact is, you know, she thought a lot of Oliver. Sat for her portrait to him once, then made me buy the thing. Well, I didn't mind doing it really, because no one could guess it's Isobel, it's all squares and triangles and she says it's good and she knows far more about that sort of thing than I do.'

Mrs Craddock was spooning prawns and rice on to a plate, murmuring, 'I wonder if she likes cucumber – it disagrees with some people,' adding a slice of turkey, a small piece of ham and reaching for a bottle of wine to fill a glass for Julia.

Frightened beyond words and desperate, Frances snatched the plate and the glass from the woman's hands, said brusquely, 'I'll take them,' made for the door and while Mrs Craddock was still only looking startled at her rudeness, shot up the stairs and through the open door into Julia's bedroom.

In its silence she first began to feel the real horror of the situation. Here she was with food and wine in her hands for a woman who lay in a room downstairs with her body cooling and her head battered in. Her gaze held hypnotised by the sight of the empty bed with its dented pillows and its blankets thrown back, Frances gulped down the wine, wishing that it was something stronger, then went downstairs again and put down the plate of untouched food on the dining table.

'She drank the wine, but she wouldn't eat anything,' she said to Mrs Craddock. 'I gave her another of the pills the doctor left for her. She's very sleepy. I really think it's best to leave her alone.'

Frustrated in her desire to do good, the vicar's wife soon left, sweeping her husband along with her, and after that, one by one, the other guests departed. At last the house was empty and quiet again.

Too quiet, too desolate. The last hour had been the worst nightmare that Frances had ever lived through, but at least the crowd of chattering people had been a defence against thought. Now she could not escape from it any longer. There was the problem of the photographs and the problem of the corpse in the studio. Looking at the table littered with china, wine glasses and left-overs, she had an absurd idea that she might do the washing-up before trying to cope with the murder, but recognising this for the idiocy that it was, and that her motive was only to put off doing what she must, she poured out a glass of whisky, sat down at the head of the table and tried to concentrate.

The photographs came first. She must nerve herself to go back into the studio and search for them. What she did next would depend to some extent on whether or not she found them. She could hardly bear to face the possibility that she might not. With the dreadful things in his hands, Mark would certainly be able to obtain custody of the children when he went ahead with the divorce that he wanted, and she would never submit to that. For apart from the pleasure that she took in the two dear girls, it would be intolerable to let Mark triumph over her.

She thought of the photographs, of which Oliver had only once allowed her a glimpse, of how appallingly revealing they were, and of the bitter amusement with which Mark would view them. They were, in their way, superb photographs. Oliver might not have been an outstanding painter, but as a photographer he had been highly skilled, as well as incredibly ingenious. She had had no suspicion of the presence of the camera in the room at the time when he had taken the pictures, and when he had told her how he had done it, she had almost had to laugh, it had been so clever. But now she must get them back. That was what she must do before she thought of anything else.

She went back into the studio. It was easier than she had thought that it would be to disregard Julia's body, the darkening blood and the murderous hammer. Locking the door in case anyone, that well-meaning busybody, Mrs Craddock, for instance, should think of coming back, she began on a methodical search of the drawers and cupboards. To her surprise, she found the photographs almost at once, not merely prints, but the negatives too, in a box in a cupboard which she thought had not yet been opened by the previous searcher.

She found several other photographs of a similar character. Feeling dizzy with relief, close to bursting into tears as she had when she had first read of Oliver's death, she studied these, which were of three women, and wondered which of them was of Isobel Sowerby. Frances knew nothing about her except that her husband did not think that she looked as if she consisted of squares and triangles. But none of the women did. They all had more curves than angles. And two of them looked rather young to be married to Major Sowerby, though that was not the sort of thing about which it was ever possible to be sure. Men of sixty sometimes married girls in their teens. However, Frances thought that Julia's murderess was probably the third woman, who was about her own age, big, heavy-breasted, rather plump, with a look of passion and violence about her. In fact, a formidable-looking woman, surely capable of murder. After studying her face for some minutes, Frances put her photographs, the prints and the negatives, back into the cupboard, took those of herself and the two younger women to the sitting room, put them down on the hearth and set fire to them.

The negatives spat, blazed briefly and disappeared, making a pungent smell in the room. The prints curled at the edges and caught fire more slowly, but as she prodded them with the poker, they flared up, then smouldered into ash. Watching them, sitting on her heels, she waited until there was not a spark left, then stood up and went to the telephone.

She had a plan now, a plan of sorts. It was a gamble, but then what could she do that was not? Picking up the directory, she looked up the Sowerbys' number and dialled it.

To her satisfaction, it was a woman's voice that answered. Frances did not introduce herself.

'I've found what you were looking for,' she said softly.

There was a silence. Frances suddenly became aware of how her heart was thudding. For this was the moment when she would discover whether or not her gamble had paid off. She might have guessed totally wrongly. Mrs Sowerby might be an innocent woman who had been in bed all day with 'flu, feeling very ill, and if that were so, Frances would have to start thinking all over again. It seemed to her lunacy now that she had not called the police as soon as she had found Julia's body. If only she had known how simple it was going to be to find the photographs, she would have done so, and would have had plenty of time to destroy them before the police arrived. But there was not much point in thinking on those lines now. It was too late. She waited.

At last an almost whispering voice said in her ear, 'Who are you?'

She drew a shuddering breath. So she had been right. Her plan was working.

'A friend of Julia's, she said. 'I think you'd better come here as soon as possible.'

'What do you want?' the voice asked.

'Your help,' Frances said.

'I can't come. I'm ill.'

'I think it would be advisable to make a quick recovery.'

'But I can't. My husband wouldn't hear of my going out.'

'That's your problem. I'll wait here for a little, but not for long.'

There was another silence, then the voice said, 'All right, I'll see what I can do.'

The telephone at the other end was put down. Frances put down the one that she was holding, realising that the hand that had been gripping it was clammy with sweat and had left damp marks on the instrument. She wondered if that mattered, but decided that it did not. She would have another call to make presently, which would account for the fingerprints.

She waited an hour before there came a ring at the front door bell. The early dusk of the February afternoon was already dimming the daylight. She had spent some of the time while she had had to wait stripping Julia's body of the dressing-gown and nightdress that she was wearing and redressing it in pants and bra, jeans and sweater. It had been a terrible undertaking. In the middle of it she had felt faint and had had to go back to the sitting room to give herself a chance to recover her self-control. But she had been afraid to wait until the other woman arrived and could help her in case the body stiffened too much to make the undressing of it possible. She knew nothing about how long it took for rigor mortis to set in. The blood-stained clothes that she removed were a problem and so was the hammer. She had not thought about that until after she had started undressing Julia, but in the end she made a bundle of them, took them out to the garage and put them into the boot of the Darnells' car. Then she went back into the house to wait.

When the ring at the door came at last and she went to answer it, she found the woman whom she had been expecting on the doorstep. Her guess about the photographs had been correct. Isobel Sowerby was a middle-aged woman, tall and thick-set, with thick dark hair to her shoulders, intense dark eyes and jutting lips. She was wearing slacks and a sheepskin jacket.

Staring at Frances with deep enmity, she said, 'What am I supposed to do now?'

'We're going to arrange a suicide,' Frances answered.

'I don't understand.' the other woman said. 'If you know so much, why haven't you turned me in?'

'Because I'm involved myself. I made the mistake of not calling the police as soon as I found the body. I wanted to find some photographs of me that Oliver had and I didn't think until it was too late how difficult it was going to be to explain how I'd managed not to find Julia as soon as I got back from the church. So I'm in almost as much trouble as you are. And I think the best thing for both of us to do is to put Julia into her car and send her over the cliffs into the sea. Suicide while the balance of her mind was disturbed by the death of her husband. I couldn't arrange it alone because she's too heavy for me to carry. I have to have help.'

'All right, whatever you say,' Isobel Sowerby said. 'But give me the photgraphs first.'

'Afterwards,' Frances said.

'No, now, or I won't help you.'

'Afterwards,' Frances repeated.

They looked at one another with wary antagonism, then Isobel Sowerby shrugged her shoulders.

'Let's get on with it then,' she said. 'I persuaded my husband to go to the golf club to get over the funeral, and he'll stay there for a time and have a few drinks, but he'll be home presently and it won't help us to have him asking me questions.'

'How did you get into the house this morning?' Frances asked. 'I've been wondering about that.'

'The back door was unlocked, as I knew it would be. We aren't particular about locking up round here.'

'And you left in a hurry when you heard me come in.'

'Yes. Now let's get on.'

It was almost dark by then and the garage doors could not be seen from the lane outside. There was no one to see them as they carried Julia's body from the house to the car, put it in the seat beside the driver's, covered it with a rug, got into the car themselves and with Isobel Sowerby driving, since she knew the roads, started towards the coast. She drove cautiously along the twisting lanes until at last they reached the cliff-top and saw the dark chasm of the sea ahead of them.

Stopping the car close to the edge of the cliff, she and Frances got out and between them moved Julia's body into the driving seat. After that it was only a case of turning on the engine again, putting the car into a low gear, slamming the doors and standing back while it went slowly forward to the brink, seemed to teeter there for an instant, then went plunging down, the sound of the crash that it made as it hit the rocks below carrying up to them with a loudness which it seemed to Frances must carry for miles.

But afterwards there was no sign that anyone else had heard it. The darkness around them was silent. They started the long walk back.

They did not talk to one another as they walked and had reached the Darnells' cottage before Isobel Sowerby said, 'I don't know what I'm going to say to my husband. He'll have got back from the golf club long ago.'

'You'll think of something,' Frances said. She did not think that Major Sowerby would be difficult to delude. 'You could always say you've been wandering around in a state of delirium.'

'Which is what I think I've been doing,' Isobel Sowerby said. 'Now give me the photographs.'

Frances took her into the sitting room and showed her the heap of ashes in the grate.

'I burnt them.'

Isobel Sowerby stared at them incredulously, then broke suddenly into hysterical laughter.

'What a fool I am!' she cried. 'I've always been a fool. I needn't have come at all!'

'But I needed your help, so naturally I wasn't going to tell you that,' Frances replied.

'Are those really my photographs? You really destroyed them?'

'Along with some of my own. I'd get home now as soon as I could if I were you, because I'm going to telephone the police and tell them Julia's missing.'

Still laughing, Isobel Sowerby turned and plunged out into the darkness.

Frances went to the telephone, called the police and told them that she was very concerned because she had just discovered that Mrs Darnell, who was suffering from a high fever and was in a state of shock after the death of her husband, had disappeared. Her car was missing too. Frances said that she had only just discovered this, because after the lunch that had been held in the house after the funeral, she had felt so tired that she had gone to her room to lie down and had fallen asleep and had only just woken up, gone into Mrs Darnell's room to see how she was and found it empty. She said that she knew that Mrs Darnell had been in her room at about half past one, when she had taken some food and wine up to her and Mrs Darnell had drunk a little wine but had refused the food. But at what time she had got up and gone out Frances had no idea, because she had been so sound asleep. She had heard nothing. Anything might have happened in the house without her being aware of it.

The man who answered her call said that someone would be out to see her shortly. Putting the telephone down, Frances fetched a dustpan and brush, swept up the ashes in the grate and flushed them down the lavatory. Then in truth feeling as tired as she had told the policeman that she had felt earlier, she began to clear up the dining room and had started on the washing-up when the police arrived.

After that everything went surprisingly smoothly. The police soon found the wreck of the car on the rocks at the foot of the cliffs and the hammer and the blood-stained nightdress and dressing-gown in the boot. They also found fingerprints on the steering-wheel which were later identified as Mrs Sowerby's and they found some highly obscene photographs of her in a cupboard in Oliver Darnell's studio. It had happened too that Major Sowerby, in a state of great anxiety at finding his wife missing when he returned from the golf club, had telephoned several friends to ask if she was with them, so without his intending it, he had destroyed any chance that she might have had of concocting an alibi. She told an absurd story about having been summoned by Mrs Liley to help her get rid of the body of Julia Darnell, whom she and not Isobel Sowerby had murdered, but the story was not believed. There was a little doubt as to whether she could have handled the body by herself, but she was a big, powerful woman and it was thought that she could and she was charged with the murder. Frances stayed on in the

Darnells' cottage until after the inquest, then when her presence was no longer required, telephoned Mark and started for home.

As she drove, she fell into one of her rare moods of self-examination. She was not a nice person, she thought. Some people might even say of her that she was rather horrible. She did not really blame Mark for wanting to leave her and marry that little pudding of a woman who had been infatuated with him for the last five years. And if only he would give up his claim to the children, Frances would be quite willing to let him go. But they were the only people for whom she had ever felt any deep and lasting love. Or what she took to be love. It did not involve questioning whether it would be better for them to stay with her or with Mark, or which of their parents the girls themselves loved most. Even in her present mood of introspection, she did not ask herself that. She simply knew that they were hers, a possession from which it would be intolerable to be parted.

And horrible as perhaps she was, was she not an instrument of justice? Had she not arranged the arrest of Julia's murderess, without herself or those two foolish young women, whose photographs she had good-naturedly burnt, becoming involved? No mud would stick to any of them. None of it would splash devastatingly on to the children. Only the guilty would suffer. So why should anyone criticise her? In a state of quiet satisfaction, she drove homewards to Mark.

ADDY

Mrs Burton was in a taxi on her way to a dinner when she realised with horror that Addy, her old dog, was dying.

For some time she'd noticed that Addy was behaving strangely. It was as if she had become senile. When Mrs Burton took her out into the street for her evening walk, she now felt obliged to put her on a lead. Addy had once been traffic-trained. Mrs Burton used to be able to open the front door of her building and wait while the dog sniffed at the lamp-post and the railings and then stepped into the gutter to do what Mrs Burton called 'her business'. Addy never would have dreamt of defiling the pavement. She did her 'business' with such grace and her movements were so feminine and delicate she looked as if she was dropping a discreet curtsey. Having accomplished what was expected of her, she used to come trotting back obediently into the house.

Recently Addy's behaviour had become very peculiar whenever she was let out into the street. If any strangers passed her, she started to follow them. It upset Mrs Burton to see the way she would go limping after their shoes as if she was devoted to them. She had always been a very loving dog, but now when she trailed the heels of strangers her lovingness seemed undiscriminating and deranged.

Mrs Burton would call her name, but Addy seemed unable to recognise it. Mrs Burton had to run after the old dog and carry her back to the house otherwise she'd have followed the feet of strangers wherever they happened to take her.

Mrs Burton no longer trusted Addy's traffic-sense. She feared she might suddenly see a stranger on the other side of the street and decide she wanted to follow him. There was a danger she might step into the road without looking to the left or right and go under the wheel of a car.

Three days ago when Mrs Burton got back from work she noticed that Addy did not come bouncing and wagging to the door of her flat to greet her. She barked a welcome, but she remained sitting on her favourite sofa. Addy had very beautiful gold-brown eyes and when Mrs Burton went over and patted her, she noticed they had an imploring expression. It was as if she wished to apologise for a discourtesy.

Addy's head still looked young and it no longer matched her body. She was a border sheep-dog and she still had an aquiline aristocratic head, but with age she had lost her figure and it spread over the sofa like a fat cushion of brown fur.

Mrs Burton had decided she ought to take the old dog out for a walk. 'Come on,' she clicked her fingers at Addy whose portly body gave a helpless shudder. She seemed unable to move from the sofa.

Mrs Burton picked her up and carried her downstairs and took her into the street. When she was put down, Addy's hind-legs collapsed under her. She struggled bravely, but she was unable to take a step. If she wanted to follow strangers, she was no longer able to do so.

Mrs Burton became alarmed. What could have happened to Addy? She picked her up and carried her to the gutter and supported her and she managed to do her 'business'. She hated the look in the dog's eyes. It was too like the expression Mrs Burton's mother used to have when she had to be lifted on to the bedpan. Addy's eyes were yellow with humiliation. Once she'd carried her back up into her flat, Mrs Burton put her down on her favourite sofa. It was then that Addy had started panting.

Mrs Burton had wondered if she ought to get the vet. But she couldn't see what he could do for Addy. The dog was really now very ancient and her old age had caught up with her. From now on Addy would have to be treated like a crippled invalid. Mrs Burton brought her some water which she accepted. She offered her some dog meat which she refused. Mrs Burton felt it was all right to leave her and she went out to see a play with a woman friend. There seemed to be nothing very wrong with Addy except that she kept on panting.

When Mrs Burton returned around midnight, Addy was asleep. She looked quite peaceful. Mrs Burton went to bed, but she suffered from insomnia. She tossed around, restless and anxious. It was as if she was waiting for something unpleasant to happen and yet she wasn't quite certain what it was.

It was around three o'clock in the morning when Mrs Burton heard an odd sound from her living-room. It was the noise of violent scratching. She got up and went next door to investigate and she saw that Addy was no longer on the sofa. She had somehow managed to get down on to the floor and she had dragged herself into a corner behind an armchair.

Addy was squatting there on her collapsed haunches and with her front paws she was digging the thick wall-to-wall carpet of the living-room. She didn't stop when Mrs Burton found her doing this. Her claws continued to tear at the carpet as if she was a rabbit digging a burrow.

'Addy! What on earth are you doing!' Mrs Burton found herself speaking very sharply as if she expected an answer. Addy went on with her digging and there was a desperation in the way that her claws ripped the fluffy pile from the carpet. 'Stop it!' Mrs Burton shouted at her. 'Stop it at once, Addy! You are ruining the carpet!'

She stopped immediately. She had always been very obedient. Mrs Burton picked her up and gave her a soft little smack of disapproval. She saw the look of reproach in Addy's eyes. Mrs Burton was very aware of the softness and the vulnerability of her fat old body as she carried her back to the sofa. Once Mrs Burton had made Addy comfortable, she kissed her nose to show she had forgiven her. She noticed that it felt very dry. Addy, was still panting and suddenly she gave such a loud pant it sounded like an agonised sigh. Mrs Burton patted her soothingly and left her to go back to bed.

The next day Addy seemed neither better nor worse. Mrs Burton took her out before she went to work and went through the same routine of lifting the weak old animal while she urinated.

When Mrs Burton returned in the evening, Addy was still sitting on the sofa. There seemed nothing very much the matter with her except that she still kept on quietly panting. Mrs Burton was tired and she felt a certain resent-ment when she had to carry her outside. Once Addy had drunk some water and refused some food, Mrs Burton put on an evening dress and went off to a dinner party. As she closed the front door behind her and left her on her own, she decided that if the dog still refused to eat in the morning, she would ask the vet to come and look at her.

It was not until she was in a taxi that Mrs Burton wondered if Addy had been trying to tell her something important. Had she refused to understand the poor animal's message because she didn't want to accept it? Could Addy be dying? Did she want Mrs Burton to know it? When she was digging the living-room carpet, had she been trying to dig her own grave? She had been trained not to cause an inconvenience or mess.

When Addy had followed strangers, had it been an act of despair? She couldn't tell Mrs Burton that she was dying. Even when she made signals that tried to convey this fact, Mrs Burton remained deaf to them. Maybe Addy had hoped that strangers could recognise that she was dying and treat her accordingly. Had she followed their heels with this blind devoted hope?

Mrs Burton knew that she ought to tell the cab-driver to turn round and take her straight back to her house. If Addy was dying, it was extremely cruel to let her die all on her own. She had always been so loving and obedient, first to Mrs Burton's daughter, Devina, and then to Mrs Burton. One of them should hold the poor old creature in her arms and give her some affection and comfort as she died. Addy was only a dog, but she deserved this human tribute.

Mrs Burton felt like a criminal, but she did not tell the driver to turn back. Mrs Fitz-James, the woman who had invited her to dine, had once been a pupil at the same school. They had once been great friends as little girls but the years had passed and their lives had gone in different directions and they had not kept in touch. Recently they'd met at a cocktail party, and Mrs Burton had been intimidated by the self-assurance with which Mrs Fitz-James met the world. She had turned into a very striking and elegant woman, but Mrs Burton disliked the way she had become both snobbish and brittle. Mrs Fitz-James was married to a wealthy London banker and she boasted about her husband as if she'd won him like a trophy. Mrs Burton remembered that Mrs Fitz-James had once won the high-jump on sports day. When she'd been handed a gold cup, she seemed unable to let go of it, but had stood there hugging it to her chest with cheeks that were pink with triumph.

When the two women met again, Mrs Fitz-James asked Mrs Burton a few condescending questions and soon made it apparent that she pitied her old school-friend for having made a mess of her life and wasted her opportunities. Her arched eyebrows had risen with sarcastic sympathy when she heard that Mrs Burton had ended up as a divorcee without sufficient alimony. She looked appalled when she heard that Mrs Burton had been forced to get a job in London in order to support herself.

Hoping to wriggle out of the uncomfortable spot-light of her old friend's condescension, Mrs Burton reminded her of a silly episode that had taken place when they were both at school. Did Mrs Fitz-James remember how they had made paper pellets and flicked them at the behind of the geography teacher, Miss Ball? Mrs Fitz-James remembered and she gave a tinkle of affected pleasure.

Miss Ball was most probably dead by now, but she had once been important to Mrs Fitz-James and Mrs Burton, and her voluminous behind was still vivid to them and they were each glad to find another human being who recalled it. It was on the strength of this frail bond that for a moment, they both drew closer to each other, and it was then that Mrs Fitz-James had asked Mrs Burton to come and dine.

The moment Mrs Burton accepted the invitation she regretted it. She suspected it had been issued out of competitiveness rather than affection. Mrs Fitz-James very probably wanted her less fortunate school-friend to be allowed a tantalising peep at the desirable life she felt she now led. Exactly as if they were still at school, Mrs Fitz-James wanted to show-off.

Now, as Mrs Burton rode on in the taxi, she realised that if she had found Mrs Fitz-James a little more congenial, she would have telephoned her and explained that she could not come to her dinner party. She knew it would be very rude if she cancelled at such short notice. If she defected, even if she explained that her dog was dying, she doubted Mrs Fitz-James would consider it an adequate excuse. The numbers at the dinner party would be made uneven. Men would have to sit next to men. Her hostess was a woman who obviously cared very much about such matters. If Mrs Burton suddenly refused the invitation, Mrs Fitz-James would be extremely annoyed. Women like Mrs Fitz-James frightened Mrs Burton. Their self-confidence and elegance and their patronising attitudes made her feel inadequate and uncouth. Mrs Burton despised herself for her cowardice, but she knew she was not going to turn back to look after Addy. She tried to persuade herself the dog was not really dying. Addy had become weak and wheezing, but she could probably go on for years in the same condition.

When Mrs Burton walked into Mrs Fitz-James's drawing-room, her hostess came swaying gracefully to greet her, holding out a beautifully manicured hand that gleamed with valuable rings. Mrs Fitz-James was looking even more handsome than when her old friend had last seen her, and her honey-coloured hair was looped around her ears and held in place by diamond clips. She was wearing a tight-fitting satin gown which showed off her supple and well-exercised figure. The very sight of her made Mrs Burton feel dumpy, middle-aged and badly dressed.

Mrs Fitz-James kissed her and was very gushing and friendly. She made a joke about Miss Ball, the geography teacher. She was trying to put Mrs Burton at her ease. But they had exhausted that subject and neither found it all that funny. Mrs Fitz-James then admired Mrs Burton's evening sandals and asked her where she had been clever enough to find them. Mrs Burton had owned them for years, but never before had she felt her shoes were quite so shabby, old-fashioned and down-at-heel.

'I'm really thrilled you could come.' Mrs Burton disliked the way Mrs Fitz-James was like an actress, word-perfect in her social lines.

A group of guests were standing round the ornate marble mantelpiece in the drawing-room. The men looked prosperous and upper-class, and they were wearing dinner-jackets.

Mrs Fitz-James introduced her to her banker husband. He looked much like all the other men in the room, but his mouth seemed just a little more cruel than theirs, and he had a slightly more supercilious and world-weary eye. When he was told that Mrs Burton had been at school with his wife, he looked surprised. 'How amusing!' he said.

There were also several women in long, glamorous

dresses, but Mrs Burton hardly dared to look at them when she had to shake their hands. She was too frightened that their beauty and stylishness would make her feel even more unattractive and dreary than she'd felt when speaking to Mrs Fitz-James.

A butler brought Mrs Burton a glass of champagne. Out of nerves she drank it in one gulp and then wished she'd had the poise and the good sense to sip it.

A scarlet-faced man started to make conversation with her. He had blue, sentimental eyes and snowy-white hair with a fluffy texture as if it had been blow-dried. He told her that he was a race-horse owner and asked if she was interested in horses. She murmured that she liked horses very much, but unfortunately, she had never had much to do with them. He said that racing was a drug, but unlike most drugs it often made you quite a lot of money! Mrs Burton smiled with fake amusement. She suspected he had made this remark many times before, and, like an old comedian, he believed that well-tried jokes always worked the best.

The butler refilled Mrs Burton's glass and she took care not to drink her champagne quite so quickly as before. She told the race-horse owner that she worked in a firm which published educational books. 'That must be very interesting.' His white head nodded knowingly. Mrs Burton felt the conversation was swaying in the wind like a rope-bridge that connected different terrains.

Mrs Burton took a third glass of champagne. She wished to God she had never come. She kept thinking of Addy. Mrs Fitz-James was describing a house she was having built in Sardinia. She complained of the problems she was having getting the plumbing installed and the laziness of the local work-men.

'Have you ever been to Sardinia?' the florid race-horse owner asked her. He was valiant with his good manners. He kept trying to find the perfect topic that would stimulate her.

'No, I've never been to Sardinia.'

'I hear it is very beautiful.'

'That's what they say.'

The butler announced that dinner was ready. The table gleamed with perfectly polished silver and its mahogany shimmered in the candlelight. Mrs Burton knew from the look of Mrs Fitz-James's table that the food was going to be delicious. This made her feel unhungry.

Mrs Fitz-James placed Mrs Burton between the racehorse owner and another depressed-looking man with grey hair. When the butler filled Mrs Burton's glass with white wine, she once again gulped it down as if it was water. By now, she was feeling too drunk to care if the other guests at the table looked at her with horror, fearing she was an alcoholic.

'I'm feeling very upset tonight,' she suddenly announced to the race-horse owner. She wanted to prevent him from embarking on any meaningless general conversation. He seemed to be a boring and mindless man, but at least he could be her listener. She was angry that she had come to this deadly dinner party and she felt quite unable to find the strength to weave any more threads of social chit-chat. She would speak only about the subject that haunted her.

Her neighbour looked concerned. 'I'm very sorry to hear you are upset. What has happened?' She had already noticed he seemed to have a sentimental streak and now his watery blue eyes had become sympathetic and avuncular.

'I'm worried about my old dog. This evening I had the awful feeling that she is dying.'

'How old is your dog?' he asked her.

'In human terms she must be about eighty-eight, maybe eighty-nine.'

'So she's really a very ancient lady.' Her neighbour nodded gravely.

'Yes, I'm afraid that's true. And recently she hasn't seemed at all well.'

'It's funny how attached one gets to the old things,' he

said. 'I remember I was very cut up when my old Labrador died.'

The butler served Mrs Burton some creamy white soup which she looked at with a feeling of nausea. The race-horse owner leant towards her as if he was confiding a secret.

'If your dog is very old, I'm afraid she is bound to die quite soon. You will just have to accept it. When she passes on you must look on it philosophically. I'm sure your dog has had a very happy life with you. When she goes – you must comfort yourself with that.'

Mrs Burton looked at her soup and it seemed to have turned a hideous grey. She kept thinking of Addy digging the carpet. Her neighbour kept repeating that she had to be philosophical. He seemed to get a relish from saying that word, just as he was relishing the soup she couldn't eat.

Addy's life had not been as pleasant as the race-horse owner assumed. There had been a few years when she had been well-treated. That was when Devina loved her and they had lived in the country. At that time Devina was always kissing Addy. She played with her all day long and she had exercised her properly and let her run hunting rabbits in the fields.

It was as if Devina's love for Addy had been a childish disease like measles. She had caught a violent dose of it and then when she went off to boarding school, she got rid of it. Devina had once carried snap-shots of Addy in her purse. Now she carried love letters from her boy-friend. Devina was glad to see Addy on the occasions that she visited Mrs Burton. But her gladness was luke-warm. Addy no longer had any real magic for Devina. She would be sad to hear that the old dog had died. Something that had been important to her in her childhood would have perished. But Devina was at university now and all her other interests would soon smother the news of Addy's death.

After Mrs Burton was divorced, she had moved to London and got a job. She had taken Addy with her, but she had never felt she was her dog. Often she had been quite a nuisance to Mrs Burton because she needed to be let out and fed. But having known how Devina had once doted on the dog, she had thought it disloyal to get rid of her.

Mrs Burton had never been a dog-lover and she'd not been prepared to allow her life to be ruled by Addy's needs. When she went off to work, Addy had been left alone in the house all day. Mrs Burton could never muster any excitement when she was greeted by the dog when she got back home, although she knew that Addy had been moping and pining, and waiting in a frenzy of antici-pation for her return. Addy's rapturous delight when she saw her come through the door irritated rather than grati-fied Mrs Burton. She disliked all her barking and squirming, and when she jumped up and put her front paws on her skirt, Mrs Burton had always pushed her down.

Addy's relationship with Devina had been one of mutual passion. After Devina's father left Mrs Burton, the little girl had needed to stifle her feelings of hurt and betrayal by pouring her love on to an object she saw as perfect because it was not human. Everything about the dog had delighted Devina in that period. She loved the smell inside her ears and she claimed it was like the smell of car-seats. She refused to sleep unless Addy was tucked beside her under the bedclothes. Sometimes Devina made her lie on her back with her head propped up on pillows in a position so undog-like, Mrs Burton found it almost unkind. But Addy had seemed perfectly happy so she had not protested. Mrs Burton only made a fuss whenever she found Devina licking the dog's pink tongue because she was terrified her daughter would get some dangerous disease.

Devina used to believe that Addy could understand

anything that was said to her. And when Devina spoke to her, it almost seemed to be true for she instantly obeyed the child's peculiar commands. Devina would give her a lump of sugar and order the dog not to swallow it. Addy then kept it in her mouth gazing up at Devina with an expression of slavish adoration. When the little girl told her to spit it out she immediately obeyed. After that Devina allowed her to eat the sugar lump and she squealed with delight because Addy had been so clever and abstemious. She then over-fed her with sweet biscuits to let her know how much the trick had pleased her. She would hug her and pat her until Addy got so over-excited she often seemed like a mad dog jumping around and barking as if she had been driven demented by such intense approval.

In those years, whenever anything upset Devina, her first instinct had been to run to find Addy. She clasped the dog in her arms as if she was a teddy bear and when Devina cried, she liked to bury her face in Addy's thick, reassuring fur.

Sitting at this formal and inane dinner party, Mrs Burton felt that she suddenly wanted to cry. She battled to prevent herself from doing so because her tears would be hypocritical. Very likely they would be treated with sympathy and that would make her feel all the more corrupt. If she was to cry, her neighbour would explain to the rest of the table that she was distressed because her beloved old dog was dying. It would be disgusting if she allowed all these strangers in expensive clothes to condole with her.

Addy had been used and violated by Devina and Mrs Burton. Devina had once needed Addy's love and loyalty as therapy and then she had betrayed her, for she had lost all interest in the dog once her adoration ceased to have any value for her. Addy had been too dumb to comprehend that human beings were fickle. When she was moved to the cold foster-home of Mrs Burton's ownership, she had always hopelessly tried to recreate the idyllic relationship that she had been falsely taught to accept as her due.

She had guarded Mrs Burton's flat as she should have been allowed to guard sheep. She seemed only to let herself half-sleep for, if there was any noise outside the door, she always sprang up with ears pricked in order to bark a warning. Mrs Burton suddenly remembered that she'd insisted that Addy be spayed. That was one more area where Addy had been cheated.

Although Mrs Burton had seen that she was kept alive, she now felt convinced her indifference towards the dog had been vicious. Once she'd moved from the country, she had made her lead the life of an urban prisoner. Addy had such a gregarious and friendly nature that Mrs Burton hated to think of all the hours that the poor animal had spent all alone in the flat.

'Have some croutons,' her expansive neighbour said. He was holding out some kind of china terrine. He started spooning some crisp brown squares into her soup. Mrs Burton was suddenly feeling dizzy, but she looked down at them floating. They became soggy in front of her eyes, but for a while they kept bobbing on the surface and they all seemed like desperate, drowning creatures.

Her soup no longer seemed like soup. As if she was hallucinating, she saw it as a dangerous lake and she felt she ought to dive in and try to save the drowning croutons. But somehow something stopped her and she could only stare at them in panic and watch them as they perished.

'Are you feeling all right?' the race-horse owner asked her. He was not very sensitive, but he had noticed she was looking peculiar.

Mrs Burton found she couldn't answer him. She couldn't say she felt all right. By now only one of her croutons retained any distinct shape. The rest had sunk into the liquid. It was this last lonely crouton that Mrs Burton found the most disturbing, for at moments it seemed to be her mother, at other moments it seemed to be Addy.

Before she had died, Mrs Burton's mother had been very brave and angry sitting in her wheel-chair in the home for arthritics. She had watched television most of the day until the arthritis had gone into her lids and crippled their muscles so that she was unable to keep her eyes open. After that she had just sat in her wheel-chair, so immobile she'd seemed like a statue.

Mrs Burton had gone to read to her once a week. But her visits had never been much of a success. Invariably her mother had told her she was reading too fast or complained that she was mumbling. It had never been very long before her mother irritably ordered her to stop reading because she didn't like the book that Mrs Burton had chosen.

The food in the home for arthritics had been ill-cooked and unappetising. Mrs Burton continually sent her mother various delicacies so that the old lady could have some relief from the dreariness of the diet of the institution. When she visited, she brought smoked salmon and jars of taramasalata and pâté. But her mother always left them untouched on the table beside her wheel-chair. On one occasion she had screamed at Mrs Burton like a child. Tears started pouring down her cheeks. She had reminded her that if you couldn't take any exercise, it was impossible to work up any appetite. She had also been very annoyed by some hot-house grapes that Mrs Burton had once brought her. Her mother had refused to taste one single grape. She complained that the pips would get stuck in her teeth.

Yet Mrs Burton had always felt guilty that she had not invited her mother to come and live with her. Once her mother had become a total invalid, she still insisted she couldn't bear to be a burden on the family. If this claim had been a lie, Mrs Burton had taken it literally. She knew she could never have tolerated the presence of that critical old lady who would have sat all day long like some huge accusing statue in her household.

If she'd agreed to nurse her mother, the old woman would have become magnified by Mrs Burton until she seemed colossal. Her mother's fury at her own paralysis would have paralysed Mrs Burton. It would have prevented her from giving any love and attention to Devina, for her confidence would have shrivelled like a prune, totally withered by her inability to make any reparation for the cruel disease that had stricken the old lady.

Even when her mother was in perfect health, she had always had an intensely dissatisfied nature. Her mother's bitterness had once been diffused, but her arthritis had brought all its disparate strands together, and it had found a perfect focus. Imprisoned by her pain-ridden and crippled body, she had felt she could give full vent to all her ancient indignation, seeing it as finally justified.

Mrs Burton knew she could never have allowed her home to be dominated by someone who sat in her wheelchair sometimes expressing her rage by stoical silences, sometimes releasing it in distressing little displays of demonic petulance. Even in her very best periods of bravery, Mrs Burton's mother would have sat with eyes closed in her daughter's household like some disturbing and vast grey monument that had been erected to commemorate the destruction of every human hope.

At the dinner party, Mrs Burton picked up her spoon and mashed her last lonely crouton until it became invisible. She was aware that her neighbour was staring at her in horror. She had squashed it with much too much violence. He was obviously shocked by her table manners. He thought, that like an infant, she was playing with her food.

The crouton had completely disappeared, but Mrs Burton felt freezing cold. Her neighbour found her weird, but he could not guess how restrained she was being. She would have liked to have screamed and jumped up from the table and run out of this loathsome house where ghosts had appeared in her soup and accused her of deserting them at the very moment when they'd most needed her. Mrs Burton controlled herself and she found her own control a little despicable. She felt deranged by guilts from the past and the present, but she disguised it and her need to do so seemed craven. She thought it shameful she was so frightened to arouse the disapproval of people for whom she had only scorn.

The dinner continued. More and more food was served. The courses seemed endless. Mrs Burton sat there and quietly endured this dreadful meal, imprisoned by her good manners. She picked at some duck and she dabbed her lips with her napkin in the most lady-like fashion. She did nothing further that could disturb her bovine neighbour. He chatted on to her and she kept nodding and giving him no indication that when she helped herself to a tiny portion of summer pudding she found it an agonising struggle to force herself to take even the tiniest mouthful. That evening it sickened her to taste anything that was the colour of blood.

When Mrs Fitz-James finally got up from the table after the coffee and the brandy she was followed by all the other women and she started leading them up the stairs to some bathroom where she wanted them 'to powder their noses'. The men remained in the dining-room and they continued drinking port and brandy.

And then Mrs Burton suddenly rebelled. She felt it would be insufferable to join the little feminine and perfumed cortège of Mrs Fitz-James. She refused to go up to her hostess's luxurious bedroom and sit around with all these ladies who would make her feel like a used tea-bag while they prinked and gushed and admired each others dresses, shoes and hair-styles.

No-one noticed Mrs Burton as she slipped into the hall and got her coat. She opened the front door very quietly and went out into the street. She was glad it was rude to leave without saying goodbye. She was relieved that at last she had done something impolite.

She was fortunate for she saw a taxi and hailed it. On the way back to her flat, she wondered if she had a fever. Once she got back to her building, her legs were shaking as she went upstairs. There was not a sound when she turned her key in the flat door. As she came in, she saw with horror that Addy was not on the sofa. It took Mrs Burton only a few seconds to find her. Addy had dragged herself into the corner behind the armchair very near where she'd done her digging. She was lying with her face to the wall.

Mrs Burton went over and picked her up. Addy felt heavy and rigid. Her amber eyes had gone dark. They had the sightless stare of glass eyes. There was no life in Addy's plump body and yet her fur still seemed to continue to have a life of its own. It felt soft and comforting and warm.

Mrs Burton stood very still in the centre of her flat cradling Addy. She noticed how quiet it was. She realised it would always be unpleasantly quiet in the flat now that she would be living completely on her own. She felt much less distraught than she'd felt at the dinner party. She had allowed Addy to die all alone, but it seemed futile and self-deceiving to torment herself with self-recriminations. If she had missed Mrs Fitz-James's dinner party and stayed in the flat with Addy, those few hours would have been unable to make reparation for all the days that Addy had spent locked up like a convict condemned to solitary.

Addy was released now. Addy had been too simple. She had seemed to believe that if she behaved as humans taught her, they would start to treat her as an equal, whereas they were only capable of endowing her with certain human characteristics. According to their varying self-indulgent whims they could turn her into a figure which embodied their shifting guilts and fantasies. But Addy had never managed to have any ultimate reality for the people she had been attached to. Once the veneer of their projections was stripped away, they could only see her as a dog.

Mrs Burton tightened her grip on Addy's motionless body. Through the years Addy had been a witness to so many painful moments in Mrs Burton's life. She had also been the speechless witness to many moments of happiness. Addy's relationship with Mrs Burton had lasted much longer than the latter's marriage.

Addy felt like a stuffed toy. Mrs Burton wished she could feel more regret for her death. All the wriggling life and bark had gone from Addy, but she was no longer threatened by decrepitude and pain and loneliness. Mrs Burton felt exhausted and frightened of the future. She envied Addy her stillness.

She suddenly wanted to make the dog a little gesture, and she couldn't tell whether her behaviour sprang from remorse or affection. As if she was hoping that her animal victim could help comfort her sense of desolation, she bent over and buried her face in the woolly thicket of Addy's brown fur.

HAVE A NICE DEATH

Everyone was being extraordinarily courteous to Sammy Luke in New York.

Take Sammy's arrival at Kennedy Airport, for example: Sammy had been quite struck by the warmth of the welcome. Sammy thought: how relieved Zara would be! Zara (his wife) was inclined to worry about Sammy – he had to admit, with some cause; in the past, that is. In the past Sammy had been nervous, delicate, highly strung, whatever you liked to call it – Sammy suspected that some of Zara's women friends had a harsher name for it; the fact was that things tended to go wrong where Sammy was concerned, unless Zara was there to iron them out. But that was in England. Sammy was quite sure he was not going to be nervous in America; perhaps, cured by the New World, he would never be nervous again.

Take the immigration officials – hadn't Sammy been warned about them?

'They're nothing but gorillas' – Zara's friend, wealthy Tess, who travelled frequently to the States, had pronounced the word in a dark voice. For an instant Sammy, still in his nervous English state, visualised immigration checkpoints manned by terrorists armed with machine-guns. But the official seated in a booth, who summoned Sammy in, was slightly built, perhaps even slighter than Sammy himself though the protection of the booth made it difficult to tell. And he was smiling as he cried:

'C'mon, c'mon, bring the family!' A notice outside the booth stated that only one person – or one family – was permitted inside at a time.

'I'm afraid my wife's not travelling with me,' stated Sammy apologetically.

'I sure wish my wife wasn't with me either,' answered the official, with ever increasing bonhomie.

Sammy wondered confusedly – it had been a long flight after all – whether he should explain his own very different feelings about his wife, his passionate regret that Zara had not been able to accompany him. But his new friend was already examining his passport, flipping through a large black directory, talking again: 'A writer. . . . Would I know any of your books?'

This was an opportunity for Sammy to explain intelligently the purpose of his visit. Sammy Luke was the author of six novels. Five of them had sold well, if not astoundingly well, in England and not at all in the United States. The sixth, *Women Weeping*, due perhaps to its macabrely fashionable subject-matter, had hit some kind of publishing jackpot in both countries. Only a few weeks after publication in the States, its sales were phenomenal and rising; an option on the film rights (maybe Jane Fonda and Meryl Streep as the masochists?) had already been bought. As a result of all this, Sammy's new American publishers believed hotly that only one further thing was necessary to ensure the vast, the *total* success of *Women Weeping* in the States, and that was to make of its author a television celebrity. Earnestly defending his own position on the subject of violence and female masochism on a series of television interviews and talk shows, Sammy Luke was expected to shoot *Women Weeping* high high into the best-seller lists and keep it there. All this was the firm conviction of Sammy's editor at Porlock Publishers, Clodagh Jansen.

'You'll be great on the talk shows, Sammy,' Clodagh had cawed down the line from the States – 'So little and cute and then – ' Clodagh made a loud noise with her lips as if someone was gobbling someone else up. Presumably it was not Sammy who was to be gobbled. Clodagh was a committed feminist, as she had carefully explained to Sammy on her visit to England, when she had bought *Women Weeping*, against much competition, for a huge sum. But she believed in the social role of best-sellers like *Women Weeping* to finance radical feminist works. Sammy had tried to explain that his book was in no way anti-feminist, no way at all, witness the fact that Zara herself, his Egeria, had not complained –

'Save it for the talk shows, Sammy,' was all that Clodagh had replied.

While Sammy was still wondering how to put all this concisely, but to his best advantage, at Kennedy Airport, the man in the booth asked: 'And the purpose of your visit, Mr Luke?'

Sammy was suddenly aware that he had drunk a great deal on the long flight – courtesy of Porlock's first-class ticket – and slept too heavily as well. His head began to sing. But whatever answer he gave, it was apparently satisfactory. The man stamped the white sheet inside his passport and handed it back. Then: 'Enjoy your visit to the United States of America, Mr Luke. Have a nice day now.'

'Oh, I will, I know I will,' promised Sammy. 'It seems a lovely day here already.'

Sammy's experiences at the famous Barraclough Hotel (accommodation arranged by Clodagh) were if anything even more heart-warming. Everyone, but everyone, at the Barraclough wanted Sammy to enjoy himself during his visit.

'Have a nice day, now Mr Luke': most conversations ended like that, whether they were with the hotel telephonist, the agreeable men who operated the lifts or the gentlemanly *concierge*. Even the New York taxi-drivers, from whose guarded expressions Sammy would not otherwise have suspected such warm hearts, wanted Sammy to have a nice day.

'Oh, I will, I will,' Sammy began by answering. After

a bit he added: 'I just adore New York,' said with a grin and the very suspicion of an American twang.

'This is the friendliest city in the world,' he told Zara down the long-distance telephone, shouting, so that his words were accompanied by little vibratory echoes.

'Tess says they don't really mean it.' Zara's voice in contrast was thin, diminished into a tiny wail by the line. 'They're not sincere, you know.'

'Tess was wrong about the gorillas at Immigration. She could be wrong about that too. Tess doesn't *own* the whole country you know. She just inherited a small slice of it.'

'Darling, you do sound funny,' countered Zara, her familiar anxiety on the subject of Sammy made her sound stronger. 'Are you all right? I mean, are you all right over there all by yourself – '

'I'm mainly on television during the day,' Sammy cut in with a laugh. 'Alone except for the chat-show host and forty million people.' Sammy was deciding whether to add, truthfully, that actually not all the shows were networked; some of his audiences being as low as a million, or say a million and a half, when he realised that Zara was saying in a voice of distinct reproach:

'And you haven't asked after Mummy yet.' It was the sudden illness of Zara's mother, another person emotionally dependent upon her, which had prevented Zara's trip to New York with Sammy, at the last moment.

It was only after Sammy had rung off – having asked tenderly after Zara's mother and apologised for his crude crack about Tess before doing so – that he realised Zara was quite right. He *had* sounded rather funny: even to himself. That is he would never have dared to make such a remark about Tess in London. Dared? Sammy pulled himself up.

To Zara, his strong and lovely Zara, he could of course say anything. She was his wife. As a couple, they were exceptionally close as all their circle agreed; being childless (a decision begun through poverty in the early days and somehow never rescinded) only increased their intimacy. Because their marriage had not been founded on a flash-in-the-pan sexual attraction but something deeper, more companionate – sex had never played a great part in it, even at the beginning – the bond had only grown stronger with the years. Sammy doubted whether there was a more genuinely united pair in London.

All this was true; and comforting to recollect. It was just that in recent years Tess had become an omnipresent force in their lives: Tess on clothes, Tess on interior decoration, especially Tess on curtains, that was the real pits – a new expression which Sammy had picked up from Clodagh; and somehow Tess's famous money always seemed to reinforce her opinions in a way which was rather curious, considering Zara's own radical contempt for unearned wealth.

'Well, I've got money now. Lots and lots of it. Earned money,' thought Sammy, squaring his thin shoulders in the new pale-blue jacket which Zara, yes Zara, had made him buy. He looked in one of the huge gilded mirrors which decorated his suite at the Barraclough, pushing aside the large floral arrangement, a gift from the hotel manager (or was it Clodagh?) to do so. Sammy Luke, the conqueror of New York or at least American television; then he had to laugh at his own absurdity.

He went on to the little balcony which led off the suite's sitting-room and looked down at the ribbon of streets which stretched below; the roofs of lesser buildings; the blur of green where Central Park nestled, at his disposal, in the centre of it all. The plain truth was that he was just very very happy. The reason was not purely the success of his book, nor even his instant highly commercial fame as predicted by Clodagh, on television, nor yet the attentions of the Press, parts of which had after all been quite violently critical of his book, again as predicted by Clodagh. The reason was that Sammy Luke felt loved in

New York in a vast wonderful impersonal way. Nothing was demanded of him by this love; it was like an electric fire with simulated red-hot coals even when it was switched off. New York glowed but it could not scorch. In his heart Sammy knew that he had never been so happy before.

It was at this point that the telephone rang again. Sammy left the balcony. Sammy was expecting one of three calls. The first, and most likely, was Clodagh's daily checking call: 'Hi, Sammy its Clodagh Pegoda . . . listen, that show was great, the one they taped. Our publicity girl actually told me it didn't go too well at the time, she was frightened they were mauling you . . . but the way it came out . . . Zouch!' More interesting sounds from Clodagh's mobile and rather sensual lips. 'That's my Sam. You really had them licked. I guess the little girl was just over-protective. Sue-May, was it? Joanie. Yes, Joanie. She's crazy about you. I'll have to talk to her; what's a nice girl like that doing being crazy about a man, and a married man at that. . . '

Clodagh's physical preference for her own sex was a robust joke between them; it was odd how being in New York made that too seem innocuous. In England Sammy had been secretly rather shocked by the frankness of Clodagh's allusions: more alarmingly she had once goosed him, apparently fooling, but with the accompanying words, 'You're a bit like a girl yourself, Sammy', which were not totally reassuring. Even that was preferable to the embarrassing occasion when Clodagh had playfully declared a physical attraction to Zara, wondered – outside the money that was now coming in – how Zara put up with Sammy. In New York however Sammy entered enthusiastically into the fun.

He was also pleased to hear, however lightly meant, that Joanie, the publicity girl in charge of his day-to-day arrangements, was crazy about him; for Joanie, unlike handsome piratical frightening Clodagh, was small and tender.

The second possibility for the call was Joanie herself. In which case she would be down in the lobby of the Barraclough, ready to escort him to an afternoon taping at a television studio across town. Later Joanie would drop Sammy back at the Barraclough, paying carefully and slightly earnestly for the taxi as though Sammy's nerves might be ruffled if the ceremony was not carried out correctly. One of these days, Sammy thought with a smile, he might even ask Joanie up to his suite at the Barraclough . . . after all what were suites for? (Sammy had never had a suite in a hotel before, his English publisher having an old-fashioned taste for providing his authors with plain bedrooms while on promotional tours.)

The third possibility was that Zara was calling him back: their conversation, for all Sammy's apologies, had not really ended on a satisfactory note; alone in London, Zara was doubtless feeling anxious about Sammy as a result. He detected a little complacency in himself about Zara: after all, there was for once nothing for her to feel anxious about (except perhaps Joanie, he added to himself with a smile).

Sammy's complacency was shattered by the voice on the telephone: 'I saw you on television last night,' began the voice – female, whispering. 'You bastard, Sammy Luke, I'm coming up to your room and I'm going to cut off your little – ' A detailed anatomical description followed of what the voice was going to do to Sammy Luke. The low violent obscenities, so horrible, so surprising, coming out of the innocent white hotel telephone, continued for a while unstopped, assaulting his ears like the rustle of some appalling cowrie shell; until Sammy thought to clutch the instrument to his chest, and thus stifle the voice in the surface of his new blue jacket.

After a moment, thinking he might have put an end to the terrible whispering, Sammy raised the instrument again. He was in time to hear the voice say: 'Have a nice death, Mr Luke.'

Then there was silence.

Sammy felt quite sick. A moment later he was running across the ornate sitting-room of the splendid Barraclough suite, retching; the bathroom seemed miles away at the far end of the spacious bedroom; he only just reached it in time.

Sammy was lying, panting, on the nearest twin bed to the door – the one which had been meant for Zara – when the telephone rang again. He picked it up and held it at a distance, then recognised the merry interested voice of the hotel telephonist.

'Oh, Mr Luke,' she was saying. 'While your line was busy just now Joanie Lazlo called from Porlock Publishers, and she'll call right back. But she says to tell you that the taping for this afternoon has been cancelled. Max Syegrand is still tied up on the Coast and can't make it. Too bad about that, Mr Luke. It's a good show. Anyway, she'll come by this evening with some more books to sign. . . . Have a nice day now, Mr Luke.' And the merry telephonist rang off. But this time Sammy shuddered when he heard the familiar cheerful farewell.

It seemed a long time before Joanie rang to say that she was downstairs in the hotel lobby, and should she bring the copies of *Women Weeping* up to the suite? When she arrived at the sitting-room door, carrying a Mexican tote bag weighed down by books, Joanie's pretty little pink face was glowing and she gave Sammy her usual softly enthusiastic welcome. All the same Sammy could hardly believe that he had contemplated seducing her – or indeed anyone – in his gilded suite amid the floral arrangements. That all seemed a very long while ago.

For in the hours before Joanie's arrival, Sammy received two more calls. The whispering voice grew bolder still in its description of Sammy's fate; but it did not grow stronger. For some reason, Sammy listened to the first call through to the end. At last the phrase came: although he was half expecting it, his heart still thumped when he heard the words: 'Have a nice death now, Mr Luke.'

With the second call, he slammed down the telephone immediately and then called back the operator: 'No more,' he said loudly and rather breathlessly. 'No more, I don't want any more.'

'Pardon me, Mr Luke?'

'I meant, I don't want any more calls, not like that, not now.'

'Alrighty.' The operator – it was another voice, not the merry woman who habitually watched television, but just as friendly. 'I'll hold your calls for now, Mr Luke. I'll be happy to do it. Goodbye now. Have a nice evening.'

Should Sammy perhaps have questioned this new operator about his recent caller? No doubt she would declare herself happy to discuss the matter. But he dreaded a further cheerful impersonal New York encounter in his shaken state. Besides, the first call had been put through by the merry television-watcher. Zara. He needed to talk to Zara. She would know what to do; or rather she would know what *he* should do.

'What's going on?' she exclaimed, 'I tried to ring you three times and that bloody woman on the hotel switchboard wouldn't put me through. Are you all right? I rang you back because you sounded so peculiar. Sort of high, you were laughing at things, things which weren't really funny, it's not like you, is it, in New York people are supposed to get this energy, but I never thought – '

'I'm not all right, not all right at all,' Sammy interrupted her; he was aware of a high rather tremulous note in his voice 'I was all right then, more than all right, but now I'm not, not at all.' Zara couldn't at first grasp what Sammy was telling her, and in the end he had to abandon all explanations of his previous state of exhilaration. For one thing Zara couldn't seem to grasp what he was saying, and for another Sammy was guiltily aware that absence from Zara's side had played more than a little part in this temporary madness. So Sammy settled for agreeing that he had been acting rather oddly since he had arrived in New York, and then appealed to Zara to advise him how next to proceed.

Once Sammy had made this admission, Zara sounded more like her normal brisk but caring self. She told Sammy to ring up Clodagh at Porlock.

'Frankly, Sammy, I can't think why you didn't ring her straight away.' Zara pointed out that if Sammy could not, Clodagh certainly could and would deal with the hotel switchboard, so that calls were filtered, the lawful distinguished from the unlawful.

'Clodagh might even know the woman,' observed Sammy weakly at one point. 'She has some very odd friends.'

Zara laughed. 'Not *that* odd, I hope.' Altogether she was in a better temper. Sammy remembered to ask after Zara's mother before he rang off; and on hearing that Tess had flown to America on business, he went so far as to say that he would love to have a drink with her.

When Joanie arrived in the suite, Sammy told her about the threatening calls and was vaguely gratified by her distress.

'I think that's just dreadful, Sammy,' she murmured, her light hazel eyes swimming with some tender emotion. 'Clodagh's not in the office right now, but let me talk with the hotel manager right away. . . .' Yet it was odd how Joanie no longer seemed in the slightest bit attractive to Sammy. There was even something cloying about her friendliness; perhaps there was a shallowness there, a surface brightness concealing nothing; perhaps Tess was right and New Yorkers were after all insincere. All in all, Sammy was pleased to see Joanie depart with the signed books.

He did not offer her a second drink, although she had brought him an advance copy of the *New York Times* book section for Sunday, showing that *Women Weeping* had jumped four places in the best-seller list.

'Have a nice evening, Sammy,' said Joanie softly as she closed the door of the suite. 'I've left a message with Clodagh's answering service and I'll call you tomorrow.'

But Sammy did not have a very nice evening. Foolishly he decided to have dinner in his suite; the reason was that he had some idiotic lurking fear that the woman with the whispering voice would be lying in wait for him outside the Barraclough.

'Have a nice day,' said the waiter automatically who delivered the meal on a heated trolley covered in a white damask cloth, after Sammy had signed the chit. Sammy hated him.

'The day is over. It is evening.' Sammy spoke in a voice which was pointed, almost vicious; he had just deposited a tip on the white chit.

By this time the waiter, stowing the dollars rapidly and expertly in his pocket was already on his way to the door; he turned and flashed a quick smile: 'Yeah. Sure. Thank you, Mr Luke. Have a nice day.' The waiter's hand was on the door handle.

'It is evening here!' exclaimed Sammy. He found he was shaking. 'Do you understand? Do you agree that it is *evening*?' The man, mildly startled, but not at all discomposed, said again: 'Yeah. Sure. Evening. Goodbye now.' And he went.

Sammy poured himself a whisky from the suite's mini-bar. He no longer felt hungry. The vast white expanse of his dinner trolley depressed him, because it reminded him of his encounter with the waiter; at the same time he lacked the courage to push the trolley boldly out of the suite into the corridor. Having avoided leaving the Barraclough he now found that even more foolishly he did not care to open the door of his own suite.

Clodagh being out of the office, it was doubtless Joanie's fault that the hotel operators still ignored their instructions. Another whispering call was let through, about ten o'clock at night, as Sammy was watching a movie starring the young Elizabeth Taylor, much cut up by commercials, on television. (If he stayed awake till midnight, he could see himself on one of the talk shows he had recorded.) The operator was now supposed to announce the name of each caller, for Sammy's inspection; but this call came straight through.

There was a nasty new urgency in what the voice was promising: 'Have a nice death now. I'll be coming by quite soon, Sammy Luke.'

In spite of the whisky – he drained yet another of the tiny bottles – Sammy was still shaking when he called down to the operator and protested: 'I'm still getting these calls. You've got to do something. You're supposed to be keeping them away from me.'

The operator, not a voice he recognised, sounded rather puzzled, but full of goodwill; spurious goodwill, Sammy now felt. Even if she was sincere, she was certainly stupid. She did not seem to recall having put through anyone to Sammy within the last ten minutes. Sammy did not dare instruct her to hold all calls in case Zara rang up again (or Clodagh, for that matter; where was Clodagh, now that he needed protection from this kind of feminist nut?). He felt too desperate to cut himself off altogether from contact with the outside world. What would Zara advise?

The answer was really quite simple, once it had occurred to him. Sammy rang down to the front desk and complained to the house manager who was on night duty. The house manager, like the operator, was rather puzzled, but extremely polite.

'Threats, Mr Luke? I assure you you'll be very secure at the Barraclough. We have guards naturally, and we are accustomed . . . but if you'd like me to come up to discuss the matter, why I'd be happy to. . . .'

When the house manager arrived, he was quite charming. He referred not only to Sammy's appearance on television but to his actual book. He told Sammy he'd loved the book; what was more he'd given another copy to his eighty-three-year-old mother (who'd seen Sammy on the Today show) and she'd loved it too. Sammy was too weary to wonder more than passingly what an eighty-three-year-old mother would make of *Women Weeping*. He was further depressed by the house manager's elaborate courtesy; it wasn't absolutely clear whether he believed Sammy's story, or merely thought he was suffering from the delightful strain of being a celebrity. Maybe the guests at the Barraclough behaved like that all the time, describing imaginary death threats? That possibility also Sammy was too exhausted to explore.

At midnight he turned the television on again and watched himself, on the chat show in the blue jacket, laughing and wriggling with his own humour, denying for the tenth time that he had any curious sadistic tastes himself, that *Women Weeping* was founded on an incident in his private life.

When the telephone rang sharply into the silence of the suite shortly after the end of the show, Sammy knew that it would be his persecutor; nevertheless the sight of his erstwhile New York self, so debonair so confident, had given him back some strength. Sammy was no longer shaking as he picked up the receiver.

It was Clodagh on the other end of the line, who had just returned to New York from somewhere out of town and picked up Joanie's message from her answering service. Clodagh listened carefully to what Sammy had to say and answered him with something less than her usual loud-hailing zest.

'I'm not too happy about this one,' she said after what – for Clodagh – was quite a lengthy silence. 'Ever since Andy Warhol, we can never be quite sure what these jokers will do. Maybe a press release tomorrow? Sort of protect you with publicity *and* sell a few more copies.

Maybe not. I'll think about that one, I'll call Joanie in the morning.' To Sammy's relief, Clodagh was in charge.

There was another pause. When Clodagh spoke again, her tone was kindly, almost maternal; she reminded him, surprisingly, of Zara.

'Listen, little Sammy, stay right there and I'll be over. We don't want to lose an author, do we?'

Sammy went on to the little balcony which led off the sitting-room and gazed down at the street-lights far far below; he did not gaze too long, partly because Sammy suffered from vertigo (although that had become much better in New York) and partly because he wondered whether an enemy was waiting for him down below. Sammy no longer thought all the lights were twinkling with goodwill. Looking downward he imagined Clodagh, a strong Zara-substitute, striding towards him to save him.

When Clodagh did arrive, rather suddenly, at the door of the suite – maybe she did not want to alarm him by telephoning up from the lobby of the hotel? – she did look very strong, as well as handsome, in her black designer jeans and black silk shirt; through her shirt he could see the shape of her flat muscular chest, with the nipples clearly defined, like the chest of a young Greek athlete.

'Little Sammy,' said Clodagh quite tenderly. 'Who would want to frighten you?'

The balcony windows were still open. Clodagh made Sammy pour himself yet another whisky and one for her too (there was a trace of the old Clodagh in the acerbity with which she gave these orders). Masterfully she also imposed two mysterious bomb-like pills upon Sammy which she promised, together with the whisky, would give him sweet dreams 'and no nasty calls to frighten you'.

Because Clodagh was showing a tendency to stand very close to him, one of her long arms affectionately and irremoveably round his shoulders, Sammy was not all that unhappy when Clodagh ordered him to take both their drinks on to the balcony, away from the slightly worrying intimacy of the suite.

Sammy stood at the edge of the parapet, holding both glasses, and looked downwards. He felt better. Some of his previous benevolence towards New York came flooding back as the whisky and pills began to take effect. Sammy no long imagined that his enemy was down there in the street outside the Barraclough, waiting for him.

In a way of course, Sammy was quite right. For Sammy's enemy was not down there in the street below, but standing silently right there behind him, on the balcony, black gloves on her big capable strong hands where they extended from the cuffs of her chic black silk shirt.

'Have a nice death now, Sammy Luke.' Even the familiar phrase hardly had time to strike a chill into his heart as Sammy found himself falling, falling into the deep trough of the New York street twenty-three stories below. The two whisky glasses flew from his hands and little icy glass fragments scattered far and wide, far far from Sammy's tiny slumped body where it hit the pavement; the whisky vanished altogether, for no one recorded drops of whisky falling on their face in Madison Avenue.

Soft-hearted Joanie cried when the police showed her Sammy's typewritten suicide note with that signature so familiar from the signing of the books; the text itself the last product of the battered portable typewriter Sammy had brought with him to New York. But Joanie had to confirm Sammy's distressed state at her last visit to the suite; an impression more than confirmed by the amount of whisky Sammy had consumed before his death – a glass in each hand as he fell, said the police – to say nothing of the pills.

The waiter contributed to the picture too.

'I guess the guy seemed quite upset when I brought him his dinner.' He added as an afterthought: 'He was pretty lonesome too. Wanted to talk. You know the sort. Tried to stop me going away. Wanted to have a conversation. I should'a stopped but I was busy.' The waiter was genuinely regretful.

The hotel manager was regretful too, which considering the fact that Sammy's death had been duly reported in the Press as occurring from a Barraclough balcony, was decent of him.

One of the operators – Sammy's merry friend – went further and was dreadfully distressed: 'Jesus, I don't believe it. For Christ's sake, I just saw him on television.' The other operator made a calmer statement simply saying that Sammy had seemed very indecisive about whether he wished to receive calls or not in the course of the evening.

Zara Luke, in England, told the story of Sammy's last day and his pathetic tales of persecution, not otherwise substantiated. She also revealed – not totally to the surprise of her friends – that Sammy had a secret history of mental breakdown and was particularly scared of travelling by himself.

'I shall always blame myself for letting him go,' ended Zara, brokenly.

Clodagh Jansen of Porlock Publishers made a dignified statement about the tragedy.

It was Clodagh too who met the author's widow at the airport when Zara flew out a week later to make all the dreadful arrangements consequent upon poor Sammy's death.

At the airport Clodagh and Zara embraced discreetly, tearfully. It was only in private later at Clodagh's apartment – for Zara to stay at the Barraclough would certainly have been totally inappropriate – that more intimate caresses of a richer quality began. Began, but did not end: neither had any reason to hurry things.

'After all, we've all the time in the world,' murmured Sammy's widow to Sammy's publisher.

'And all the money too,' Clodagh whispered back; she must remember to tell Zara that *Women Weeping* would reach the Number One spot in the best-seller list on Sunday.

THE NEW GIRL FRIEND

'You know what we did last time?' he said.

She had waited for this for weeks. 'Yes?'

'I wondered if you'd like to do it again.'

She longed to but she didn't want to sound too keen.'Why not?'

'How about Friday afternoon, then? I've got the day off and Angie always goes to her sister's on Friday.'

'Not *always*, David.' She giggled.

He also laughed a little. 'She will this week. Do you think we could use your car? Angie'll take ours.'

'Of course. I'll come for you about two, shall I?'

'I'll open the garage doors and you can drive straight in. Oh, and Chris, could you fix it to get back a bit later? I'd love it if we could have the whole evening together.'

'I'll try,' she said, and then, 'I'm sure I can fix it. I'll tell Graham I'm going out with my new girl friend.'

He said goodbye and that he would see her on Friday. Christine put the receiver back. She had almost given up expecting a call from him. But there must have been a grain of hope still, for she had never left the receiver off the way she used to.

The last time she had done that was on a Thursday three weeks before, the day she had gone round to Angie's and found David there alone. Christine had got into the habit of taking the phone off the hook during the middle part of the day to avoid getting calls for the Midland Bank. Her number and the Midland Bank's differed by only one digit. Most days she took the receiver off at nine-thirty and put it back at three-thirty. On Thursday afternoons she nearly always went round to see Angie and never bothered to phone first.

Christine knew Angie's husband quite well. If she stayed a bit later on Thursdays she saw him when he came home from work. Sometimes she and Graham and Angie and David went out together as a foursome. She knew that David, like Graham, was a salesman or sales executive, as Graham always described himself, and she guessed from her friend's life style that David was rather more successful at it. She had never found him particularly attractive, for although he was quite tall, he had something of a girlish look and very fair wavy hair.

Graham was a heavily built, very dark man with a swarthy skin. He had to shave twice a day. Christine had started going out with him when she was fifteen and they had got married on her eighteenth birthday. She had never really known any other men at all intimately and now if she ever found herself alone with a man she felt awkward and apprehensive. The truth was that she was afraid a man might make an advance to her and the thought of that frightened her very much. For a long while she carried a penknife in her handbag in case she should need to defend herself. One evening, after they had been out with a colleague of Graham's and had had a few drinks, she told Graham about this fear of hers.

He said she was silly but he seemed rather pleased.

'When you went off to talk to those people and I was left with John I felt like that. I felt terribly nervous. I didn't know how to talk to him.'

Graham roared with laughter. 'You don't mean you thought old John was going to make a pass at you in the middle of a crowded restaurant?'

'I don't know,' Christine said 'I never know what they'll do.'

'So long as you're not afraid of what I'll do,' said Graham, beginning to kiss her, 'that's all that matters.'

There was no point in telling him now, ten years too

late, that she was afraid of what he did and always had been. Of course she had got used to it, she wasn't actually terrified, she was resigned and sometimes even quite cheerful about it. David was the only man she had ever been alone with when it felt all right.

That first time, that Thursday when Angie had gone to her sister's and hadn't been able to get through on the phone and tell Christine not to come, that time it had been fine. And afterwards she had felt happy and carefree, though what had happened with David took on the colouring of a dream next day. It wasn't really believable. Early on he had said:

'Will you tell Angie?'

'Not if you don't want me to.'

'I think it would upset her, Chris. It might even wreck our marriage. You see. . . .' He had hesitated. 'You see, that was the first time I – I mean, anyone ever. . . .' And he had looked into her eyes. 'Thank God it was you.'

The following Thursday she had gone round to see Angie as usual. In the meantime there had been no word from David. She stayed late in order to see him, beginning to feel a little sick with apprehension, her heart beating hard when he came in.

He looked quite different from how he had when she had found him sitting at the table reading, the radio on. He was wearing a grey flannel suit and grey striped tie. When Angie went out of the room and for a minute she was alone with him, she felt a flicker of that old wariness that was the forerunner of her fear. He was getting her a drink. She looked up and met his eyes and it was all right again. He gave her a conspiratorial smile, laying a finger on his lips.

'I'll give you a ring,' he had whispered.

She had to wait two more weeks. During that time she went twice to Angie's and twice Angie came to her. She and Graham and Angie and David went out as a foursome and while Graham was fetching drinks and Angie was in the Ladies, David looked at her and smiled and lightly touched her foot with his foot under the table.

'I'll phone you. I haven't forgotten.'

It was a Wednesday when he finally did phone. Next day Christine told Graham she had made a new friend, a girl she had met at work. She would be going out somewhere with this new friend on Friday and she wouldn't be back till eleven. She was desperately afraid he would want the car – it was *his* car or his firm's – but it so happened he would be in the office that day and would go by train. Telling him these lies didn't make her feel guilty. It wasn't as if this were some sordid affair, it was quite different.

When Friday came she dressed with great care. Normally, to go round to Angie's, she would have worn jeans and a tee shirt with a sweater over it. That was what she had on the first time she found herself alone with David. She put on a skirt and blouse and her black velvet jacket. She took the heated rollers out of her hair and brushed it into curls down on her shoulders. There was never much money to spend on clothes. The mortgage on the house took up a third of what Graham earned and half what she earned at her part-time job. But she could run to a pair of sheer black tights to go with the highest heeled shoes she'd got, her black pumps.

The doors of Angie and David's garage were wide open and their car was gone. Christine turned into their driveway, drove into the garage and closed the doors behind her. A door at the back of the garage led into the yard and garden. The kitchen door was unlocked as it had been that Thursday three weeks before and always was on Thursday afternoons. She opened the door and walked in.

'Is that you, Chris?'

The voice sounded very male. She needed to be reassured by the sight of him. She went into the hall as he came down the stairs.

'You look lovely,' he said

'So do you.'

He was wearing a suit. It was of navy silk with a pattern of pink and white flowers. The skirt was very short, the jacket clinched into his waist with a wide navy patent belt. The long golden hair fell to his shoulders, he was heavily made-up and this time he had painted his fingernails. He looked far more beautiful than he had that first time.

Then, three weeks before, the sound of her entry drowned in loud music from the radio, she had come upon this girl sitting at the table reading *Vogue*. For a moment she had thought it must be David's sister. She had forgotten Angie had said David was an only child. The girl had long fair hair and was wearing a red summer dress with white spots on it, white sandals and around her neck a string of white beads. When Christine saw that it was not a girl but David himself she didn't know what to do.

He stared at her in silence and without moving and then he switched off the radio. Christine said the silliest and least relevant thing.

'What are you doing home at this time?'

That made him smile. 'I'd finished so I took the rest of the day off. I should have locked the back door. Now you're here you may as well sit down.'

She sat down. She couldn't take her eyes off him. He didn't look like a man dressed up as a girl, he looked like a girl and a much prettier one than she or Angie. 'Does Angie know?'

He shook his head.

'But why do you do it?' she burst out and she looked about the room, Angie's small, rather untidy living room, at the radio, the *Vogue* magazine. 'What do you get out of it?' Something came back to her from an article she had read. 'Did your mother dress you as a girl when you were little?'

'I don't know,' he said. 'Maybe. I don't remember. I

don't want to *be* a girl. I just want to dress up as one sometimes.'

The first shock of it was past and she began to feel easier with him. It wasn't as if there was anything grotesque about the way he looked. The very last thing he reminded her of was one of those female impersonators. A curious thought came into her head, that it was *nicer*, somehow more civilised, to be a woman and that if only all men were more like women. . . That was silly, of course, it couldn't be.

'And it's enough for you just to dress up and be here on your own?'

He was silent for a moment. Then, 'Since you ask, what I'd really like would be to go out like this and. . .' He paused, looking at her, 'and be seen by lots of people, that's what I'd like. I've never had the nerve for that.'

The bold idea expressed itself without her having to give it a moment's thought. She wanted to do it. She was beginning to tremble with excitement.

'Let's go out then, you and I. Let's go out now. I'll put my car in your garage and you can get into it so the people next door don't see and then we'll go somewhere. Let's do that, David, shall we?'

She wondered afterwards why she had enjoyed it so much. What had it been, after all, as far as anyone else knew but two girls walking on Hampstead Heath? If Angie had suggested that the two of them do it she would have thought it a poor way of spending the afternoon. But with David. . . . She hadn't even minded that of the two of them he was infinitely the better dressed, taller, better-looking, more graceful. She didn't mind now as he came down the stairs and stood in front of her.

'Where shall we go?'

'Not the Heath this time,' he said. 'Let's go shopping.'

He bought a blouse in one of the big stores. Christine went into the changing room with him when he tried it on. They walked about in Hyde Park. Later on they had dinner and Christine noted that they were the only two women in the restaurant dining together.

'I'm grateful to you,' David said. He put his hand over hers on the table.

'I enjoy it,' she said. 'It's so – crazy. I really love it. You'd better not do that, had you? There's a man over there giving us a funny look.'

'Women hold hands,' he said.

'Only *those* sort of women. David, we could do this every Friday you don't have to work.'

'Why not?' he said.

There was nothing to feel guilty about. She wasn't harming Angie and she wasn't being disloyal to Graham. All she was doing was going on innocent outings with another girl. Graham wasn't interested in her new friend, he didn't even ask her name. Christine came to long for Fridays, especially for the moment when she let herself into Angie's house and saw David coming down the stairs and for the moment when they stepped out of the car in some public place and the first eyes were turned on him. They went to Holland Park, they went to the zoo, to Kew Gardens. They went to the cinema and a man sitting next to David put his hand on his knee. David loved that, it was a triumph for him, but Christine whispered they must change their seats and they did.

When they parted at the end of an evening he kissed her gently on the lips. He smelled of Alliage or Je Reviens or Opium. During the afternoon they usually went into one of the big stores and sprayed themselves out of the tester bottles.

Angie's mother lived in the north of England. When she had to convalesce after an operation Angie went up there to look after her. She expected to be away two weeks and the second weekend of her absence Graham had to go to Brussels with the sales manager.

'We could go away somewhere for the weekend,' David said.

'Graham's sure to phone,' Christine said.

'One night then. Just for the Saturday night. You can tell him you're going out with your new girl friend and you're going to be late.'

'All right.'

It worried her that she had no nice clothes to wear. David had a small but exquisite wardrobe of suits and dresses, shoes and scarves and beautiful undercloths. He kept them in a cupboard in his office to which only he had a key and he secreted items home and back again in his briefcase. Christine hated the idea of going away for the night in her grey flannel skirt and white silk blouse and that velvet jacket while David wore his Zandra Rhodes dress. In a burst of recklessness she spent all of two weeks' wages on a linen suit.

They went in David's car. He had made the arrangements and Christine had expected they would be going to a motel twenty miles outside London. She hadn't thought it would matter much to David where they went. But he surprised her by his choice of an hotel that was a three-hundred-year-old house on the Suffolk coast.

'If we're going to do it,' he said, 'we may as well do it in style.'

She felt very comfortable with him, very happy. She tried to imagine what it would have felt like going to spend a night in an hotel with a man, a lover. If the person sitting next to her were dressed, not in a black and white printed silk dress and scarlet jacket but in a man's suit with shirt and tie. If the face it gave her so much pleasure to look at were not powdered and rouged and mascara'd but rough and already showing beard growth. She couldn't imagine it. Or, rather, she could only think how in that case she would have jumped out of the car at the first red traffic lights.

They had single rooms next door to each other. The

rooms were very small but Christine could see that a double might have been awkward for David who must at some point – though she didn't care to think of this – have to shave and strip down to being what he really was.

He came in and sat on her bed while she unpacked her nightdress and spare pair of shoes.

'This is fun, isn't it?'

She nodded, squinting into the mirror, working on her eyelids with a little brush. David always did his eyes beautifully. She turned round and smiled at him. 'Let's go down and have a drink.'

The dining room, the bar, the lounge were all low-ceilinged timbered rooms with carved wood on the walls David said was called linenfold panelling. There were old maps and pictures of men hunting in gilt frames and copper bowls full of roses. Long windows were thrown open on to a terrace. The sun was still high in the sky and it was very warm. While Christine sat on the terrace in the sunshine David went off to get their drinks. When he came back to their table he had a man with him, a thickset paunchy man of about forty who was carrying a tray with four glasses on it.

'This is Ted,' David said.

'Delighted to meet you,' Ted said. 'I've asked my friend to join us. I hope you don't mind.'

She had to say she didn't. David looked at her and from his look she could tell he had deliberately picked Ted up.

'But why did you?' she said to him afterwards. 'Why did you want to? You told me you didn't really like it when that man put his hand on you in the cinema.'

'That was so physical. This is just a laugh. You don't suppose I'd let them touch me, do you?'

Ted and Peter had the next table to theirs at dinner. Christine was silent and standoffish but David flirted with them. Ted kept leaning across and whispering to him and David giggled and smiled. You could see he was enjoying himself tremendously. Christine knew they would ask her and David to go out with them after dinner and she began to be afraid. Suppose David got carried away by the excitement of it, the 'fun', and went off somewhere with Ted, leaving her and Peter alone together? Peter had a red face and a black moustache and beard and a wart with black hairs growing out of it on his left cheek. She and David were eating steak and the waiter had brought them sharp pointed steak knives. She hadn't used hers. The steak was very tender. When no one was looking she slipped the steak knife into her bag.

Ted and Peter were still drinking coffee and brandies when David got up quite abruptly and said, 'Coming?' to Christine.

'I suppose you've arranged to meet them later?' Christine said as soon as they were out of the dining room.

David looked at her. His scarlet-painted lips parted into a wide smile. He laughed.

'I turned them down.'

'Did you *really*?'

'I could tell you hated the idea. Besides, we want to be alone, don't we? I know I want to be alone with you.'

She nearly shouted his name so that everyone could hear, the relief was so great. She controlled herself but she was trembling. 'Of course I want to be alone with you,' she said.

She put her arm in his. It wasn't uncommon, after all, for girls to walk along with linked arms. Men turned to look at David and one of them whistled. She knew it must be David the whistle was directed at because he looked so beautiful with his long golden hair and high-heeled red sandals. They walked along the sea front, along the little low promenade. It was too warm even at eight-thirty to wear a coat. There were a lot of people about but not crowds for the place was too select to attract crowds. They walked to the end of the pier. They had a drink in the Ship Inn and another in the Fishermen's Arms. A man tried to pick David up in the Fishermen's Arms but this time he was cold and distant.

'I'd like to put my arm round you,' he said as they were walking back, 'but I suppose that wouldn't do, though it is dark.'

'Better not,' said Christine. She said suddenly, 'This has been the best evening of my life.'

He looked at her. 'You really mean that?'

She nodded. 'Absolutely the best.'

They came into the hotel. 'I'm going to get them to send us up a couple of drinks. To my room. Is that OK?'

She sat on the bed. David went into the bathroom. To do his face, she thought, maybe to shave before he let the man with the drinks see him. There was a knock at the door and a waiter came in with a tray on which were two long glasses of something or other with fruit and leaves floating in it, two pink table napkins, two olives on sticks and two peppermint creams wrapped up in green paper.

Christine tasted one of the drinks. She ate an olive. She opened her handbag and took out a mirror and a lipstick and painted her lips. David came out of the bathroom. He had taken off the golden wig and washed his face. He hadn't shaved, there was a pale stubble showing on his chin and cheeks. His legs and feet were bare and he was wearing a very masculine robe made of navy blue towelling. She tried to hide her disappointment.

'You've changed,' she said brightly.

He shrugged. 'There are limits.'

He raised his glass and she raised her glass and he said: 'To us!'

The beginnings of a feeling of panic came over her. Suddenly he was so evidently a man. She edged a little way along the mattress.

'I wish we had the whole weekend.'

She nodded nervously. She was aware her body had started a faint trembling. He had noticed it too. Sometimes before he had noticed how emotion made her tremble.

'Chris,' he said.

She sat passive and afraid.

'I'm not really like a woman, Chris. I just play at that sometimes for fun. You know that, don't you?' The hand that touched her smelt of nail varnish remover. There were hairs on the wrist she had never noticed before. 'I'm falling in love with you,' he said. 'And you feel the same, don't you?'

She couldn't speak. He took her by the shoulders. He brought his mouth up to hers and put his arms round her and began kissing her. His skin felt abrasive and a smell as male as Graham's came off his body. She shook and shuddered. He pushed her down on the bed and his hands began undressing her, his mouth still on hers and his body heavy on top of her.

She felt behind her, put her hand into the open handbag and pulled out the knife. Because she could feel his heart beating steadily against her right breast she knew where to stab and she stabbed again and again. The bright red heart's blood spurted over her clothes and the bed and the two peppermint creams on the tray.

THE MOUSE WILL PLAY

Mrs Bellew surveyed her neighbours through the large picture window of her living-room at number 17, Windsor Crescent. Across the road, the fair young man with the beard was getting into his Sierra, briefcase already placed in the rear. Two small children and their mother watched him leave, all waving. Up and down the street, other morning rituals were taking place. Some husbands sprang into their cars and drove away without a visible farewell; at several houses both partners – you could not be certain they were married nowadays – left home daily. Soon the Crescent would settle into its weekday mode as the children left for school, the younger ones with their mothers, others alone, a few in groups. Then the toddlers would come out to play – a few, to Mrs Bellew's horror, in the street. Mrs Bellew's own son had never played in the street.

She was, as far as she could tell, the only senior resident on the estate, and she had been accustomed to a very different life.

Mrs Bellew's husband had died a year ago, suddenly, of a heart attack while in Singapore on business. Until then, hers had been a busy, fulfilling existence, acting as his hostess as his own business expanded. Frequently, guests who were in fact his customers were entertained at Springhill Lodge to dinner, or even for an entire weekend, with a round of golf or a swim in the Bellews' kidney-shaped azure pool. Deals were mooted and concluded around the Bellews' mahogany dining-table while Mrs Bellew and the visiting wife chatted of this and that in the drawing-room and the hired Cordon Bleu cook cleared up in the kitchen. Mrs Bellew planned the menus but never prepared them.

Occasionally, in her turn, Mrs Bellew travelled abroad with Sam and was, herself, entertained, but not on that last journey.

And now it had ended, with Sam heavily in debt.

After his death their son had decided that his mother must be resettled in a small, easy-to-manage house on a bus route and within walking distance of a general store, for she would not be able to afford a car. Thus it was that she had been uprooted from her large house with its two acres of garden in Surrey and despatched to this commuter village where she knew no one.

She could catch the train to London easily, her son had pointed out, to visit him and her grandchildren, and it was not far from his own weekend cottage in the Cotswolds.

Mrs Bellew would have agreed that the distance was not great if she could have been whisked there in Sam's Rover, or even in her own Polo, but there was no way of getting to Fettingham from Windsor Crescent by public transport without two changes of bus involving a long wait between them, so she stayed away. Giles had said he would often fetch her for a visit, and this had happened once, but Mrs Bellew had not enjoyed the weekend spent in the damp stone cottage which Giles and his wife were renovating. While they spent their time decorating or in the pub, Mrs Bellew was expected to mind the children and to cook the lunch. Chilled and miserable, Mrs Bellew was thankful to return to 17 Windsor Crescent, with its central heating.

But her days were long and solitary. She kept to a routine of housework, as she had done throughout her life before she had anyone to help her with it, but she could not dust and polish all day long. Meals were dull. She missed not Sam so much as what went with him – the bustle of his life and its purpose, as well as the comforts she had now grown used to, which his money bought; and she felt bitter anger at his failure to leave her properly provided for. Now she was no one, just an elderly woman living in a modern house – one of the smallest on the estate – among other anonymous houses in an area where there was no sense of community. Mrs Bellew did not require the services of Meals on Wheels or the old people's day centre. It did not occur to her that she could have usefully lent her aid and experience to either of these organisations.

When Sam died, the deal that he had been negotiating had been intended to put his business back in profit, but meanwhile his credit was extended, funds borrowed and despatched, like Antonio's argosies, to earn reward, and like those, some were lost. He had pledged his main insurance on this last project.

'You've got to face it, Mother. Father was a speculator and his gamble came unstuck,' Giles had told her sternly. 'If he hadn't died, he'd have been in serious trouble.' It had taken all Giles's own considerable ingenuity to rescue what he had from the collapse of his father's ventures, and he had been unable to spare his mother the discovery that the old man had died as he had lived, dangerously, in bed with a young Chinese woman.

Now, nothing broke the monotony of Mrs Bellew's days. No Sam, red-faced and cheerful, returned with tales of successfully concluded deals.

How many of such stories had been lies? Like his protests that he missed her when he went abroad?

These thoughts were unendurable. Mrs Bellew would not entertain them and instead she concentrated on her neighbours. Which of them, superficially so self-satisfied and smug, with their rising incomes and, in many cases, their second car and salary, were living lies?

Wondering about them, Mrs Bellew began to notice things. There was the dark blue Audi which left number 32 each morning at half-past seven and was sometimes absent for several days at a time. One day she saw the owner, a man in his late thirties, carrying an overnight bag to the car. Like Sam's, his job obviously involved travel.

She watched the house while he was gone and saw a green Porsche parked outside it until very late at night. Mrs Bellew soon identified the driver, a young man with fair curly hair.

The cat's away, she thought, and that mouse is playing.

She noticed other things: an impatient, angry mother cuffing her small son about the head as they walked along the road bound for the nursery school; older children on roller skates who swung on trees that overhung the pavement, breaking branches and skating off, giggling, before they were discovered. She began to keep a record, writing down the habits of her neighbours in a notebook. She knew no one's name, but within the compass of her vision from her window she observed which wife was visited by her mother every Tuesday; who was called on by a man in a Triumph Spitfire every Wednesday afternoon; who cleaned and polished – such women were seen in pinafores cleaning windows – and who employed someone to help them. She recognised her neighbours in the supermarket in the local town and saw how they laid out their money: who bought frozen food in bulk; who spent vast sums on pet food; who was frugal. Walking along the street on winter afternoons, she could see through the large lighted windows into rooms where women spent hours eating chocolates and watching television.

Some of them had secrets, and she began to learn them.

Mrs Bellew prepared the letters carefully, cutting the words from a magazine and pasting them on to plain sheets of Basildon Bond. She planned every operation with the same meticulousness that had made her dinner parties so successful, choosing each victim when she was confident of her facts, and finding out their names from the voters' list.

She wrote to the social security office about the child she saw cuffed in the street, and soon had the satisfaction of seeing an official-looking woman calling at the house.

Later, the child's mother went away. The window-cleaner
– almost her only contact apart from the postman and the
milkman – told her that the father, left alone with the child
and a job to do, could not cope and the small boy had
been taken into care.

'A shame, I call it,' said the window-cleaner. 'Been
knocking the kid about, it seems – the mother had. Girls
don't know they're born, these days. But I don't know –
poor little lad. It makes you think.'

Mrs Bellew agreed that indeed it did. She was surprised
at the outcome of her intervention; still, the boy would
be looked after now.

She did not fear discovery; the recipients of her letters
would not broadcast their own guilt. On trips to London,
which were cheap because she used her old person's rail
card though she did not like to think that she looked old,
Mrs Bellew mailed her serpent missives. Then she would
indulge herself in tea at Harrods before catching her train
home. She would prepare the next offensive whilst
awaiting the outcome of the last.

One Wednesday, the husband of the woman visited by
the Triumph Spitfire driver came home unexpectedly. He
caught his wife *in flagrante* with the young man from the
estate agent's who had sold the house to them, and went
straight round to see the young man's wife who had also
been ignorant of what was going on. Eventually, both
couples separated. Four school-age children were
involved, two in each family.

Mrs Bellew soon had the interest of watching new neighbours move into Number 25.

The window-cleaner expressed dismay that there had
been so much unhappiness on the estate lately. He'd heard
that Mrs Fisher's mother, who came to see her daughter
every Tuesday, had been asked by her son-in-law to
restrict her visits because it was time Mary Fisher pulled
herself together and stood on her own feet after her fourth
miscarriage. She ought to get a job, her husband had told

her, and stop brooding. She'd told the window-cleaner all about it when he went round and found her weeping bitterly.

Mrs Bellew was surprised to hear about the miscarriages. Her letter to Mr Fisher had mentioned his wife's child-like dependency on her mother and suggested she was idle. To the window-cleaner, she opined that sitting about indulging in self-pity was not constructive.

Mrs Bellew went on a summer visit to her son and his family in their cottage. This began as a better experience than the last; she sat in a deckchair for an hour reading *Good Housekeeping*, but was expected to cook the Sunday lunch while her son and his wife met their friends, fellow weekenders, in the local pub. The children were delighted as their grandmother had been left a leg of lamb to roast; on other Sundays a precooked pie, bought from the local butcher, was their lot. It was a grandmother's pleasure to cherish her family, Giles's wife stated firmly; her own mother liked nothing better than to cook for any number.

'Get her to do it, then,' said Mrs Bellew, demanding to be taken home early.

She was in time to see an ambulance drawn up outside the Fishers' house, but she did not learn what had happened until the next visit of the window-cleaner. He told her without any prompting.

Mrs Fisher had tried to kill herself. She had swallowed various pills, drunk a lot of sherry, and gone to bed with a plastic bag over her head. Woozy with the sherry and the drugs, she had used a bag already perforated for safety and so she had survived, though she was deeply uncon-scious when discovered by her next-door neighbour. Mary's mother had known that Tim Fisher, an enthusiastic golfer, was playing a double round that day. Unable to reach her daughter on the telephone, she called the neigh-bour. Tim had come back from the golf course grumbling about neurotic women.

There was a satisfactory amount of coming and going

to please Mrs Bellew for several days after this. She knew that Tim Fisher would never show her original letter to a soul, and she did not make the mistake of following it with a second. She had a new target lined up in her sights now.

In the local supermarket, she had noticed the woman from Number 43 buying gin and sherry – such a lot of it, several bottles every week. The woman's face was flushed; she was one of those who watched television in the afternoons.

Neatly and painstakingly, Mrs Bellew cut the words from *Homes and Gardens*. The paper was pleasanter to work with than ordinary newsprint, which made one's fingers inky.

Does your wife take her empty gin bottles to the bottle bank? Mrs Bellew enquired, in careful composition. Her messages were always terse, just enough to sow disquiet.

Dick Pearson showed his wife the letter when he tackled her. There were tears and recriminations as Barbara confessed to feeling useless and lonely while the children, both now teenagers, were at school all day. Dick didn't want her to go to work; his was an income adequate for their needs and a mother's place was in the home; besides, she had no proper qualifications.

Now he felt shame. Busy chasing orders for his firm, which dealt in manufacturing equipment, he had failed to think of her, even to talk to her when he was at home. But for the anonymous letter, he was thinking, she could have ended up like Mary Fisher.

Had there been a letter there?

He could not ask, but both he and Barbara wondered.

Mary Fisher left the hospital at last. When she came home, her mother resumed her visits, and Barbara Pearson, trying to redeem herself, also took to calling round. The two women began to discuss launching a joint enterprise, catering for private parties – even, perhaps, business lunches in the local town. Both were skilful cooks.

The idea burgeoned. They had cards printed and put notices in the local paper. Then they distributed leaflets.

'That woman at number 17,' said Barbara. 'She always looks so elegant, but she must be getting on. I wouldn't mind betting she'd appreciate a bit of help when she entertains. And she might have well-off friends who'd use us, too. Let's go and see her.'

Mary, wrapped in her own misery, had barely noticed Mrs Bellew. She thought she looked stuck-up.

She went to call, with Barbara.

Mrs Bellew, unaccustomed, now, to company, recognised them both and at first she did not want to let them in. But Barbara said they needed her advice, and so, reluctantly, she admitted them.

In her elegant living-room, Barbara described their plan.

Mrs Bellew said she never entertained now, but had done a lot during her husband's lifetime. She waxed eloquent about *milles feuilles* and Chicken Supreme.

'You should join us,' Barbara enthused. 'Your experience would be invaluable.'

Six months ago, Mrs Bellew might have considered it; she knew all about well chosen, balanced menus. But now she was already wondering how she could bring them down, for she had learned to hate success.

Mary had problems concentrating these days. Her attention wandered, and she picked up a magazine from the coffee table in front of her, leafing idly through it. Mrs Bellew saw what she was doing, rose swiftly and removed the magazine from her grasp as if she was a child touching a forbidden object. Without a word of explanation, she put it in a drawer and soon the interview had ended.

'Wasn't that odd of her?' said Mary as they left. 'But it was rude of me, I suppose, to look at it when we were meant to be talking. Sorry.'

'She was ruder,' Barbara said.

'There were holes in it,' said Mary.

'Holes?'

'Sort of like windows. Pieces cut from different pages.'

'Recipes cut out?'

'No. Bits in the middle of a story,' Mary said.

Barbara had seen the letter sent to Dick. He alone of all the recipients in Windsor Crescent had shown it to its subject.

Next Friday, Mrs Bellew went, as usual, to the supermarket in the local town. Barbara was also there. She had often seen the older woman buying her one packet of butter, her small portion of frozen food, and had vaguely pitied her. Now, she was curious; she'd thought a lot about the mutilated magazine. Whoever had written that letter to Dick had either seen her buying drink or disposing of her empties and so was local, though the letter had had a London postmark. So many small tragedies had happened lately in the area; other people might have been receiving letters too.

Watching Mrs Bellew study prices on some chops, Barbara selected two pairs of tights she did not want. She scarcely thought about it as she passed behind Mrs Bellew who was stooping forward, peering into the freezer chest, her wicker basket gaping on her arm. Barbara, not even worrying in case she was observed herself, dropped the tights into it and moved on.

They might not be discovered. Nothing might be done about it if they were, especially if Mrs Bellew proclaimed her ignorance of how they got there.

Far off among the cereals, Barbara missed the small commotion at the door as Mrs Bellew was led away for questioning.

Biographical Notes

MARGERY ALLINGHAM (1904–1966) was born in London. Her first story was published soon after she left school at the age of 16 and she then became a writer for pulp magazines. She began to write novels after her marriage to Philip Youngman Carter, upon whom her fictional character, Albert Campion, is said to be based. She wrote prolifically throughout her lifetime, and among her best-known novels are *Black Plumes* (1940), *Traitor's Purse* (1941), *The Fashion in Shrouds* (1938) and *The Tiger in the Smoke* (1952).

CAROLINE BLACKWOOD was born in Ulster. Her novels include *The Stepdaughter* (1976), *Great Granny Webster* (1977) and *The Fate of Mary Rose* (1981). Her non-fiction work about Greenham Common, *On the Perimeter*, was published in 1984.

AGATHA CHRISTIE (1890–1976) was born in Devon and is one of the best-known figures of crime literature. She married twice, and with her second husband (archaeologist Max Mallowan) travelled all over the world. She wrote in a unique style, with a splendid ear for dialogue, and among her numerous classics are *The Man in the Brown Suit* (1924), *Murder on the Orient Express* (1934), *Death on the Nile* (1938), *By the Pricking of My Thumbs* (1968) and *Sleeping Murder* (1976). She was created a Dame Commander of the Order of the British Empire in 1971 and at her death had written well over fifty novels.

ELIZABETH FERRARS (1907) was born in Rangoon, Burma. She trained as a journalist and began writing crime novels in 1940. She was one of the founder members of the Crime Writers Association in 1953 and received a Crime Writers Association Award in 1981. She has written over fifty books, among which are *Enough to Kill a Horse* (1955), *Witness Before the Fact* (1979), *Experiment with Death* (1981) and *Root of All Evil* (1984).

ANTONIA FRASER (1932) was born in London where she still lives. Already well-established as a biographer and historian, she began writing crime novels in 1977. Among her novels are *Quiet as a Nun* (1977), *A Splash of Red* (1981), *Cool Repentance* (1982) and *Oxford Blood* (1985), all featuring the detective, Jemima Shore. Her most recent historical work, *The Weaker Vessel: Women's Lot in Seventeenth-Century England* (1984) won the Wolfson Prize.

PATRICIA HIGHSMITH (1921) was born in Fort Worth, Texas, and has lived in Europe since 1963. Her most famous character, Tom Ripley, features in several of her novels and is notable as a figure who is profoundly amoral yet fascinating. She has won several awards, including the Grand Prix de Littérature Policière (1957) and the Crime Writers Association Silver Dagger (1964). Among her novels are *The Talented Mr Ripley* (1955), *Strangers on a Train* (1950), *The Boy Who Followed Ripley* (1980) and *Found in the Street* (1986). Among her short story collections are *Eleven* (1970), *The Black House* (1981) and *Mermaids on the Golf Course* (1985).

ELIZABETH JANE HOWARD (1923) was an actress and reviewer before turning to fiction. Her novels include *The Long View* (1956), *The Sea Change* (1959), *After Julius* (1965) and *Getting It Right* (1982). She has also published two collections of short stories, including *Mr Wrong* (1975).

P D JAMES (1920) was born in Oxford and has worked in the theatre, National Health Service, Home Office, police department and as a Justice of the Peace. Her first crime novel, *Cover Her Face* (1962) introduced her central character, Inspector Adam Dalgliesh. Her other works include *Shroud for a Nightingale* (1971), *An Unsuitable Job for a Woman* (1973), *The Skull Beneath the Skin* (1982) and *A Taste for Death* (1986). She received a Crime Writers Association Award in 1967 and was awarded an O.B.E. in 1983.

and is a

speaker

a period

chshunds

well as

n *Ellery*

st *Detec-*

but now

mystery

n in the

Brothers

he Beast

ing Walls

ar Allan

oman of

egan her

on With

rd, who

o written

orks are

r (1975),

and *Live*

rt stories

ed under

ford and

dvertising

rote her

rst intro-

n *Whose*

ts in the

troduced

veller in

ovels are

The Five

Red Herrings (193

(1936). She also wro

moon (1936), as well

and literature.

MARGARET YO

in the W.R.N.S. d

Dead in the Morn

Patrick Grant. How

discarded Grant and

novels, including *T*

(1982), a novel in

rape, *The Smooth*

(1986). She has been

ation and in 1982 r

Award.

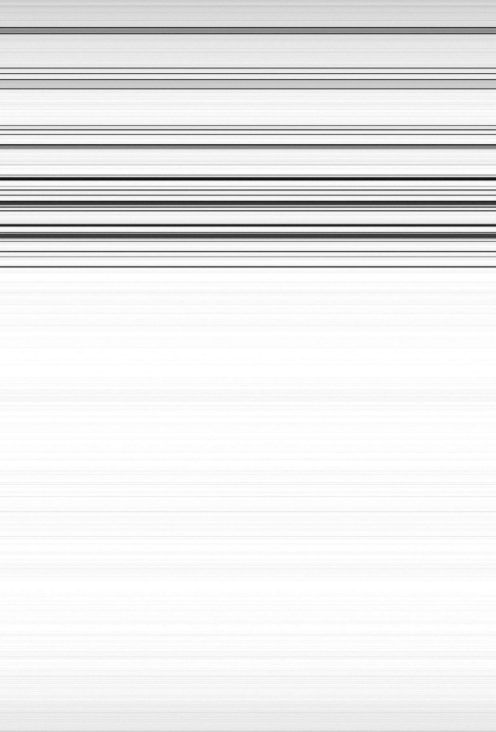

Acknowledgements

Acknowledgements are due to the following for permission to include the stories which appear in this book:
Aitken Stone Ltd for 'Tape-Measure Murder' by Agatha Christie from *Miss Marple's Final Cases* (Collins 1979); Patricia Highsmith and William Heinemann Ltd for 'The Snail-Watcher' from *Eleven* (William Heinemann Ltd 1970), first published in *Gamma*; A D Peters & Co Ltd for 'The New Girlfriend' by Ruth Rendell from *The New Girlfriend and Other Stories* (Hutchinson 1985); P D James and Elaine Green Ltd for 'Great-Aunt Allie's Flypapers'; Margaret Millar and David Higham Ltd for 'McGowney's Miracle'; Florence Maybèrry for 'Woman Trouble', first published in *Ellery Queen's Mystery Magazine*; Antonia Fraser and Curtis Brown Ltd for 'Have a Nice Death' from *Jemima Shore's First Case and Other Stories* (Weidenfeld & Nicolson 1986), first published in *The Fiction Magazine*, 1983; Elizabeth Ferrars and David Higham Ltd for 'Instrument of Justice' from *Winter Crimes* 13 (Macmillan London Ltd, 1981); Margaret Yorke and Curtis Brown Ltd for 'The Mouse Will Play'; David Higham Ltd for 'The Incredible Elopement of Lord Peter Wimsey' by Dorothy L Sayers from *A Treasury of Sayers Stories* (Gollancz 1958); Caroline Blackwood and William Heinemann Ltd for 'Addy' from *Goodnight Sweet Ladies* (William Heinemann Ltd 1983); Elizabeth Jane Howard and Jonathan Cape Ltd for 'Mr Wrong' from *Mr Wrong* (Jonathan Cape 1975); P & M Youngman Carter Ltd and Curtis Brown Ltd for 'The Black Tent' by Margery Allingham.

1954 Margaret Millar, renewed 1982 by Margaret Millar Survivors Trust; 'Woman Trouble' © 1973 Florence Mayberry; 'Have a Nice Death' © Antonia Fraser 1983; 'Instrument of Justice' © Elizabeth Ferrars 1981; 'The Mouse Will Play' © Margaret Yorke 1987; 'The Incredible Elopement of Lord Peter Wimsey' © Dorothy L Sayers 1958; 'Addy' © Caroline Blackwood 1983; 'Mr Wrong' © Elizabeth Jane Howard 1975; 'The Black Tent' © P & M Youngman Carter Ltd 1987.

For the very best in crime fiction,
both new and classic

KINGSLEY AMIS
The Crime of the Century

Bridget Ainsworth, aged 20, lay dead in Barn Elms Park. She
had been stabbed five times in the back. The next night
another girl was found murdered – and then another. The
police were baffled. Lawyers, psychologists and even a rock
star joined the hunt. But the biggest crime of all was yet to
come . . . *The Crime of the Century* is a hugely entertaining
novel, full of surprises and stamped with Kingsley Amis's
unmistakable brand of waspish satire.

NICHOLAS BLAKE
End of Chapter

A Nigel Strangeways mystery, in which he enters the cut-
throat publishing business, and finds a corpse. 'The Nicholas
Blake books are something quite by themselves in English
detective fiction' (*Elizabeth Bowen*).

The Private Wound

In the West of Ireland a young novelist rents a lonely cottage
to write his new book. He is soon seduced by the wife of the
local squire, a hot-tempered older man who once fought for
the Black and Tans. A powerful story of love, passion and
murder, this is Nicholas Blake's last book and a fine novel in
its own right.

SIMON BRETT
A Shock to the System

'A new book by Simon Brett is always an event' *P.D. James*
Paperbacked in Mastercrime for the first time, this is the
chilling story of an executive whizzkid who turns to murder
when promotion passes him by and family life sours.
'Superior of its kind, with an excellent sense of pace, tension
and encroaching panic, and a genuine surprise ending'
(*The Times*)
'More enthralling than any whodunit' (*Books & Bookmen*)
'Very good indeed. I don't know if Mr Brett has ever done
anyone in, he seems to understand murderers so well.' (*Daily
Telegraph*)

Dead Romantic

For the first time in paperback – the gripping story of a
woman who has been saving herself for Mr Right, and
chooses Mr Wrong. 'Tantalizing . . . the end is unguessable
and very sharp' (*Oxford Times*)

JAMES M. CAIN

Two novels from 'the twenty-minute egg of the hard-boiled
school' (David Madden)

Cloud Nine

First time in paperback. A tough, sexy crime novel set in
America's mean streets. 'As moving and unnerving as *Double
Indemnity* or *The Postman Always Rings Twice*' (*Chicago
Tribune*).

The Magician's Wife

Back in print after nearly two decades – a Cain classic set in an urban jungle of sharks and swindlers, drifters and gold-diggers.

MICHAEL GILBERT
Smallbone Deceased

Scandal, suspicion and murder follow the discovery that a deed-box held by a highly respectable legal firm contains not the expected document but the body of a certain Mr Smallbone. This is top-class entertainment from 'the best living master of the classic English murder mystery' (*The New Yorker*). 'One of the best detective novels of recent years' (*The Observer*).

JAMES MELVILLE
Death of a Daimyo

This is the paperback debut of Superintendent Otani, 'the Japanese answer to Maigret' (*Observer*). East meets West when he visits Cambridge University and stumbles on the corpse of a Japanese tycoon. Meanwhile, back in Kobe, a policewoman disguised as a mahjong madam risks her life to spy on the power struggle between Kobe's criminal elite for the position of *daimyo* (gangland boss). Fascinating background detail, authentic Japanese flavour and Melville's ironic touch makes his crime novels sheer delight.

Further details about Mastercrime and about all Dent Paperbacks, including Classic Thrillers, Everyman Classics and Everyman Fiction, may be obtained from the Sales Department, J.M. Dent & Sons Ltd, 33 Welbeck Street, London W1M 8LX. We welcome readers' opinions on our range of titles and suggestions for additions to our list.

ORDER FORM

.... **ALLINGHAM:** The Fashion in Shrouds	£3.95
.... **AMIS:** The Crime of the Century	£2.95
.... **BENTLEY:** Trent Intervenes	£3.95
.... **BLAKE:** Head of a Traveller	£3.95
.... **BLAKE:** End of Chapter	£3.95
.... **BLAKE:** The Private Wound	£3.95
.... **BRETT:** A Shock to the System	£3.95
.... **BRETT:** Dead Romantic	£3.95
.... **CAIN:** Cloud Nine	£3.95
.... **CAIN:** The Magician's Wife	£3.95
.... **GILBERT:** Smallbone Deceased	£3.95
.... **HUXLEY:** The African Poison Murders	£3.95
.... **ILES:** Malice Aforethought	£3.95
.... **MELVILLE:** Death of a Daimyo	£3.95
.... **MELVILLE:** The Ninth Netsuke	£3.95
.... **RINEHART:** The Circular Staircase	£3.95

All these books may be obtained through your local bookshop, or can be ordered direct from the publisher. Please indicate the number of copies required and fill in the form below.

Name .... BLOCK
Address .... LETTERS
.... PLEASE
....

Please enclose remittance to the value of the cover price *plus* 40p per copy to a maximum of £2, for postage, and send your order to:
BP Dept, J.M. Dent & Sons Ltd, 33 Welbeck Street, London W1M 8LX

Applicable to UK only and subject to stock availability
All prices subject to alteration without notice